CW01004975

The Diary of a Has-been

The Diary of a Has-been

William Humble

urbanepublications.com

First published in Great Britain in 2016 by Urbane Publications Ltd
Suite 3, Brown Europe House, 33/34 Gleaming Wood Drive, Chatham, Kent ME5 8RZ

A CIP catalogue record for this book is available from the British Library.

ISBN 978-1-911129-60-8
EPUB 978-1-911129-61-5
MOBI 978-1-911129-62-2

Design and Typeset by Julie Martin
Cover by Julie Martin

Printed in Great Britain by
CPI Group (UK) Ltd, Croydon, CR0 4YY

urbanepublications.com

The publisher supports the Forest Stewardship Council® (FSC®), the leading international forest-certification organisation. This book is made from acid-free paper from an FSC®-certified provider. FSC is the only forest-certification scheme supported by the leading environmental organisations, including Greenpeace.

For Caroline

Foreword

After the 2010 general election my father Arnold Appleforth finally found happiness and reluctantly agreed to move out of his squalid west London flat (thereby causing adjoining property prices to rocket overnight) and at the same time gave up his life-long struggle to be the most admired left-wing hack of his generation. I well remember that September morning, as Dad stood watching his much-loved home being simultaneously dismantled and fumigated. I felt so sorry for him that I even kept quiet as he drank his way through the last bottle of the hideous 3 for £10 wine he was so inexplicably fond of. After he'd drained the last drop he looked me right in the eye – or tried to – and said he had something he wanted to give me.

"What is it, Dad?"

"It's my diary."

"Oh God," I heard myself say.

"It's an important historical document, Roger, and a searingly honest personal one as well."

"That's what I was afraid of."

"Let me finish! I wrote it during the last election and it offers a unique insight into all sorts of stuff. And you know lots of rich and powerful Tories, don't you? So I was thinking, maybe you could chat them up while you're playing golf or whatever it is you get up to together and get it published for me. I'll split it fifty-fifty."

Faced with such a mixture of flattery and desperation, what could I do but try? And five years later, I succeeded (mainly thanks, I think, to the OBE I was recently deeply honoured to receive).

So here it is. Prescient, pithy, outspoken. To be honest, not my sort of book at all. But a suitable memorial all the same for my dear old Dad, Arnold Appleforth – writer, dreamer, idealist, sponger.

Roger Appleforth OBE
October 2016

Easter Sunday 4th April 2010.

11.00 a.m.

Lie in bed, very depressed. Am over 60 and life is pointless because not-quite-glittering journalistic career is in tatters and haven't had sex for three months and have sod-all money (mainly because of extraordinary generosity to ex-wives and sundry other women). Then hear church bells ringing to celebrate the Resurrection of our Lord, and reflect that at least I've survived 28 years longer than Jesus and I've certainly had a lot more totty. This cheers me up. Decide I won't stay in bed all day after all. Get up and get dressed and google "Jesus how old" just to make sure I've got the figures right. I have! (Crucified aged 33). Pop down the road to the Galloping Gastro for a quick drink to celebrate being 61 and alive and to read The Sunday Times without paying for it. (This is not only because I refuse to subsidise the iniquitous Murdoch press but because I object to helping pay the inflated salaries of the wankers who write for it. It's the least I can do.) Over third glass of house Rioja decide I'm ten times as witty as any Sunday Times reviewer and if my journalistic career hadn't been prematurely derailed I too could be earning a fortune writing snooty crap that makes people like me want to throw up. Decide to do something meaningful with my life instead.

After fourth glass decide what it's going to be. I'm going to keep a diary. Yes, a diary!

A life-enhancing moment – I have a purpose again!

7.20 p.m.

Celebrate some more by drinking several glasses of the 3 for

£10 Tesco reddo and fall asleep in front of a re-run of a Doc Martin Christmas special. When I wake up Martin Clunes has disappeared and there's no sign of the sexy secretary I watch it for, but it's still snowing – and it seems to be the 1950s. Strange. I wonder if Doc Martin has gone all Life on Mars in one of ITV's typically pathetic attempts to keep up with the times. Then I realize it's a re-run of a different Christmas special. Clearly ITV3 are having a themed evening of old Christmas specials! Brilliant! What an imaginative idea! Specially for Easter!

Then I catch sight of Geraldine McEwan camping about like a poor man's Maggie Smith. Oh Christ, it's Miss Marple. I believe the accepted view among Agatha Christie congnoscenti is that the Geraldine McEwan Marple isn't a patch on the good old BBC Joan Hickson one. Personally I think they're both crap and so was Margaret fucking Rutherford.

Make an effort to focus on the nice scenery and costumes, but G McEwan's voice is swoopy and grating both at the same time and gives me a headache and I turn her off.

Make a quick Cointreau frappé before turning in and wonder – not for the first time – why they call it "Marple" now instead of "*Miss* Marple". Is it to make it sound cooler and more cutting-edge? What are they hoping to do, put her in The fucking Wire? By the time I get to bed the equanimity I need in order to have any hope of getting to sleep has vanished. Take a herbal sleeping pill made of lettuce and it has no effect at all.

Easter Monday 5th April

12.30 a.m.

Get up and go for pee. Stay up to continue writing diary.

Immediately start to feel calmer, in fact strangely content, until a sneery little voice starts in my head. "So what's there to celebrate about being 61? Let's face it, every day now is a day closer to death. And what can you possibly write a diary about – nothing ever happens to you!"

Pour another tiny Cointreau (no ice this time, certainly not frappé, it's half past one, can't be arsed) and refuse to respond to Sneery Voice because he's talking rubbish of course. Flippant, nihilistic one in the morning rubbish. But I ought to thank him, because it helps me focus the mind and work out what the point of this diary really is. Clearly astute left-of-centre political comment and pungent philosophical musings will be crucial, but what else?

Is it a celebration of getting older?

Partly. But more than that. *Much* more.

But *what?*

Am having fourth pee of the night when it hits me.

The point of this diary is to show by detailed observation of my still-vigorous lifestyle that nowadays age is meaningless. Just numbers. Meaningless numbers. You're only as old as you feel!

Rush back to write it down before I forget. *You're only as old as you feel.* Brilliant!

Adrenalin now flowing and itching to write some more!

2.50 a.m.

Seem to have dozed off. Am feeling knackered so make black coffee (Gold Blend) and have two Kit-Kats to give me energy. The dark-chocolate ones that are on special offer at Tesco. Gives me a much needed boost and have further in-depth thoughts on diary.

Political and philosophical manifesto for my diary

I promise to use this diary to express my frustration and disgust at globalisation, the media and the terminal state of the so-called Labour Party. I write this with much sadness as a former Marxist and unreconstructed Old Labour idealist who still proudly brandishes his profoundly held socialist credentials. Because let's face it if people like me don't brandish them, who will?

I suddenly hear Sneery Voice again (maybe it's the Kit-Kats). "For God's sake why not go to bed and forget about it? It's just a *diary*, no-one's ever going to read it anyway."

For the second time that night he provokes the opposite response to the one he wants. I realize that a lifetime spent at the crumbling coalface of journalistic hackery has left me with the overwhelming need to leave something permanent behind.

Not that I mean to under-sell myself. Not everything I've written has been ephemeral. For example, there are the six witty travel guides I wrote to countries I never visited (Out of print but available from my website www.arnoldappleforthmarxistwriter.co.uk). There's also "Everybody out, Siegfried", my witty but not entirely successful episode for All Creatures Great And Small in which Christopher Timothy (or was it Peter Davison?) toys with starting a workers' rebellion in picturesque Darrowby (available as personally signed VHS from my website, or as part of overpriced, unsigned DVD box sets everywhere else).

Of course I mustn't forget my greatest claim to immortality – the living memorial I've achieved through the DNA that courses through the veins of my three or four adorable children. (The DNA of the fourth is still in contention, hence the vagueness. I don't mean to sound callous).

But needless to say none of this compares to the unique memorial of a proper hardback book that would be preserved forever on the sparkling aluminium shelves of the British Library (NB – don't get me wrong, the kids bit compares to it, of course it does!). Or come to think of it an e-book that would be preserved forever on the virtual shelves of cyberspace. Or an app, that would be kept wherever it is apps are kept.

As the point of a diary is to be searingly honest, had better make guilty confession here. What I want most of all is for the diary (henceforward known as my magnum opus) to be discovered by a thrusting young, but not too young, publisher. Ideally one who has fond teenage memories of my famous early tirades in Private Eye in the 80s – specially the ones about the Falklands and the Brighton bombing that led the Daily Mail to christen me Arnold The Antichrist (God, those were the days). He would of course recognise at once the incisive wit and perceptiveness and sensitivity of diary and get me mega advance. Reckon this would help solve women problem too.

Have just had to pee again. Think I have peed three more

times since whenever it was I said I'd peed four times.

Then prepare biography for publicity purposes for so-far imaginary young-but-not-too-young publisher.

Arnold Appleforth – journalist, diarist, idealist

Arnold Appleforth is a writer who learned his craft the hard way, not from soft-option media studies courses but from endless underpaid years writing am dram reviews and the nature column for the Market Harborough Gazette, followed by more endless underpaid years writing the nature column and second-string opera reviews for the Brixton Herald even though he hated opera (but not quite as much as his readers did). Fun-loving former Marxist, Arnold has never quite received the recognition he deserved. But there have been many highlights even so. Some of us still fondly remember that all-too-brief but glorious period when he wrote viciously hate-filled think-pieces for the Mail on Sunday, in that hot sultry summer when their regular hate-filled writers all suddenly ran out of things to be hateful about.

I pause and wipe a tear from my eye. Christ those *were* the days.

Eventually get back to bed and to sleep. Wake up to pee twice more but sleep through till eleven, then feel totally and utterly fucked. Thank God it's a bank holiday.

Get out of bed but can barely get to the kitchen to pour a beer. Preoccupied by thoughts of mortality so drink beer to take my mind off it but it doesn't work, so try to think who else in the world is my age. Mind goes blank. In desperation google Jeremy Clarkson and discover he's 50. *Only 50 – Jesus!* Try to cheer myself with thought that all he does is write stupid crap about cars while I'm deep into the magnum opus. But it doesn't work at all and sink into deep depression and have another beer.

3.15 p.m.

Fall asleep over a Midsomer Murders repeat.

Wake up an hour later wondering if anyone in the whole of human history has ever stayed awake through an entire episode of Midsomer Murders. Also wonder if I usually pee as often as I did yesterday.

Tuesday 6th April

Gordon Brown announces date of general election will be 6th May.

Gordon and I go way back, of course. Well, Sarah and I, really. Ten years at least, to when I was working with Piers Morgan on the Mirror. I loved Piers, he obviously realized I was multi-talented but chronically undervalued because he gave me a rich variety of work. One day he'd get me doing op-ed pieces about the broken society, the next I was standing in for whichever of the 3am girls was indisposed at the time. Fantastic. They had this Wicked Whispers column which I was ace at, though I say it myself. Witty gossipy bits like "Which ageing female pop star prefers dating boys her son's age? Does she think it's something to Shout about???" And "Which Scottish Chancellor of the Exchequer's curvacious wife likes starting the day by sticking her fingers in her husband's till???" Piers liked the first but said the second one was tasteless and childish. I gave him a bit of straight-talking about the Swiftian power of comedy and added that if he wanted to be an establishment toady I fucking didn't. All water off a duck's back. So I went on about journalistic integrity and he listened with that pursed little smile that makes you think he's desperate for a pee. The only reason he gave in was because one of the 3am girls had just set him up with a D-list celeb's sister and he was desperate to get away.

When I bumped into Sarah at a Woman Of The Year do several years later I asked her if she remembered my little jibe.

"I've no idea what you're talking about," she said icily, and turned her back on me.

I was struck by her rear view (not literally). I polished off my glass of tasteless 10 per cent proof Chenin Blanc (very Woman of the Year) and set off after her. I caught her up as she was trying to avoid Esther Rantzen, and said I'd always thought she was an attractive woman and Gordon must be really busy nowadays and did she fancy lunch?

"No thank you," she said, in an even icier tone than before.

I suppose that should have been that. But indignation added something to the way she walked and I just stood there transfixed by her furious arse as she strode off. She clearly sensed something because she quickly turned round and saw me staring awestruck at the space where a second before her glorious posterior had been, and in a now triple-icy tone asked me what I was staring at. "I've always liked a bit of meat on a woman," I said, without even thinking.

Over the years I've found complete honesty can often achieve in moments with a woman what weeks of wining and dining fail to do. And after all even a future prime minister's wife is still a woman, and surely longs to be admired and flattered just like the rest of her sex. So part of me expected Sarah to become putty in my hands, just like the fifty-year-old binge-eating divorcee I befriended at Notting Hill Nando's a few months back.

I have to admit I misjudged the situation. When I picked myself up off the floor and asked if I could interview her for a piece for the Guardian about gender politics and New Labour she snarled and said something that was probably Scottish and she'd got from Gordon, but I certainly didn't understand.

Anyway, that's enough of the political background stuff. Back to the big news of the day!

Actually, Gordon's announcement has been predicted by everyone in the world so there's absolutely nothing to say about it. But I phone all my children (except for the DNA one, who's too young to vote) to remind them not to vote Labour on any account and if they have even a flicker of doubt not to forget the following –

1 *They took us to war in Iraq*
2 *They're hypocritical class traitors who don't really care about the poor (eg me) at all*
3 *If they had any real belief in equality they'd have banned private education years ago*
4 *They're still up the bankers' arses whatever they pretend*
5 *The third runway at Heathrow will really screw up my idyllic bit of village London.*

None of them answers, so I leave messages.

Then go for a delightful constitutional around the aforementioned idyllic bit of village London. A characterful tucked away corner of west London with ready access to the West End by tube and bus, it's so authentically villagey it even has a villagey name – Brook Green. Full of Telegraph readers of course, all no doubt scenting victory. But as I pass them in the street we exchange polite smiles and nod vaguely, just like they do in the country (so I'm told). And at least they're tasteful and cultured and discreetly hide their Sky dishes from view in much the same way as they wouldn't dream of banging on about their hideous political views. As I stroll along the peaceful early Victorian streets I try to put politics and social injustice out of my mind and focus on nicer things. I wonder whether once my magnum opus is a best seller I could revive interest in my travel guides to places I've never visited. Maybe I'll be able to use my new success to rejig them as travel guides to places you'd never *want* to visit. Just the thing for staycation post-recession Britain, surely. They'd also make excellent apps for the growing number of twelve-year-old book-phobic wankers I see on the tube and on buses (thanks to my trusty freedom pass) prodding away at their iPhones and Blackberries.

As I turn back into my road I see a couple of them sitting outside the Galloping Gastro. Two smartly dressed young chaps with fags in their mouths, squinting through the smoke as they tap away, doubtless members of the front line of David Cameron's toffs for Britain campaign. Either that or they're texting daddy to ask for a few thou to see them through the rest of the week.

Not for the first time I wonder why I drink there. But I'm determined to avoid negative thoughts and force a friendly smile. One of them gives me a pained look and hands me a couple of quid. I give him a deeply affronted look, on the point of telling him exactly what I think of him and of his Cameronian bum-chum. But the bum-chum notices and looks uneasy and scrabbles in his wallet and gives me a fiver and a nervous smile. "Now fuck off grandad, OK old chap?"

I am so shocked that a rare thing happens – I'm speechless. As it happens I do have grandchildren. Four of them. (At least). And I adore them and they're the apples of my eye. But I don't *see* myself as a grandad.

Perhaps it's a generational thing. After all, my father was a natural grandad. He looked like a grandad years before he was one. And I'm sure *his* father looked like one even earlier, at birth probably. But it's not just that. It's a fashion thing, too. I mean neither of them wore jeans. Or T-shirts or trainers. I mean *ever.*

The question is – which came first, the generational or the jeans thing? No one will ever know. But in my opinion 60-year-old wit Martin Amis was spot on when he cut through the crap and wisely said that being a grandfather is seriously uncool.

Anyway, I'm so shocked by this insult that I forget to stick the seven pounds right up the young men's condescending public school arses and continue on my way. By the time I remember, it would be too embarrassing to go back (plus there's an element of redistribution of wealth involved too).

As I approach my modest ground-floor flat another shock awaits me. I see something in the next door ground floor window.

It's a Tory poster. Unbelievable! Don't they know that people round here are too tasteful to put up posters that publicly proclaim their monstrously reactionary views? And how the hell did they get hold of one so quickly?

I look at it again...Oh my God...Yes I'm right. The Tory candidate is *black*. What's happening with the world?! A black Conservative candidate! What's the thinking behind that? Does the devious Etonian scumbag who's hoping to take over this country think that liberal guilt in this leafy enclave is so pervasive that even Labour and Lib Dem voters will flock to a Tory candidate if he's black? Or perhaps he's right. Or perhaps – most disturbing thought of all – Tories really *do* like black people nowadays. I feel out of date and irrelevant. All my hard-earned certainties are crumbling. If I can't cling to the prejudices I've nurtured all these years, what's left of me? Perhaps the world has just passed me by and I've failed to notice!

I struggle to get indoors to hide from this threatening new Britain. As I double-lock the front door the phone rings. Maybe it's one of the kids returning my call! God that'd be even more extraordinary than having a black Tory candidate! If I get any more shocks today, I'll have a heart attack and die without having time to leave anything for posterity after all (except for the kids and grandkids of course).

"Hi, this is Wills. How are you keeping?"

Wills is my oldest and dearest friend. We go way back. All the way back to Time Out in 1974 in fact, to the early days of that bourgeois distraction feminism, when you had to be *really* careful what you said. "Hi, Cuntface," I say. "I'm fine."

"No you're not, you're not fine, I can tell."

"OK. I'm in deep trauma."

"Me too."

What's going on? We don't talk about his problems – that's what makes the friendship work! The deal is I'm the one with spunk and integrity, which always makes life difficult for me (entirely true), while Wills has sold out more times than I've had hot totty and as a direct result has done a million times better professionally. Put it like this: he's quite rightly guiltily in awe of my integrity, and as conscience money I generously let him buy lunch. It works really well.

"So are you still on for tomorrow?" he asks.

"Look do you want to hear about my fucking trauma or not?!"

"Tomorrow, yes. Got to go now. See you then."

Before I can say anything he puts the phone down. Like I

just said, I adore Wills and he's my oldest and dearest friend and I'd trust him with my life, but it's amazing how quickly you can go off someone.

Wednesday 7th April

8 a.m.

Get up and turn on the radio. Silence. The battery's run out. This cheers me up because it means I won't have to find an excuse not to listen to the smug public school bastards on the Today programme (NB – I exempt my old mate John Humphrys, who left school at 15 just like me. Johnno and I were educated the hard way, dragged up through the gritty unforgiving school of journalistic hard knocks. An unbeatable apprenticeship which made us what we are today. We sometimes laugh about how much we have in common! Both prickly, both uncompromising!)

Anyway, haven't been up this early for ages and don't plan to make a habit of it. But the black Tory poster kept me awake half the night. Spent most of the time wondering if the ugly bridge-playing Tory lesbian next door put it up to get back at me. Maybe she heard me yelling at her dogs to shut the fuck up the other day when I thought she was out.

But why would she assume putting up a Tory poster would annoy me? How could she know what my politics are?

Ponder this over pleasant breakfast of pitta bread and syrup washed down with Gold Blend and condensed milk (forgot to make proper list for last Tesco shop), and come to the conclusion that I might just *look* a little bit left wing.

This thought cheers me even more than not being able to listen to the Today programme. *Even though I'm 61, maybe I don't look like a Tory!*

I get dressed in my usual clothes and have a look in the mirror to check.

Decide that must be it. But which bit of my attire in particular alerted her? Is it the jeans? Though my Dad and his Dad never wore jeans, surely lots of Tories do nowadays? Or is it the fact that they're *torn jeans?* But don't lots of Tories wear torn jeans too? The only difference being that in my case they're torn because they're old, not as a decadent upper-class SamCam-type fashion statement.

Finally decide that the obvious explanation is probably the right one. It's most likely my "DICK CHENEY – Before He Dicks You!" T-shirt that alerted her – though I could perfectly well be wearing it ironically.

If I'm right, it's further evidence to confirm my life-long theory that Tories don't have a sense of humour (except for Peter Cook. And Keith Floyd, come to think of it. And a few other of my heroes too, unfortunately).

It immediately strikes me there's an article in this. (In the looking-left-or-right-wing bit, not the still-not-quite-proven lack of sense of humour bit). Decide to pitch it to Wills when I see him for lunch. It'll be great for the new lifestyle-cum-gossip mag he's secretly developing for that Russian guy Lebedev. A mixture of fashion and left-wing politics – perfect!

12.35 p.m.

Am about to set off to meet Wills up west when I realize I haven't got my freedom pass. Disaster. I look everywhere but can't find it. (It's at times like this I really regret not being in a relationship – if I was I could blame her for tidying it away). Finally find it under pile of unopened mail.

Glance at the dates on the unopened mail and realize I haven't used the freedom pass for several weeks. Which means

I haven't left my hood (which I ironically call my delightful bit of village London) for several weeks.

Ask myself if this is good or bad. Am I living the life of the mind or just rotting?

I think again about my hero Peter Cook, of whom it was said in his later years that he never travelled further than the nearest off-licence or newsagent unless it was vitally necessary. Is his a good or a bad example? Finally decide it's a rare example of contentment with one's lot and with the small pleasures of life from which we could all learn a considerable amount.

Am on my way out again when I remember Peter Cook was an unfit overweight alcoholic who died at 58.

3 years younger than me!

Promise myself I will run down the down escalator at Shepherds Bush tube and up the up one at Covent Garden, and not drink too much at lunch. Then remember Covent Garden doesn't have escalators only a lift, and how can I not drink too much as Wills is buying?

Am finally leaving the flat when an election pamphlet pops through the letter box. The first since Gordon's anti-climactic announcement yesterday. It's a smaller version of the black Tory poster next door!

Decide radical action is called for. Means I'll be late for Wills but have learnt that at certain times in life the political has to take precedence over the personal. You have to stand up and be counted. I find the crayons I once bought for the grandchildren (can't remember why, a drunken burst of sentimentality I guess), and a sheet of A4 and draw a big thick red triangle on it like they do on the road signs. Then in black letters I print – "WARNING – TORIES AT LARGE!" and sellotape it to the living room window in roughly the same place as the ugly bridge-playing lesbian's poster next door.

Am really late now, but once I'm in the street can't resist stepping back to inspect my work.

Brilliant.

It's good to feel politically engaged again. Feel so invigorated that I even remember to run down the down escalator at Shepherds Bush. And get off at Leicester Square instead of Covent Garden or Holborn because it's further away than both and run all the way up the up escalator without stopping.

Have terrible stitch and feel like shit. Pause to get rid of stitch and reflect that I've already lived four years longer than Peter Cook, so clearly my lifestyle is better than his, so decide not to overdo draconian fitness regime and get taxi (that I can't afford) to Joe Allen, the mildly trendy Covent Garden eaterie where Wills and I always meet.

1.25 p.m.

As I walk down the steps into the familiar subterranean gloom I get the comforting feeling I always do. A bit like going back to the womb (I imagine). And a lot like returning to somewhere that has hardly changed since the 70s – just like me!

Guiltily realize I'm twenty-five minutes late. But it's just a passing twinge. After all I'm always late for Wills. I reckon he'd be disappointed if I was on time – it'd mean I'd become as boringly conventional and suburban as him.

As I approach our usual table I'm taken aback that he doesn't instantly leap up and come and high-five me in the middle of the room – our customary amusingly ironic form of greeting.

In fact, he's not even at the table. And I start to feel pissed off.

"Hi Arnie – over here!"

I pretend I haven't heard him and sit down and look at the menu.

"*Hey! Arnie!* Come and meet Trevor!"

Am now starting to feel distinctly jangly. If I have a fault it's that I do like routine and familiarity, and I freely confess I might not be quite as good at change as I should be. Lifelong radical and subversive though I am, the unexpected does tend to bring me out in a sweat. Some people might say – indeed certain of my ex-wives have said – that this is a problem. But some people are insensitive twats – specially ex-wives – and my answer is always that Peter Cook was even more routine-bound than me.

I quickly do the deep-breathing exercises my third wife's yoga teacher taught me while we were having our little fling, and start to feel calmer. I peer over the menu and see Wills is standing a couple of tables away chatting to a mephistophelian looking man with a beard and a long black wig (very Joe Allen – probably an extra in "Wicked").

Wills sees me peering at him and grins and bounces over. "What's the problem? Why did you ignore me? I wanted you to come and meet Trevor!"

"Who's Trevor?"

"Trevor Nunn!"

"Who's Trevor Nunn?"

"You're kidding me? Actually he's only an amazingly famous theatre director!"

I hate the theatre because it's elitist rubbish so I'm none the wiser. But Wills *is* my oldest and dearest friend and I don't want to spoil his obvious excitement, it's sweet really, so I play along and smile as if I've just remembered who he's talking about. "Yeah of course. He directed 'Wicked', didn't he?"

"No of course he didn't direct 'Wicked'. But he's directed virtually everything else! And he ran the National and the RSC and –"

"The what?"

Wills stares at me. Even after all these years he's not quite sure when I'm taking the piss. This is the great thing about being cleverer than your best mate, it's so easy to wind him up. "OK," he says patiently, "you've heard of Andrew Lloyd Webber? Well he's directed loads of his stuff."

Now I know who he's talking about. Sir Trevor of Chiswick. Lots of wives and shitloads of money. "So why are you talking to him?"

"Because we're mates."

This upsets me. "*I'm* your mate, Wills."

"Yes, of course you are! But he's my *new* mate. Didn't I tell you? We met at Lebedev's garden party last week."

"*Last week?* Who has garden parties in March?!"

"Lebedev does. Well he's Russian, you see. He's not quite got the hang of things yet."

"I do know he's Russian, Wills." I have to stop myself reminding him that *I* was the one who taught him about Russia in the first place. I remember explaining to him in '74 about Lenin and Kerensky and what a fucking samovar was. This was before Time Out sold out and turned into another meaningless consumer magazine and it still required some political commitment from its contributors. (Or the pretence of it, in Wills's case).

"Why are you being so tetchy? Are you jealous?"

I don't deign to answer this. "Why did you call me Arnie in front of him? You know I hate being called Arnie!"

Will smiles. "Oh I *see*... Because you're my oldest and dearest friend and I really wanted Trevor to be aware of that right from the start, and I thought calling you Arnold might make it sound like we didn't know each other as well as we do. Sorry!"

That's the thing about Wills. He might be bourgeois and thick and an even worse arse-licker than John Humphrys, but sometimes he just takes my breath away with his simple warmth and openness and emotional generosity. To be frank, he can make me feel a bit of a cunt.

At that moment I'm distracted by the sight of Trevor getting up from his table. I watch as he adjusts his hair and prepares to leave and murmurs something through his suspiciously black beard at the hot-looking blonde he's been having lunch with. She might well be his beautiful third wife Imogen Stubbs who I recall reading about recently online (probably in "E! Online" or "People.com" while doing in-depth research for new markets for my work). On the other hand, she might not be.

"Of course she is!" Wills indignantly assures me. He's such a romantic.

Trevor catches sight of Wills and me staring at him and waves and blows a kiss and puts his arm round the hot blonde, wife or not, and drifts off with her. Probably to have a sexy afternoon plastering each other with his thanks-to-Andrew-Lloyd-Webber millions.

"No I'm *not* jealous," I say, "about anyone!"

By the time Wills and I have necked a couple of litres of the vino reddo de la maison things between us are getting back to normal. We don't even mention the election.

"So what have you been up to since I saw you last?" Wills asks.

"Apart from wanking, you mean?" I pause and wait for him to laugh. One of us always does the wanking joke – usually me. We've been doing it since '74, it's one of our little rituals. When he's finished laughing I carry on. "Not a lot," I say. I'm not going to tell him about my magnum opus, oldest friend or not. Bitter experience has taught me that you can trust your nearest and dearest *too* much. "But I've got a great idea for a piece for that heap-of-shit fashion-cum-gossip magazine you're developing for Lebedev. Want to hear it?"

"Oh right..." he says vaguely. "Well, to be perfectly honest I'm not sure I –"

"OK I'll tell you." So I launch into the story about the lesbian and the Tory poster and my Dick Cheney T-shirt (which I'm still wearing – just to prove I'm not making it up!) but instead of being amused and engrossed like he's meant to, he starts looking fidgety and embarrassed. So I go straight to the pitch – how it's going to be a witty but hard-hitting piece about the subtly hidden politics of clothes. Then when even that doesn't clinch it I add that if it's too lightweight I can chuck in stuff about the sickness of western materialism and the decline of capitalism that an old Commie like Lebedev will just love.

"Actually, I'm not sure that Alexander really sees himself as a communist."

"Who?"

"Mr Lebedev. And as he happens to be a billionaire he might not be quite as keen on the decline of capitalism angle as you imagine."

"Picky, picky, picky."

He looks ashamed, as well he might. "You're right, I'm sorry! You're a million times better read than me and know so much more about politics and stuff, it's just –"

"Thank you." I sit back in my chair and smile tolerantly. "So you'll commission it?"

"I'd love to – in theory – yes of course."

"Great!" I wave at a waiter to order another litre of the house poison to celebrate. Usually when I pitch Wills an idea he says it's brilliant and intelligent and fantastic, but unfortunately just *too* brilliant and intelligent and fantastic for the crappy standards of Pantyhose Weekly or Beautiful Brides or whichever rag he happens to be prostituting himself on at the time. So this is progress at least.

The waiter doesn't seem to see me so I wave again. But he's clearly got macular degeneration because he looks right through me.

"The trouble is..." says Wills. "Look you remember the trauma I mentioned yesterday?"

"What trauma?"

"I mentioned it to you on the phone."

It does ring a very faint bell. "Yes of course – brilliant!"

"It's not brilliant. To be honest, I've been having a little problem with Lebedev."

I nod sympathetically. This works well, so I add a smile then an understanding chuckle. "Well, what I always say is, if it's only little, why worry about it?"

For some reason he looks irritated. "Because it's not little really, Arnold!"

"Then why did you say it was?"

"Have you been listening properly to what I've just said?"

"Of course I have."

"*Good.* The point is I might have to move on."

"Move on?" Jesus, you can't trust anyone any more. They all betray you in the end – why do I never learn? "What about my article?!"

"I'm really sorry, Arnold, but if I'm not working there, I can hardly publish it, can I?"

I feel the sweaty panicky feeling coming on and try the deep-breathing exercises again. Wills looks worried and pours the last dregs of the carafe into my glass, which helps. "Look, Wills, OK you find this Lebedev guy difficult but you've got to try to see it from his point of view. The poor bastard's completely out of his depth, stuck in a foreign country with no English and no friends and nothing to do –"

"Actually, he speaks perfect English and he's got a private jet."

"Picky, picky, picky. I'm just saying it's understandable if he's difficult. We all know how moody Russians are, look at Chekhov! But for Christ's sake he does his best. He invites you to his garden party – he introduces you to the guy who did 'Wicked' – doesn't that mean anything? Don't you feel any loyalty at all? What about love thy neighbour? And all the other stuff we heard when we went to church that time with Richard Ingrams when we were trying to get that first gig on Private Eye?"

Wills looks chastened. "You think I should stay?"

I shrug, suddenly weary. I can see the first commission I've ever got from him floating off to join the million other polite refusals on his reject pile.

He avoids my gaze and waves at the waiter, who sees Wills immediately and hurries off to get another carafe.

Wills turns back to me, smiling apologetically. "The thing is, it's too late. I've already accepted another job."

The waiter returns and I quickly fill both our glasses, while Wills just keeps smiling his sickening smile at me. "But what I can say is, I can really give you work this time. Really I can. Promise."

I don't answer.

"Did you hear me, Arnold?"

I know he hates me ignoring him.

"Arnold...?"

I stare into the middle-distance. Which turns out to be exactly where Sir Trev was sitting. But now Dawn French is there. At least I think it's Dawn French. And she stares straight back at me. I give her a smile and a playful wink as it crosses my mind she must be desperate for it now Lenny's gone. For a moment I forget about Wills – which is easily done – and wonder if I should get up and saunter over and tell her about the black Tory poster. I'm sure she'd laugh herself stupid over it. Either that or she'd kick me in the bollocks. It's hard to tell with these alternative so-called comedians. What the hell. She's still looking at me, and she's smiling now, definitely smiling, so I grin again and raise my eyebrows and she does that sexy pretend-disgusted grimace she does and snorts with laughter and looks away and I know she's really up for it, no question. I start to get up.

"Arnold please..."

"Get lost."

"Look, you've got red wine over your mouth and chin and it's dripping over your T-shirt. I don't want to interfere but why don't you go to the lav and see if you can wash it off?" He looks over to where I was looking and waves. "Hi, Dawn! Hi! Great to see you!"

3.40 p.m.

Stand in Joe Allen's gents and stare into the mirror as I scrub at my wine-stained T-shirt with a wet hankie. I scrub really hard. In the end I'm left with a wet stain all the way down the T-shirt and the red wine stains are just as visible.

I return to the table and see Wills is standing chatting and giggling with Dawn French and Jennifer Saunders. He waves for me to come over but I ignore him and sit down and pretend to be engrossed in the menu. I try to blot out the gales of laughter that come wafting over from the three of them. Thank God I'm not a shameless sycophant like Wills. Having to force himself to laugh at so-called jokes from their latest so-called sitcom probably.

Eventually Wills comes back, chuckling to himself.

"What's so funny?"

This sets him off again. I patiently wait till he stops. "I suppose you met them at Lebedev's garden party too, did you?"

"No. Actually, I met them at a little welcoming party for my new job."

Something very worrying has happened to Wills. In the old days he was just like me, he only wanted to meet famous people if they were famous for changing the world, like Arthur Scargill (well trying to change it, in his case). Or perhaps he was lying to me all along, because he's the ultimate starfucker now, the sort of person who behaves as if rubbing shoulders with the famous actually validates your personality! Still, if your personality is as non-existent as his then it very well might.

"So what *is* the new job?" I ask politely. "And what sort of work are you intending to offer me?" I smile wearily to show how profoundly uninterested I am.

"Look I don't want to bore you. Anyway I've got to go in a tick, Dawn and Jen asked if they could pop into my new office and –"

"Just tell me what you're fucking working on!"

"Sudoku Weekly."

I give him a look.

"Dawn and Jen love Sudoku, you see, in fact they're obsessed by it, that's how come we met at the –"

"Do you seriously think I'm so desperate for work I'd be interested in making up *Sudoku puzzles?* Do you not know anything about me at all, Wills? Do you? For God's sake what have we talked about together all these years?!"

"You mainly."

"What did you say?!"

He grins. "Just joking! Anyway got to go! Don't worry I paid the bill while you were in the lav." He waves at Dawn and Jennifer. "OK girls – coming!"

"Girls?!"

"See you next Wednesday, Arnold." And before I can work out something really cutting to say he's up and off with his new so-called friends.

"You certainly will not!" I shout, but he's too busy laughing sycophantically with the much-loved comedy duo, and doesn't seem to hear.

4.25 p.m.

Plough my way through the manically jolly throng in Covent Garden piazza, appalled as ever by humanity's insatiable appetite for junk food, fizzy drinks, anything it can stuff down its disgusting throat. Buy a 99 at the Mr Whippy van because we didn't get round to having usual chocolate pudding and ice cream at Joe Allen's, then pick up billionaire Lebedev's free Evening Standard and start reading it going down the lift at Covent Garden tube. Young woman tells me to stop nudging her with my flake, and I wittily respond that I wouldn't nudge her with my flake if she paid me, whereupon a large boyfriend appears and takes remains of 99 and threatens to stick it in my face. Decide he's part of the lumpen proletariat that Marx was so dismissive of, and that reason and logic will be wasted, so say "Please keep the 99 I've had enough anyway," then stand back to make sure they get out of the lift before me. Am so determined not to enter into a vulgar fracas that the lift door shuts again, and I have to go up and down in the lift again.

At last walk to the platform. Unfortunately, the lumpen proletariat couple are still there, so stand back and wait for them to get on the next train, then at the last minute run up to the far end of the platform and get on too.

All this excitement takes my mind off treacherous friend Wills, and I fall asleep on the tube and dream about David Niven (another hero) becoming Prime Minister at the election, much to Gordon Brown's and David Cameron's fury. In the dream everyone (except them) loves him and he's the most popular PM in history because he's so urbane and witty, just like me. In reality nearly miss my stop.

Walk past the Galloping Gastro on way home reading

Lebedev's Standard. Delighted to see that Lib Dem leader Nick Clegg has said that voting either Labour or Conservative would be a "vote for corrupt policies". Think how amazing – someone in British politics who tells the truth at last! Perhaps I won't vote for Respect after all.

So engrossed in Nick Clegg story that almost step in pile of dog shit outside my front door. I mean *right* outside my front door. Calculate that no dog would voluntarily reverse right into my doorway to take a dump, so conclude that human agent is responsible. But who?

I ask myself who has a motive and a dog or dogs.

Yes, it was clearly the ugly bridge-playing lesbian next door in a childish bit of tit for tat.

I step past the dog shit and go indoors. This is war.

I look for something to scoop it up. Can only find Teflon spaghetti server with slots in it for water to drain through. Using this it takes several journeys to move the pile of dog shit from my front doorstep onto next door's. Am really impressed that none of it slips through the slots and wonder whether to write to Teflon to congratulate them on the versatility of their product.

Decide against it while washing spaghetti server and pondering whether to vote Lib Dem or not.

5.45 p.m.

Google "Trevor Nunn how old" *He's 70!!!* And still wearing cool jeans (forgot to mention that earlier) and denim jacket (ditto) and pulling sexy blondes (even if it is his wife, about which I reserve judgement).

Put him down as my new hero, partly because unlike most of my other heroes he's still alive. Work out I have nine years left to become like him. Bit of a stretch, but who knows?

Fall asleep watching Deal Or No Deal and have disturbed Joe-Allen induced dreams. So often like this when I go to Joe Allen with Wills – toxic mixture of minor celebrities and house reddo and Wills trying to show off and impress me.

Dream about David Niven running the country and showing his impressive penis to world leaders.

Wake up feeling disturbed and wondering if it means I'm gay. Have a headache and get three Nurofen Plus, and as I swallow them see David Niven's photo beaming up at me from my bedside table. It's on the cover of a biography I'd forgotten I was reading, which goes into his penis in some depth, so to speak. Relief that I'm not gay is mixed with anxiety in case my magnum opus isn't as successful as the urbane and (according to the biog) enormously well-endowed Niven's "The Moon's A Balloon". Google him. Work out he was 61 when it was published. *Sixty-one – the same age as me! Fantastic!*

Read on and get depressed because it took him years to write and I've only just started and if I'm not careful I'll be as old as Trev by the time it's a bestseller. (NB – looking on the bright side, if seriously decrepit by then could buy long black wig, it clearly works wonders).

Back to Niven's penis. Can I do something with it?

7.20 p.m.

Write letter to Lebedev about proposed Niven article.

Dear Mr Lebedev,

As a fellow ex-commie and newspaper junkie, you'll no doubt know my work, but I attach a CV in case it's slipped your mind. As you can see, it ranges all the way from my famous hate-filled pieces for the Mail on Sunday to the more recent "How To Be A Left-Wing Mum" series in Woman's Own (sadly cancelled after the first article). Your ex-employee Wills Gradley tells me you're secretly developing a new glossy lifestyle-cum-gossip magazine. What a great thing to do in a period of financial and political uncertainty! Are you by any chance looking for material? Are you in the market for celebrity-themed articles with a touch of sauciness? If you are, I've got one that might be just the job.

PS It's about a dead celebrity, but I hope that isn't a problem. Believe me, it'll really appeal to the older demographic who are sadly sidelined in the current glossy mag market (specially in the area of harmless sexual innuendo) and I can assure you are desperate for this sort of thing. Not all of us are brain-dead pricks who only read OK and Hello!

7.40 p.m.

Write celebrity-themed article for Lebedev magazine (and a modified version for Saga magazine too, just in case).

Dead but still sparkling

Dead though he sadly is, David Niven lives on. Twinkly and witty and charming without being creepy, he was compulsively unfaithful and effortlessly pulled women throughout his life, even when "happily" married. Clearly an example that any healthy but not-quite-so-young red-blooded bloke would be desperate to emulate!
So how did he do it?

What was his secret?
Simple, I hear you say. It was the legendary wit and charm and sophistication and an enormous fund of hilariously funny stories.
There is, however, another possible explanation.
The actor Patrick Macnee (former Avengers star, now a scary 88) claims the real secret of his old friend Niv's success was the eye-watering size of his member, which Macnee chanced to catch sight of when they were filming together one day. Enviably lacking in actor's ego, Macnee describes it as about three times the size of his own appendage – i.e. one foot long and enormously wide. "And it's the width that matters, you know," he adds wisely.
At this point I must pause to ask something many of you might be thinking. Is this of anything other than prurient interest? Why tarnish the memory of a much-loved star and archetypal English gentleman with tacky talk about the size of his penis? Is this the inevitable consequence of too much reality TV and a general decline in moral standards? Is the Daily Mail right after all?

Above all, does it in any way help the over-sixties in their quest to work out how to get old properly, or even better improperly? (Note to editor – the last sentence is only for Saga magazine).
One might well think that however much we might all yearn (well, half of us) to possess a member of such imposing proportions, the sad reality is there's not a lot one can do if one has, so to speak, drawn the short straw.
But as so often in life, the truth is more complicated. Men and women everywhere adored him and found his company irresistible even when they knew nothing about his special

secret. But why? What made him so poised and irresistible, even when well past his prime?

After a quick look through the works of Sigmund Freud, I suggest David Niven possessed a profound inner confidence that came from the knowledge that wherever he went his magnificent tool would come bobbing along too, an ever-loyal source of psychic reassurance.

The lesson is surely clear. Even if no longer in our first flush, we all need a secret something to give us that extra boost to help us through the difficult times – whether it's a particularly large trouser snake or a small but reassuring drug habit or even a building society account the wife knows nothing about.

To each his own. The secret is immaterial.

11.50 p.m.

Read through finished article and enjoy warm satisfied glow. Decide to send article off right away before warm satisfied glow vanishes. So print letter, do different version for Saga mag, print that, print two copies of article, google Lebedev and Saga and write addresses on envelopes and find last two first-class stamps I possess and stick them on and set off to post letters.

11.59 p.m.

Skid in fresh heap of dog shit right outside front door and fall over nearly breaking back, while letters land in nearby picturesque Brook Green puddle.

Lie on ground, enraged. Get up, grab sodden letters and go back in flat and grab spaghetti server and return to scene of crime and scrape up remains of pile of dog shit and run to next door's window and hurl it as hard as can at black Tory poster.

Spatters satisfyingly all over Tory candidate's smug over-fed face. Feel better at once.

"What on earth are you doing?" comes a posh voice from behind. I spin around, to see the ugly bridge-playing Tory lesbian descending indignantly from a taxi, furiously lugging her tartan luggage while her three dogs leap out after her and stand yapping at me accusingly.

I'm surrounded.

Realize this could be tricky.

Thursday 8th April

Here's the good news. Once I've got a bowl of hot soapy water and washed all the crap off next door's window, the ugly bridge-playing Tory lesbian turns out to be OK after all. Wouldn't go so far as to say she actually admired my political activism, but once we'd had a little chat she was quite understanding. Turns out she's a libertarian Tory and professed herself outraged by anything that tries to suppress freedom of speech, e.g. crapping dog outside front door.

The bad news is I'm going to have to stop calling her the ugly bridge-playing Tory lesbian. One, because she plays poker, not bridge. Two, because she insists we should be on first name terms. The reason being – wait for this – that we're neighbours!

Her name is Lizzie.

Lizzie also insists that as a libertarian Tory it's her public duty to do all she can to help me track down the phantom crapper and its owner.

What a turn up for the books. Lizzie the Lezzie and I are mates. Whatever next!

Maybe a new spirit of village-London neighbourliness has taken root in my soul and is about to blossom forth, astonishing everyone.

And maybe I'll take up fucking basket-weaving.

1.15 p.m.

Wake up on sofa to sound of phone ringing and Nick Berry on ITV3 dressed as a 1960s policeman talking to the man who had his hand up Basil Brush (Derek Fowlds – just googled "Basil Brush Heartbeat" to check). Briefly wonder if Nick Berry is related to John Nettles because they share similar breadth of expression and histrionic versatility, but my musings are disturbed by the phone ringing.

"Why aren't you here?"

It's my wonderful, talented, beautiful daughter Alice. She's 33 and the apple of my eye. I know you shouldn't have favourites, but I just can't help it. Maybe it's because she's creative like me. "Hello darling, great to hear your dulcet tones. So what gives?"

"Why aren't you here?"

"Why do you keep saying that? Why aren't I where?"

"At the snobby little local you seem to like so much…"

She's got the same sense of humour as me too, that's another reason we get on so well. "Why should I be? Look I don't live there, you know!"

"Because we arranged to meet at one, and it's one-fifteen."

"Oh shit."

"And I've got a meeting at two-thirty and it takes me ten minutes to get back, so unless you …"

"Be right there, baby!"

"Please don't call me baby. Not even in fun."

I decide I'd better look my best for my darling daughter so I take off my "Dick Cheney – Before He Dicks You!" T-shirt (actually it's getting a bit whiffy, not to mention the wine stain) and put on a brand new T-shirt in her honour. Then dash off up the road to the Galloping Gastro.

And there she is, crouched over her Blackberry tapping away like there's no tomorrow, her usual Diet Coke by her side. I come over and she half gets up and I give her a kiss and a hug and wonder, like I always do, why she doesn't respond a little more enthusiastically. Still, we all have our faults, and she's adorable even so, so I give her another hug before she manages to wriggle away and I wave at Michelle behind the bar. "The usual, darling, OK?!"

I settle opposite Alice and beam at her. She gives her usual uptight smile back. "How are the kids?"

"They're great thank you Dad."

"And the BBC?"

"Oh, you know..." She makes an unhappy face. It's funny how everyone I've ever known who works for the BBC does the same face. I'm talking about creatives of course. Don't know whether it's embarrassment at being paid so much to do sod-all or embarrassment at being a lickspittle of the establishment. Still, the great thing is, it makes me realize I was so right to have backed off and let John Humphrys get the Today job all those years back. Not that I ever really doubted it, I mean poor old Johnno was so desperate I'd have needed a heart of steel to stand in his way. But just occasionally, like when I'm lying there unable to sleep at three in the morning worrying that I've got no pension and no money and no career, I do wonder if things might have been easier if I'd been a little more ruthless, and also how much Johnno gets paid for crap like Mastermind.

"So what are you working on at the moment?" I ask her. "Is it still the Dr Who spin-off where the Dalek gets married to Zoe Wanamaker?"

"No no that's gone into turnaround."

"Oh, right. By the way, what happened to my comedy-drama idea about the new Respect MP for Surbiton?"

"It wasn't funny, Dad – it was rubbish."

"It would have been funny if you'd got Caroline Quentin to do it."

"No it wouldn't, it was embarrassing."

"Did you actually *show* it to anyone?"

"I didn't need to, it was awful!"

I don't pursue the matter. What's the point? In fact, I only mention it as yet another example of the artistic and political censorship that's so prevalent at the BBC. And from my own supposedly left-wing daughter!

To be fair, she's got a lot on her plate. Not just kow-towing to the repressive powers-that-be but juggling a "successful" career with bringing up two kids – by different dads! – all on her own.

"So how's your love life?" I ask. Alice has always had a rich and varied love life, which is yet another thing we have in common. (Not that I've got a rich and varied love life at the moment, but I do usually. So I've been a positive role model for her in so many areas, which is great).

Alice doesn't answer my question but watches as Michelle brings over a bottle of Rioja and pours a glass and I take a swig and give Michelle a matey wink. I offer Alice a glass, but she shakes her head like I knew she would and takes a little sip of her Diet Coke like a silent reprimand. I refill my glass.

"You drink too much."

She sounds just like her mother so I smilingly ignore her.

"I was asking you about your love life." Now she's staring at the slogan on my T-shirt. "Do you really think that's appropriate, Dad?"

"What do you mean appropriate? It's brand new. I put it on specially for you, baby."

She reads it out. "Che Guevara wears David Cameron T-shirts."

"Yeah!"

"Is that supposed to be funny?"

"Just a bit."

"You're sixty-one, Dad."

"So?"

She looks at me for a moment, then shakes her head wearily. "Nothing."

"Have you been seeing your mum a lot recently? You sound very like her nowadays."

"So do you think your T-shirt is making a political statement of some sort?"

"Everything I do is a political statement in one way or another, Alice, don't you know that by now?"

"Then have you considered whether it's making quite the political statement you assume it is?"

You know, sometimes her condescending Oxbridge way of talking to me irritates me a tiny bit, but I love her dearly and can forgive her anything so I laugh merrily. "OK – so what do *you* think it's saying?"

She smiles at me. "It's not what I *think* it's saying, Dad, it's what it clearly *is* saying. It's saying that an Argentinian Marxist revolutionary leader who you deeply admire supports the current leader of the Conservative Party."

"No it isn't."

"I'm afraid it is."

"It isn't!"

"Of course it is. Why else would Che Guevara be wearing David Cameron T-shirts if he didn't support him?!"

"Because it's *ironic.*"

"In what way? Where exactly is the irony? I can't quite see it."

To be honest, she's *really* irritating me now. "Because it just is."

Yes, you keep saying," she smiles, "but how?"

"OK I'll tell you how! Because Che Guevara died in 1967, when David Cameron was still shitting his nappies, so he wouldn't even have known about him, would he? That's why it's ironic!"

"No, Dad, sorry, that's possibly mildly amusing, or possibly not, but how exactly is it ironic?"

"Don't keep saying *how,* it just is!"

"*Ah!* Now I understand!"

"About fucking time!"

I sit there congratulating myself on being able to hold my ground in an argument even though I left school at 15 and she went to Oxbridge. She leans forward. "By the way I do wish you wouldn't swear so much, Dad. It's very unappealing, especially in someone your age."

As I said before, Alice is my darling daughter, the apple of my eye, so I refuse to take this personally. After all, she can't help her bitchy streak, it's just part of her DNA – the part that comes from her mother. Besides, I know my lovely daughter so well I can always tell when something's going on. And today I sense a neediness in her, a vulnerability beneath the brittleness. So I smile warmly. "You OK then, baby?" I ask.

She purses her lips (just like her mum!) "Please don't call me that," she says.

"Look, I know you're angry and upset about something. But I'm your dad and any problems you've got, you've got to feel you can offload them on me. Because the bottom line is, you've only got one dad, even when you're thirty-two. And I don't want to blow my own trumpet, but I have been around the block a few times, even more than you probably, so I'm unshockable. So if there's anything you want to get off your chest I'm here for you, baby."

"I said don't!"

"Sorry."

She glares at me, then finishes her diet Coke and sniffs. I'm amazed to see something glistening in her eyes. "Actually, it's true..."

"What's true?"

"I am finding things rather difficult at the moment." Suddenly she isn't the big successful BBC producer any more, she's my baby daughter and she's crying and all I want is to look after her and keep her safe, do anything I can to protect her from whichever bastard is making her unhappy.

"Who's done this to you? It's a man, isn't it? I know it is..." I'm not entirely lacking in self-awareness – being a man myself I do understand the unhappiness they can accidentally cause sometimes.

She nods tearfully.

"Just tell me all about it."

I gently put my hand on hers, but she yanks her hand away as if I've got the pox. As I said before, I do sometimes wonder why she can't be a little more affectionate but I push this selfish thought from my mind and smile supportively. "So who is he, baby?"

"It's you."

"What?"

"I've been deeply depressed at my inability to have proper relationships with men, and it's all because of you."

"All because of me?! What's it got to do with me?" I laugh. "Anyway, *what* inability, what are you talking about, you've had lots of relationships! And I say that entirely non-judgmentally because it's great for women to sleep around when they're young – it's called sexual equality! It's brilliant!"

"In the end I got so depressed I decided to go into therapy."

I can't help laughing. *"Therapy? You didn't?!"*

"I knew you'd be sympathetic..."

"No, look," I say sympathetically, "if you want to perpetuate that tired old bourgeois lie, it's up to you, I mean if you want to blame everything on childhood trauma instead of acknowledging it's society that makes people unhappy, if that really floats your boat..."

"I told my therapist that it'd be a complete waste of time talking to you."

"I just wish I had that sort of money!" I laugh.

"But she was very insistent I should at least *try*."

I ponder this for a minute, or pretend to. "So how old is she? Is she single?"

She gives me a withering look that reminds me uncannily of her mother. "Just joking! So why is she so keen you should talk to me about it?"

She stares at me. "I just told you why."

"Did you? I must have missed it. Sorry – tell me again."

"She wants me to talk to you – or *try* to – because you're the reason I go for unsuitable, immature, emotionally unavailable men – men who aren't capable of sustaining a long-term relationship! You set the pattern! Don't you understand?! It's your fault I'm fucked up!"

God I hate women swearing. But I try not to wince because I can see she's stressed. So I sit there silently, like that shrink woman in Sopranos who listens sympathetically while Tony S rants on – just like Alice now.

After a while she runs out of hurtful things to say about me and sits sniffing and wiping her eyes. I smile and offer her my hankie, and she takes it and is about to wipe her eyes then sees it close-up and throws it to the floor in disgust. Which I call ungrateful, but I don't show my feelings and make a mental note to wash T-shirts and hankies at the same time in future.

"And another thing! My therapist told me to tell you that she'd like you to come and see her."

I give her a look. "Call me old-fashioned, but she *definitely* sounds single..."

"And she wants you to come with *me*."

"Oh I see... So is this some scam so she can charge double?"

"No it is not!"

I laugh fondly. For all her Oxbridge education and her high-flying BBC career, my little daughter can be so naïve. "Well she wouldn't *say* it was, would she, baby?!"

She just stares at me. For a moment I see something in her eyes that makes me wonder if she really likes me that much. But then it's gone.

"She wants to meet you so that we can see if you can help me sort out my fear-of-abandonment issues."

I miss most of this because I'm under the table trying to get my hankie. "What was that?"

She repeats it angrily. The funny thing is, I've always thought we shared a sense of humour – but today I'm beginning to wonder! "But don't bother," she continues icily, "I told her she was wasting her time."

"No I'd be delighted."

"What?"

"I'd be delighted to come. Of course I would!"

"*Really?*" She looks so shaken that I wonder if she'd have preferred me to say no.

I lean across the table to her and smile. "You see – maybe I'm not so immature after all!"

I wave for another bottle of Rioja and she stares at me – she really is lost for words. And just for once her Oxbridge education doesn't come to the rescue! *Result!*

Before she has a chance to start slagging me off again I ask if she got my phone message warning her who not to vote for and why.

"Yes I did."

"So who are you going to vote for?"

"It's private."

"Let me guess. Respect?"

"Don't be stupid."

"The Greens?"

She doesn't want to answer but once she's started she can't stop herself. "Of course not, they're a complete waste of a vote."

"Lib Dems?"

"Ditto."

I'm running out of alternatives. "Christ, baby – you're not going to vote *Conservative?!*"

"God no – what do you take me for?! I'd *die* rather than vote Tory!"

I can't think of anyone else – I'm stumped. "So who on earth *are* you going to vote for?"

"Labour."

Now it's my turn to stare at her, while I struggle to find

words to express my shock at her betrayal, not just of me, but of all the working class heroes who fought against privilege and wealth, like Ken Livingstone and Arthur Scargill and Tony Benn (even though he was a Lord).

In the end I get up and make a dignified exit. Well that's what I would have done, except Michelle arrives at that moment with the second bottle of Rioja and Alice has to hurry back to work. So I'm forced to stay and drown my sorrows instead.

7.40 p.m.

After leaving numerous messages on his answerphone I finally get hold of adorable oldest son, Quentin (39 and the product of my brief first marriage, Alice being the product of my brief second one).

"So who are you going to vote for, Quentin?"

"Oh no not that again, Dad."

"I *want to know.*"

"Look we're going to see Priscilla tomorrow night –"

"Who?"

"It's not a who it's a what. Priscilla Queen of the Desert. It's a show at the Palace Theatre and a chum of Adam's let us down so we've got a spare ticket. So we wondered if you'd like to come."

"Oh God no, I hate the theatre – elitist bourgeois –"

"For heaven's sake it's not theatre, Dad, not theatre *as such,* it's a *musical!*"

"Oh. OK then."

"And I'm going to vote Tory. And before you yell at me I've got to, Georgie would never forgive me if I didn't."

"Georgie?"

"Georgie Osborne, Dad – the Shadow Chancellor! – how can you pretend you don't remember? For heaven's sake you were the one who sent me to St Pauls with him, Dad!"

"Let's get this straight once and for all, I did *not* send you to St Paul's, Quentin, you know very well –!"

"Then how come I ended up there?"

"You're really winding me up here, aren't you?"

"Am I?" I can almost see his irritatingly superior grin over the phone.

"Yes you are! If I was education secretary you know very well I'd close every public school in the land! It's your mum's fault, she sent you there behind my back! *That's* why I divorced her, if you remember, because of her ideological treachery!"

"I thought it was because she left you for Horatio?"

"Well, that too, yeah. She always had a weakness for a bit of posh. Look, OK, I'm sorry if I wasn't quite as involved as I might have been as a dad..."

"Quite?" he laughs.

"Don't start getting at me – I'm having a hard time at the moment. Anyway I was *busy* when you were young – really busy!"

"Got to go now..."

"But if I'd known you'd end up best mates with the smug podgy-faced son of a tossing wallpaper tycoon I'd have pulled my finger out, believe me..."

"See you tomorrow. Bye, Dad!"

The phone goes dead.

8.25 p.m.

Have brief phone conversation with apparently ruthless but in fact adorable youngest son Roger, who's 27 and the product of brief and briefly happy third marriage (happy when I was having fling with her yoga teacher – not happy when wife found out).

"I'm voting Tory before you ask."

"Well at least it's better than voting for class traitor Brown and his war criminal cronies."

"Yes well, maybe..."

"What do you mean, Roj?"

"I mean I don't know about all that political stuff, Dad, all I know is no one votes Labour any more, it's really passé. I went to a dinner party last week and someone said they were voting Labour and they all *laughed* – I mean I'd half thought *I* might till then but after that, well *sorry!*"

I briefly wonder why my passionate political commitment hasn't rubbed off on my sons quite as much as I'd have liked, but Roger's a busy young man so I press on with our all-too-rare father-son bonding chat. "So what have you been up to, Roj?"

"Don't call me Roj, please."

"Why not?"

"Because no one called Roj would manage a highly successful hedge fund, nor would they regularly play golf with Sir Fred Goodwin and Bruce Forsyth CBE, often both at the same time I might add..."

"I'd have thought they'd be delighted to find anyone who'd play with them!"

"Ho ho, very original. Just remember it's Roger, not Roj. Got to go."

The phone goes dead.

Friday 9th April

3.10 a.m.

Wake with combined Rioja and Tesco reddo and Cointreau frappé headache and also combined feeling of panic and hopelessness and despair. Briefly wonder if the two are connected, then work out they're not. The hangover is alcohol-induced while the feeling of panic and hopelessness and despair is because am total and utter failure – as human being (specially as father) and career-wise and financially and *en passant* as political agitator too. Realize it's only my dream of world success from my magnum opus, and the women who will fall at feet as direct result, that stops me topping myself at once.

Decide to start tackling the feeling of panic and hopelessness and despair one step at a time.

First step is to get in touch with Alice's mum Daphne. One, so we can discuss our darling daughter's unhappy state and see what we can do about it. Two, because evidence of my sensitivity and concern for our daughter's wellbeing will move her deeply and she might put out. Because frankly am getting desperate, which is part of the reason for current awful feelings of P and H and especially D for despair.

3.25 a.m.

Decide am despicable even to have such thoughts.

3.26 a.m.

Decide it's worth a try though. But a bit early in the morning to phone her, so try to go back to sleep.

11.45 a.m.

Doorbell rings and wakes me. See the time and turn over to go back to sleep again. Doorbell keeps ringing.

Realize it might be registered letter from Lebedev containing contract for David Niven article and quickly get up.

Realize dressing gown was last used to mop up something I won't go into, so put on jeans and "Che Guevara wears David Cameron T-shirts" T-shirt instead. As I reach door realize it can't be letter from Lebedev because he will only have got mine today.

But too late. It's my new friend Lizzie the Lezzie. She's holding out a cup. I look inside and it's full of brown sugar. She gurgles away as if it's the funniest thing in the world. "That's what neighbours do in Coronation Street, dear, bring round cups of sugar for each other! Well so I'm told!"

"Why do they do that?"

"No idea! Some Neanderthal northern custom I assume."

"But it wouldn't be brown sugar, surely?"

"Why not? Don't they have brown sugar up there? No I suppose they don't! Anyway, you can make me a cup of tea with it if you really insist..."

I try to think of a reason why I can't but she's already gone past me into my living room.

I take ages to make it in the hope that she'll get bored and leave, but when I come back she's still there. I hand her the tea and try to look as if I'm really busy but she calmly sips it and gazes at my T-shirt. "You know I'm surprised to see you're a Cameron supporter like me, I must say I wouldn't have thought it."

"I'm not a Cameron supporter, it's *ironic.*"

She smiles. "I don't think it is, actually."

"Of course it is! David Cameron was just a babe in arms when Che Guevara was alive so how could he be wearing a T-shirt with his face on it?!"

"Who, Cameron?"

"No, Che Guevara – it's a joke!"

"Yes but perhaps it's not the joke you think it is. For it to make the point you seem to think it's making, dear, surely it should say David Cameron wears Che Guevara T-shirts."

"Oh forget it!"

I decide there and then I'll write a withering letter to the manufacturers telling them to stop selling ironic T-shirts because they're taking customers' money under false pretences because no one in the world apart from me fucking understands what irony is (maybe they'll send me a free T-shirt too).

Lizzie seems in no hurry to finish her tea. In fact, she perches on my sofa and takes another sip of tea from my1984 "Maggie Out" mug, the overtly political content of which seems to have escaped her notice. "Is there anything I can do for you, Lizzie?" I smile.

"It's what *I* can do for *you*, Arnold." She carefully puts my "Maggie Out" mug on top of the "Socialist Worker" annual that darling Alice got me last Christmas, and without even noticing the irony of what she's done she launches into a story. It seems she was coming back from taking the doggies for walkies yesterday evening (about the time that I was failing to engage my sons in intelligent political discussion) when she saw a suspicious looking person loitering outside my front door. With a dog.

"How do you mean outside my front door?"

"*Right* outside."

"Who was it?"

"I'm afraid I didn't see. As I got nearer they must have noticed me because they scuttled off."

"Male or female?"

"I'm not sure about that either."

"What sort of dog?"

"Quite a friendly dog I think..."

"What do you mean friendly? He stopped by to give me a present, did he?"

She gurgles at my witticism. "No, no, all I mean is Rexie didn't yap, nor did Paula or Dolly, and they *always* yap if they smell an unfriendly doggie, even if it's miles away. Oh dear, I'm not being much help really – sorry! I'm not much of a Miss Marple, am I?"

No you're fucking not, I think. But I smile forgivingly. "Don't worry, it's great to know we've got our own little neighbourhood watch going, Lizzie. I appreciate it."

"If I come up with anything else, I'll tell you at once!" Then to my relief she swigs down the rest of her tea and gets up. "Now I'm off to see Boris."

"Boris?"

"Boris Johnson – our scrumptious mayor – he's giving one of his speeches. Such a clever man, don't you think? No, I suppose you don't. But even you must admit he does speak Latin beautifully, doesn't he? Even a leftie like you can't deny that!" I hope my silence speaks volumes about what I think about the iniquity of a classical education in our class-ridden society. Actually the only Latin I know is "hic haec hoc" and I don't even know what that means, so I'm wondering whether to make some witty remark about snobby Etonian twats but she hardly pauses for breath. "Personally I think it's really important that the mayor of Londinium should speak Latin and classical Greek, it gives a lovely sort of link with the past. Not like that ghastly adenoidal oik what's-his-name, you know, with the bendy buses and the newts." She looks appalled and clasps my arm apologetically. "Now I'm being rude, I'm sure you really liked him, didn't you? How *could* you though – no *really*?"

I toy with a crushing response, then realize that she's so old it might finish her off and I'd have to phone 999, then I'd have to wait in, which means I'd be late for my lunchtime linger over a small Rioja or two at the Galloping Gastro. So I decide the best solution is to maintain a dignified silence and watch her make her doddery way to the door. By the way," she says brightly when she gets there, "did you know that one of your lot has just called elderly voters *coffin dodgers,* on his what-d-you-call-it, Twitter page?"

"*My lot?*"

"The Labour lot. They *are* your lot, aren't it?"

"Not exactly, no," I say acidly.

She flaps a withered hand. "Of course they are – but you don't need to apologise to me, Arnold – I understand!"

"I wasn't –!"

"*Anyway,* the thing is, he was a Labour candidate but now they've sacked him. And good riddance. I mean really! How offensive can you get, calling people like us *coffin dodgers?*"

I freeze. "People like *us*?"

She registers my shock and comes back and squeezes my arm again. "Only elderly in *anno domini,* Arnold. In every other way we're as young as spring chickens and as fresh as daisies!"

She gives me a quick dribbly kiss on the cheek which is like being snogged by a wet sponge, then dodders out, looking eighty-five if she's a day. I'm left trying to work out how she could be so stupid as not to realize I'm clearly a quarter of a century younger than her. Maybe she's just going gaga.

1.50 p.m.

Here is an exchange of text messages between myself, at the Galloping Gastro, and Alice's mum Daphne, at whichever dive she's slumped in (she later claims she was sitting soberly at home, but I wonder).

Me – hi sugartits

Her – oh christ

Me – am worried about alice. Wd like 2 meet 2 discuss

Her – am in v happy relationship with caring man do not want 2 meet u

Me – surely in circs like this our daughters happiness comes first

(Long pause. So long that I'm on the point of ordering another tiny Rioja).

Her – ok

(Decide I need to up the pressure a bit)

Me – am v v worried about her u see

(Another long pause)

Her – ok then

Me – so how about u come 2 my place cd make bite 2 eat

Her – how about u stick ur dick in freezer then fuck off

Me – ok where then

(Another pause. About fifteen minutes. Spend the time fondly remembering our first meeting all those years ago. She was wearing a cute little waitress uniform with a tight little tank top, and leant over me with my onion soup and I gazed into her cleavage and I knew immediately she was The One. I knew at once she had everything I'd always been looking for – small but big in the right places, blonde hair, not over-educated – what more could you ask for? Am sadly pondering the transience of love and wondering where it all went wrong when she texts back)

Her – crypt of st martin in field church traf square tmrrw 3 pm no funny business

Me – am unhappy about this – dont believe in god and feel uncomfortable anywhere near christian church – christianity is even more oppressive force than Islam

Her – how about mosque in st johns wood then

Me – ho ho hilarious. Ok crypt it is

7.20 p.m.

Meet Quentin and Adam at the Palace Theatre, which is full of noisy people who look as if they go to the theatre even less often than I do. Haven't seen a musical since Quentin's mum made me see Oklahoma because we didn't "do enough things together" and got all frosty when I feel asleep. But Priscilla Queen Of The Desert has more jokes than Oklahoma (not hard) and I'm concerned to make a good impression with Quentin and his gay lover so stay awake (most of the time).

All goes well until half-time, when Quentin and Adam order a bottle of Lord Lloyd Webber's Palace Theatre shampoo. Adam "knows people in the theatre" and tells me that as his Lordship owns the place he gets a mega rake-off from the bar. They smilingly watch me sample the strictly average shampoo and adamantly refuse to have any. Adam tells me they're both on a radish and adzuki bean diet, which means strictly no alcohol.

Then Quentin says, "We've got something to tell you, Dad. Something important."

"Let me guess – you're pregnant!"

They smile politely but I get the feeling they're not genuinely amused. I'm starting to think Alice isn't the only person in the family who's lost their sense of humour. In fact, I seem to be surrounded nowadays by po-faced tosspots, including sad to say my second ex-wife Daphne, none of whom would recognise a joke if it bit them on their politically correct arses.

"Adam and I have decided that as we've been together sixteen years it's time we made a commitment. A proper commitment. We didn't do it before because neither of us thinks these things should be entered into lightly." He laughs self-deprecatingly. "You probably think we've been terribly over-cautious!"

"Not at all," I smile back.

Adam cuts in. "The thing is we didn't want to declare our love for each other publicly until we were a hundred per cent sure that we really wanted to spend the rest of our lives together."

"Are you trying to make a point here?" I ask, getting straight to the nitty-gritty.

Adam smiles uncertainly. "How do you mean?"

"*I mean* are you by any chance trying to say that you didn't want to follow my example?"

Quentin chuckles. "Exactly, Dad, how perceptive of you."

"Well that's great, Quentin. All I can say is I'm delighted I've had such an influence on you."

"Oh you have, undoubtedly!"

I put a fatherly arm round him. "You don't know what that means to me, son, you really don't."

"That's nice," he says as he tries to wriggle free. "Anyway, we're planning to have a civil ceremony. And we wanted you to be the first to know."

"Brilliant."

"Well the first after Mum and Alice, and Adam's Mum and Dad of course and his sisters."

"Fantastic. Cheers!" I swallow some more of Lord Lloyd Webber's cheapo shampoo and it gives me confidence to voice my one concern. "Can I say something?"

For some reason Quentin looks tense. "Yes, of course, Dad."

"Don't you worry that by reacting against my example you're just betraying the gay culture to which you belong? I mean what's the point in being bent if you're not promiscuous and don't play the field? And don't look at me like that please, Adam, I'm not being homophobic, not the slightest bit– believe me I'd have been a fag too if I'd had the choice. Sounds a great life to me, the only thing that stopped me is I'm not too keen on having blokes stick their –"

A fire-alarm rings and stops me in mid-explanation and I make a dash for the exit, but Quentin grabs me and says it's just the interval bell telling us we've got three minutes to get back to our seats. I finish the shampoo and notice that he and Adam both look rather stressed now, obviously because I've given them food for thought. So I tactfully change the subject.

"So what do you want for your wedding present? If you're still going ahead with it I mean? It'll have to be cheap I'm afraid because I've got sod-all money..."

"We don't need presents," Adam says tersely and stalks back into the theatre.

"That's fine by me," I say, and smile reassuringly at Quentin but he doesn't smile back. "So is smug git Osborne coming?"

"I certainly hope so as he's my very close friend."

"Is he a shirtlifter too? I've often wondered."

"For God's sake, Dad!"

"It's nothing personal, I blame St Paul's. You were all up each other, weren't you? Same with all public schools."

"No he's not, he's extremely heterosexual. And by the time Adam and I plight our troth he will I hope be helping run this country, so whether he comes or not depends on if he can spare a couple of hours from sorting out the disastrous economic mess your Labour Government has left us in!" And he turns and stalks off after Adam.

"It's not *my* Labour government!" I yell after him. "Don't you listen to a thing I say?!"

But he's gone. I turn to the girl behind the bar and give her my best smile.

"I'd like something that doesn't taste like piss this time, if that's all right with you, darling."

"Are you going back into the theatre, sir? If so, you'll need a plastic beaker."

"Is that a gay thing then?"

"Sorry?"

"Drinks in plastic beakers?"

"Excuse me, sir," she says icily. And disappears to serve someone else.

"I'll have a large Rioja!" I call after her. "And a fucking sense of humour would help too!"

Saturday 10th April

3.10 a.m.

Have nightmare. God tells me he's going to punish me for betraying my principles and allowing Quentin to be privately educated.

"How are you going to do that, God?" I ask, terrified.

"By turning him into a shirtlifter, Arnold."

"But he already is a shirtlifter. Didn't you know?"

"Oh God no, I didn't know, that's awful!" says God and looks really shocked. "Then I'm going to punish you even more for not providing a more positive role model!"

"I know, I know, gay *and* monogamous! How could I have let this happen?!"

God just folds his arms and looks at me.

"Come on, say something, God. Say something reassuring!"

God looks at me like I'm a useless piece of shit then slowly shakes his head, and vanishes.

Wake up in cold sweat.

3.35 a.m.

Drink restorative glass of Grand Marnier (discovered yesterday covered in dust behind Amaretto) and feel relieved God doesn't exist.

Then wonder if the nightmare is my unconscious trying to tell me something. But don't believe in unconscious any more than in God, so decide this is crap.

8.30 a.m.

Phone Roger and get hold of him as he's setting out for golf with Fred the Shred and Jimmy Tarbuck.

"Did I fail you as a father, Roger?"

"Of course you did."

"I'm not joking, Roger."

"Nor am I!"

"So do you blame me for the way you turned out?"

"Why should I blame you? I'm a big success, Dad..."

"You mean you really don't blame me? You're not just saying that?!"

"Why on earth would I blame you? You were never there long enough to have any effect on me at all! I'm really grateful I didn't have a father, Dad. Look got to go now, Brucie's just driven up."

"I thought you said Jimmy Tarbuck?"

"Yes but Brucie always likes to tag along, we're really close."

"So is he a father figure for you, Roger?"

"What?"

"Is Bruce Forsyth a father figure for you, Roger?"

"Look bad line, sorry – got to go..."

Or what about Jimmy Tarbuck? Or Fred the Shred for that matter?"

"Bye, Dad – bye..."

"Bye bye, Roger! And listen, I don't mind if they all are, really I don't! Just thank you – thank you so much!"

8.40 a.m.

While having second pee of the day think how much I love Roger. In a funny way he's always been my favourite. Of course I know you shouldn't have favourites, but you just can't help it sometimes (plus he gives me miniscule monthly allowance, which is more than the other two cheapskates do).

Feel so cheerful I go online instead of going back to bed till midday. First of all, check to see if Lebedev has emailed offering contract.

No he hasn't. But Saga magazine has! (emailed me I mean – not offered contract, well not yet).

Dear Sir,

Thank you for sending us your article. However, after careful consideration, we have decided that it is not right for us. We hope that you have better luck elsewhere.

Best wishes.

Yours sincerely,

Anthea Greenspan (assistant editor)

PS Hi Arnold. Am a great fan of yours, specially those hard-hitting Private Eye pieces in the 80s! Wow! But I'm afraid Niven's cock etc. is not quite our thing. It's not that we're prudish (huh!) and of course we like to think that our Third Age readers have really healthy and active sex lives (as if!) but the fact is they do seem to prefer their mag to feature less sensational stuff – eg lighthearted think pieces and anything about the Duchess of Devonshire. A drag, I know, but what can you do? So if you've got anything like that, specially life-enhancing and with an oldie angle, bung it my way.

PPS Have you tried Niven's cock on GQ?

8.55 a.m.

Write lighthearted life-enhancing think piece with oldie angle for Saga Magazine. (Spend first ten minutes trying to fit in the Duchess of Devonshire too, then give up).

What is old?

OK so you're sixty. Or is it seventy? So what? What's the difference? Yes, all right, there's ten years' difference, but what exactly does that mean? I mean really mean? It's just a number. The point is you don't have to be old any more. Age has nothing to do with how long you've been on the planet any more. Nowadays the great thing is, you're only as old as you feel.

Consider these two men.

One of them is forty-nine and he's depressed and his wife has left him and he hates himself because he's never done what he wanted in life and now it's too late and his world's about to collapse – and all because he's nearly fifty.

The other is seventy-eight and his wife has just died. So what does he do? He decides you're only as old as you feel, and he becomes a silver surfer and he sneaks into the over-fifties chatroom where he lies about his age and meets this amazing woman and now he's suddenly having the best sex of his life and feels like a teenager all over again. And he's nearly eighty!

Isn't that a life-enhancing story?

Not for the forty-nine-year-old unfortunately, because the seventy-eight-year old happens to be his Dad, and his sudden success with women only makes his son's chronic sense of failure even worse, and to add to his woes his Mum's hardly cold in her grave and she's already been replaced by this blond blowsy nurse – this truly awful, vulgar woman – and to make it even worse he just finds her totally and rivetingly sexy.

He feels horribly guilty about this and tries to stop it but he can't. And his self-loathing reaches unbearable levels because inside his head he's now being incestuous and disloyal to his Mum – both at the same time!

But the son is not our role model. He's a self-pitying loser and a weirdo. No wonder his wife left him. The one whose side we're on here is Dad, isn't it? Because the point is that eighty is the new sixty and sixty is the new forty, and life nowadays is great for all of them.

Well isn't it?

Of course it is. Just look around. Joan Collins is having hot times with her toy boy husband and Hugh Hefner is apparently still busy doing whatever he does with his bunny girls, and despite having had eleven or twelve wives and a hair transplant Silvio Berlusconi is still a total babe-magnet.

Maybe the rest of us don't live such remarkable lives. But we do our best, we haven't given in, and most important of all we still defiantly wear jeans, the badge of eternal youth – just like our kids do.

Which means we're cool and happy. According to Esther Rantzen, the baby-boomer generation are now having the time of their lives – and she should know!

Then there's the couple who recently got divorced in their eighties. What does that tell you about changing attitudes to age? An optimistic, death-defying act if ever there was one! And it seems it was the wife who divorced the husband. When asked why she had done it, she said all her husband wanted to do was watch DVDs of Heartbeat and anything with Stephen Fry in it while she wanted to travel the world and explore her inner potential.

Good for her, eh?

God what a boring stick-at-home slob he sounds, doesn't he?! I mean come on, you're only eighty-four, get a life!

So, you see, the phrase "act your age" really doesn't mean anything anymore. Straightforward chronological age no longer exists!

So stop worrying if you can no longer wear things that say "slimline" and if they're all laughing at you when you shop at Primark. Just remember to tell those unnaturally stick-thin teenagers to stick their skimpy "paedo" bikinis up their anorexic arses, and get out there and enjoy yourself!

11.25 a.m.

Briefly worry it might be more suited to The Sun than Saga magazine, but don't have time to do anything about it because last post on Saturday is at midday. Write quick letter to Anthea Greenspan. (NB – Have good feeling about her. Think she might even fulfil role of thrusting young-but-not-too-young publisher! And possibly might put out too).

Dear Anthea,

Great to hear from a fan – far too few of them around nowadays! (I jest!)

So how about this little think piece for the mag?

And if you want to chew it over with me any time – or chew anything else over come to that! – give me a bell.

Power to the people!

Arnold

11.40 a.m.

Write quick letter to Dylan Jones, editor of GQ.

Hi Dylan,

A mate of yours suggested I send you this article about David Niven's dong. For some reason he thought it might be up your street!

Hope it is. If not, fuck you! And your mate David Cameron too! (Only joking, mate).

Btw, I love the tits in your mag. No seriously!

Yours sincerely,

Arnold Appleforth

Look at it for a moment, not sure if I've got the laddish tone quite right or not. But can't see how I can improve it so what the hell.

11.50 a.m.

Print out articles and letters, sign letters, stick them in envelopes, address envelopes, look for stamps – *and realize I've run out.*

11.56 a.m.

Hurriedly exit flat in dressing gown clutching envelopes, skid over pile of dogshit and collide with Lizzie the Lezzie as she's returning to her house with her hideous yapping dogs.

"Stamps, Lizzie, have you got stamps?!"

"Oh no *look* you've got *poo* over your dressing gown! How *horrid!*"

"*Forget the fucking poo,* I need two stamps!"

"Yes of course – would you like a cup of tea? When you've got the poo off I mean..."

"*Stamps* Lizzie, *stamps,* I've got *three* minutes..."

"Roger, wilko, over and out!" And with a speed I can only describe as remarkable in an octogenarian she pops indoors and pops back out in seconds with the stamps, and I stick them on and run to the pillar box, shit-streaked dressing gown flapping in the breeze, giving my bollocks a quick airing, and post both letters just as the Royal Mail van approaches down the road.

As I turn back, I see Lizzie having a good look at my wedding tackle. Disturbs me for a moment, then realize I should feel sorry for her. After all, the poor woman's probably never seen a full set before.

Even so, don't want to overdo the altruistic bit, so hurry indoors and put on clothes.

12.15 p.m.

Over tea in her posh living room, Lizzie asks why I didn't email the articles. Realize I'm surprised she even knows what email is. Wonder if perhaps I'm underestimating her.

After second cup, say I really have to go. But she asks me to stay for lunch. Poor lonely soul, I think, desperate for company of any sort, so I tell her I'd love to stay for lunch, but I've got to go and have a difficult discussion with my troubled ex-wife about our depressed daughter. I see her heart instantly melt, in fact I can almost see it dripping over the carpet.

"What a nice man you are, Arnold, aren't you?"

"Am I, Lizzie? Well thank you. I do my best."

"Oh I can see that now. But shall I tell you what your trouble is? I hope you won't be offended by me saying this, but your trouble is you hide your niceness too well."

"Do you really think so?"

"Definitely. To be completely honest, I actually thought you were quite uncouth when we first met."

"Did you?!" I laugh.

"But you're quite sensitive and vulnerable really, aren't you?" she says earnestly. "I mean underneath the effing and the blinding and the awful T-shirts and things..."

"Well, I like to think I am," I smile modestly. "But I have to say, not everyone I've known would agree with you! In fact, some people I've known in the past have accused me of –"

"Oh *some people!* We all know what *some people* think! The trouble is, most people are stupid and insensitive and totally incapable of seeing past their own noses, which is why the rest of us have to stick together, Arnold."

"Yeah, I suppose you're right – I hadn't thought of it quite like that..."

"Really? Well it's high time that you did," she says briskly. "More tea?" She gives me a twinkly smile and leans towards me with the teapot.

Christ Almighty, you never know, do you? If she wasn't eighty-five and a lezzie I reckon I'd be having to fight her off now. I get up and give her a jolly smile. "*Anyway*, must run, really."

"On your mission of mercy – yes of course."

"See you later. No don't get up just for me!"

"One more thing," she says and tries to clasp my hand but I'm too fast for her. "Don't forget that I'm always here if you need me."

"Yeah great..." I'm at the door now.

"No I mean it – I really do."

Judging from the look on her face she really does. So I flash a smile and I'm out of there before things get any more embarrassing. Still, when you're that old I suppose you don't have any sense of shame any more. After all what's there to lose?

12.40 p.m.

Get back home and remove "Che Guevara wears David Cameron T-shirts" T-shirt and give it a sniff to see if it's OK to take back, because I've decided direct action is called for (plus I can't be arsed to write a letter to the manufacturer). I've only been wearing it since Thursday, so it's fine. I give it a quick iron and it looks almost like new, so I put it in a plastic bag then put on my wine-stained "Dick Cheney – Before He Dicks You!" T-shirt. (Note to self – remember to wash it soon, ideally at same time as shit-streaked dressing gown in order to conserve world's resources).

Go out again.

1.40 p.m.

The straight-looking guy in the political T-shirt section of Politicos Bookshop sniffs my "Che Guevara wears David Cameron T-shirts" T-shirt then looks at me suspiciously. "It's whiffy."

"No it's not."

"Yes, it is. I'm sorry, we don't exchange used T-shirts."

"I told you, I've never worn it!"

"Then why is it whiffy?"

"Probably because someone else tried it on before I bought it, some sweaty fucking Tory probably!"

He goes pursed-lipped but doesn't answer. "Anyway, why do you want to exchange it? It's one of our most popular lines."

I speak slowly and clearly because he's annoying me but I really don't want to lose my cool. "Because I thought it was ironic but it isn't."

"Of course it's ironic," he laughs. "It's one of our most ironic T-shirts! *That's* why it's so popular!"

"Then why do Tories go for it so much?"

"Who said they did?"

"You just did."

"No I didn't. I certainly didn't! We're not allowed to make overtly political comments."

"Well you didn't deny it when *I* said it. You just asked a prissy little question."

He looks round shiftily, then lowers his voice. "Well if you felt that my question implied that, perhaps it's because I do find Tories have a better sense of humour."

"You reckon."

"But please don't tell anyone I said that."

I stare at him. "OK – if you exchange the T-shirt."

"I told you, I *can't* exchange it."

"No problem." I make a move towards a senior looking bloke standing by the cash desk.

"OK OK, I'll give you twenty per cent off a new one."

"Fifty."

"Thirty."

"Forty-five."

"Forty!"

"It's a deal."

(NB – I include this otherwise trivial episode because it contains a painful lesson, which is that distasteful though it is, you just have to swallow your pride sometimes and fight the capitalists at their own game. Specially when you save six quid).

2.10 p.m.

On the way to meet Daphne in St Martin-in-the-Field crypt I pause for quick libation at the Salisbury public house up the road. Am still wearing Dick Cheney T-shirt because don't want to risk getting the new one dirty, because really want to create good impression with cute little second ex-wife who I work out I haven't seen for eleven years (I think).

3.00 p.m.

Go to pub bog to change. Am followed by man in leathers who's been trying to get my eye ever since I ordered my second crème de cacao frappé (I like to be a bit adventurous at weekends). I lock myself in the crapper and change into my new T-shirt (which was hidden away right at the back of the Politicos' T-shirt section) and stuff the whiffy Dick Cheney one in with the Che Guevara one in my plastic bag. I hear a noise and look up and am surprised to see the man in leathers peering down at me. He looks peeved to see I'm now wearing a T-shirt which reads "I love hot mums" and yells "wanker!" at me and disappears from view.

3.05 p.m.

Walk down St Martin's Lane and buy packet of Trebor Extra Strong Mints. Suck Trebor mint and have fond memories of Daphne.

Go down the steps to St Martin-in-the-Field crypt. Pop second Trebor Extra Strong Mint in mouth. No point mentioning I paused at the Salisbury, because have vague recollection of drink being tiny bone of contention between us once upon a time.

I gaze round the trendy eaterie. Where is she? I see a dumpy figure in a beret and a shapeless brown cardigan waving at me. Oh shit. Am instantly overwhelmed by thoughts about ageing and death and wonder why I didn't stay at home to watch the Inspector Dalgleish retrospective on ITV3 (the Roy Marsden one, not the one with the bloke from The Professionals who plays that po-faced vegetarian judge who shags a lot). Then remember I'm recording it and cheer up.

I even manage a smile as I approach her table. "Great to see you, baby," I say. "You're looking good." (Two lies in eight words – must be some sort of a record!)

"Thank you. It's because I'm happy – at last."

I ignore the pointed remark and sit opposite her.

"Are you happy too?" she asks.

"Yeah great." I find myself wondering if she still owns the tight little jumpers and micro-minis I once bought her and when she was last able to get into any of them.

She looks disappointed. "Are you?"

"Yeah – idyllic." I can see she really doesn't like that because she goes tight-lipped and looks me up and down as if to check what's wrong with me, and I quickly fold my arms over the "I love hot mums" T-shirt and hope to God she doesn't think I'm wearing it because I'm trying to come on to her. (Really disturbing how fast plans can change).

"Well that's nice," she says grudgingly. "Because happiness is so hard to find. Personally I thank God every day that I'm so happy at last."

Now I might not know much about women, but one thing I've learned is that when they keep telling you they're happy, they're not at all really (another thing I've learned is that when they're really hostile, like she was when I texted her, it means they're struggling with a powerful attraction they've got very little control over).

She's staring at me thoughtfully. "Well you don't look too good at all," she smiles, which takes the biscuit I reckon. But I smile pleasantly back.

"Are you still with that wimpy bloke?"

"His name's Henry. And yes I am – and he's the reason I'm so happy."

"Bit of a drip though, as I recall."

"No, Arnold, he's not. Unlike you, Henry is loving and caring and thoughtful and he can never do enough for me."

"Exactly. What's his job again?"

"He's in insurance."

"There you are, I rest my case, baby!" I chuckle but she glares at me. (Yet another woman with a sense of humour bypass. Jesus, can I pick 'em).

She almost hisses across the table at me. "He's helped me to *heal*, Arnold!"

"Why, what did you have wrong with you?"

"I mean he's helped me recover from the terrible damage that living with you caused me. He's held my hand and led me to a safe, secure place where there's warmth and affection, and where I can at last feel free to love a man properly, and feel that he can love me back properly too."

"How do you mean properly?"

"What do you mean, how do I mean properly?"

"I mean does he go down on you like I did?"

For some reason this seems to upset her. "God you're *sick* – you're just *sick!*"

"Why am I sick?! What's the matter, I was just *asking?!* You were talking about love and stuff and I thought we'd had a really pretty hot time together and –"

"Shut up."

"– and specially you know when we –"

"Shut up!"

So I do. (Another thing I've learned about women – they might love getting down and dirty when the going's good but they come over really weird when years later you want to talk nostalgically about it).

Now I see she's got tears in her eyes. "I knew I shouldn't have agreed to meet you. It was a stupid, stupid mistake..."

"No. no it's great to see you!"

"All you ever wanted from me was sex. I'm sure that's all

you've ever wanted from any woman! You probably don't even really want to talk about Alice, it's probably just an excuse!"

I look wounded and indignant. "That's hitting below the belt, Daphne – that's really unfair!"

"I *know* you, remember."

"People do change, Daphne."

"Yes, I bet. So far as I can see, you've changed from being a drunken sex-obsessed young man into a drunken sex-obsessed old one. And if you think that sucking Trebor Extra Strong Mints hides the alcoholic fumes, well they didn't thirty years ago so why on earth would it work now?"

A cheap jibe, but I rise above it. "Oddly enough, my lezzie neighbour was saying only this morning how sensitive and vulnerable I was."

"I don't want to hear about your lezzie neighbour, thank you."

"That's really sexist of you, Daphne. I hope Henry isn't turning you into an intolerant suburban reactionary. So which way are you voting on May the 6th?"

She looks at me with an undisguised venom that fills me with fond memories. "How I vote is none of your business and leave Henry out of this."

"No problem at all."

"God, I can't imagine what I ever saw in you, I really can't."

"Can't you?" I smile. "I bet you can if you think back hard enough."

She's obviously not even up for a bit of harmless flirtation. "For heaven's sake, you're sixty-one, Arnold. Some of us grew out of this sad adolescent obsession you still have *years* ago!"

"What are you talking about?"

"The *sex thing*. It's meant to be a temporary stage, Arnold. Henry's read me articles about it. It's meant for youngsters, not filthy wrinkly old people, because it's *biological* – it's all to do with having *babies!* But I wouldn't expect a disgusting old man like you to understand that. You really are just gross and loathsome and hideous!"

I feel a stirring in my loins. She might look like a dumpling but she can still do scorn and abuse like no one else and even nowadays it really does it for me. I give her an annoying smile. "When you say some of us grew out of it years ago, don't you mean some *women* grew out of it?"

I'm hoping this will make her even more vitriolic but unfortunately it doesn't. She looks at me for a moment, then smiles patiently. "No not just women, Arnold. That's the wonderful thing about Henry, if you must know – well one of the many wonderful things..."

"What is?"

She leans forward so no one else can hear. And it takes me right back to when she first leant over me all those years back, almost spilling out of her little tank top into my soup, and I instantly get the horn, just like I did then. "He understands there's more to a relationship than sex," she whispers. "In fact he understands that too much sex can really get in the way of a meaningful relationship, just like it did with us, if you remember."

"Did it?" Thank God I haven't got to stand up, I'm like the Eiffel Tower down there now. "Did it really?" I manage to smile back.

"What do you mean, *did it really?* All that endless sex, sex, sex, yes of course it did."

"Right, OK."

"Which is why I'm so much happier with Henry."

I nod understandingly. "Tell me why again exactly?"

For a second she looks embarrassed at being forced to spell it out, but she's on a mission now, determined to spread the word. "You really can't imagine the depths of intimacy and love you feel when you've finally thrown the sex stuff out of the window. It's so liberating, I just can't describe it."

"And how does old Henry feel about this?"

"He feels exactly the same, of course he does, he loves it too." She laughs. "It wouldn't work very well if he didn't, now would it?!"

"No of course not. So how does he get by? A quick one off the wrist when you're out of the room, is that it?"

She leans back and smiles again. "You can't shock me, Arnold, not any more. I know you just have to cheapen and defile everything, you do don't you, everything you come in contact with. It's just the way you are."

I sense I might have gone too far. "Let me buy you a drink," I beam at her but she's already on her feet.

"No thank you. I need to go up into the church to cleanse myself. I feel like my soul has just been sullied."

She never used to use words like cleansed and sullied when she was with me. It's Henry's fucking fault, he's been teaching her things.

I realize drastic action is needed. "Before you go, there's something I really need to ask you."

"No I'm not having a threesome with you and your lezzie neighbour thanks all the same."

"This is serious, Daphne."

"I thought that *was* your idea of serious."

"I was going to ask if you'd come along with Alice and me to see her shrink. I think the three of us going together would be really helpful for her, but of course if all you can do is make flippant homophobic jokes..."

She looks at me warily then wraps her shapeless cardigan around herself. "She told me it was her relationship with you that was the problem. What's it got to do with me?"

"That's what she told me too," I smile patiently. "But if you really think life is that simple..."

"In this case yes I do. In fact, I'd say it's quite obvious it is!"

I look at her calmly and thoughtfully (which is getting pretty difficult). "Do I hear a note of defensiveness in there somewhere?" I smile again.

"I'm going to go upstairs now and pray for your soul, Arnold. Sixty years too late of course, but..."

"If you change your mind and decide to come with us, baby, I know Alice will be so happy." I can feel my smile getting rictus-like. "But if you really can't open yourself to such an exposing situation – well – we're all only human. I certainly won't hold it against you – and I'll do all I can to make sure Alice doesn't."

She hesitates. "All right a tomato juice."

Result!

"That's great. A tomato juice and...?

"All right, with vodka in it."

Double result!

She sits down again and I quickly look round for waiters and there aren't any, so with a sinking heart I go and join a queue. I try to get to the front by flashing my freedom pass and saying I'm a bit rocky on the old pins and I might collapse any second but no one gives a shit. Then when I do get to the front they refuse to serve me alcohol without food as well. After an exhausting time haggling they reluctantly agree a green salad constitutes food, then make me order two of them, and I finally return to our table carrying a tray of overpriced rabbit food plus drinks and trying very hard to contain my rage.

We sip our Bloody Marys and I breathe deeply and focus on becoming calm and serene while Daphne eats her salad and then mine. Conversation is a little stilted, mainly because her mouth's constantly full of lettuce. So I tell her my nightmare about God (an edited version). This goes down pretty well, like I thought it would, so I go for broke by stumblingly confessing my worries about failing as a Dad and as a human being too (as if!) By the time I've finished her eyes are moist and I can almost feel the heat coming out from her shapeless cardie at me. She puts out her hand and squeezes mine consolingly and I try to put out of my mind the thought of a threesome with her and Lizzie the Lezzie (that Daphne put there in the first place I might add) but the total grossness of the idea exerts a really powerful appeal.

"OK I'll come with you and Alice to the shrink," she says softly, and it takes me a second to remember what she's talking about.

"That'd be great."

5.20 p.m.

After a couple more Bloody Marys we surface from the crypt and say our farewells on the pavement. We have an affectionate goodbye hug, like I've read long-divorced couples sometimes do after an open and honest chat about their offspring, and I get a boner and she jumps away and shoots me a look.

"Sorry but it's out of my control, baby," I apologise. "It's got a life of its own. And I guess maybe it's trying to tell you that it's always there for you, you know, just for old times' sake, any time that you need it, no strings attached."

Both Mr Stiffie and I know full well she's gagging for it. How could she not be, a hot-blooded woman like her, specially after three large Bloody Marys and now that Henry's not riding the old bony pony anymore? Still, I pride myself on being sensitive to a woman's moods and decide that probably now isn't the best time to discuss her sexual needs. So I move to give her another goodbye hug but she leaps away, still pretending she's not desperate for it, and quickly says she'll fix a time with Alice and hurries off down the street.

I can't go after her because of the boner. So I stand there waiting for it to subside, incidentally feeling pretty good that I can still get a major hard-on at 61. After a few minutes it's on its way south and I start to relax. Of course it's then that Julie Burchill approaches and before I know it it's standing to attention again (NB – Julie is another of my heroes, along with Arthur Scargill and Ken Livingstone and Tony Benn among others, though none of the last three give me boners I hasten to add).

"Hey Julie, I just want to say how much I admire you! What a firebrand and iconoclast you are, eh?!"

"Who are you?"

"And I've always thought your Dad sounded pretty cool too – a proper old leftie just like me!"

"Is that meant to be an erection or have you stuffed a hankie down your pants?"

"Let's talk about the political not the personal, shall we?

You know I'm a bit of a firebrand and iconoclast too. The name's Arnold Appleforth, journalist of this parish!"

"I don't go for old guys, my husband's thirteen years younger than me, now sod off."

"OK you might not remember the name, but I'm sure you remember my famous tirades in Private Eye in the 80s. Unless of course you were too coked out of your box at the Groucho, which is perfectly possible!"

She's looking at me oddly. I wonder if I've gone too far with the coke and the Groucho. "Were you the one who wrote about the Falklands and the Brighton bombings?" she asks.

"Yeah that's me, yeah! Arnold The Antichrist the Daily Mail called me! Great that you remember!"

"Well for your information I *love* Margaret Thatcher, she's my total hero, even more than Princess Diana! And weak men like you always hate strong women, you're just so threatened by them because you're a decrepit slimeball and a cunt."

God I love it when women swear at me, this is even better than Daphne, I can feel Mr Stiffie almost bursting out of my boxers, so I do all I can to provoke her. "No Julie *you're* the slimeball and the cunt and your leftie Dad'd be ashamed of you for supporting Margaret Thatcher!"

"No he wouldn't! What do you know about anything?!"

"And by the way Tony Parsons is a *million times* better writer than you and I happen to know he thanks God every day he's not married to you anymore!"

"Well, screw you, Arnie, and sideways!"

I have to keep my hands over my crotch now to stop myself getting arrested. "And another thing Julie, your militant so-called feminism you're so proud of is irrelevant bourgeois bollocks as any Marxist will tell you!"

I'm sure this will *really* get her going, but to my frustration she snorts derisively and gives me the finger and walks off. Christ, it's like coitus interruptus but worse. And thanks to Mr Stiffie I can't even run after her. All I can do is yell – "And I fancied you much more when you were a fat fucking lesbian too!"

This stops her in her tracks. Fantastic. She's turns round. Come on, Julie – come on ... A bit more of your famously fearless abuse please! Please please!

But she doesn't move. Not for ages. Then she turns away again and bends over.

"What's the problem, Julie?!" I yell again. "Out of breath, are you? It's all that moving to Brighton isn't it, you've become a fully paid-up pampered member of the bourgeoisie! What price feminism now, eh?!"

Then I see she's doing something weird. She's shaking with laughter. Why is she doing that? Whatever the reason, it causes instant detumescence and I turn and walk away and reflect that meeting your heroes in real life is so often sadly disappointing.

7.15 p.m.

Get home and turn on the TV and collapse in front of it. It's Brucie on Strictly Come Dancing. What a trooper – he's played a quick eighteen holes with son Roger and Tarbie and Fred the Shred this morning then zoomed off to TV Centre to crack a few lame jokes and do a few geriatric twirls and whatever else he does.

Amazing for someone of a hundred and ninety-two. Amazingly boring to watch too, so turn on PVR (generous

Xmas present from darling son Roger) and begin watching six-hour recorded Inspector Dalgleish retrospective. But am exhausted by struggle to win over ex-wife and failure to get nookie and by searing political debacle with Julie Burchill, and fall asleep watching Roy Marsden in toupée strolling at sedate pace round East Anglian countryside sedately talking to suspect.

11.40 p.m.

Wake to see Roy Marsden still strolling at sedate pace round East Anglian countryside sedately talking to different suspect. Wonder if reason he walks like that in famously blowy part of the world is because if he goes any faster his toupée will fall off.

Watch for ten minutes and he chases someone, but as usual only for a few yards. Wonder if John Nettles pinched his running style from Roy, and if David Jason did too. Or did they all pinch it from the original geriatric copper, Dixon of Dock Green? Am wondering about all this because as always can't follow plot. (Alice "jokily" says that it helps if you stay awake throughout, but surely that's asking too much of any human being?)

Turn off PVR (generous Xmas present for which I had to ask three times) and the BBC so-called news comes on. Hate watching BBC establishment propaganda thinly disguised as news and am about to turn it off when Lib Dem leader Nick Clegg appears alongside Spanish wife Miriam.

Am immediately struck by gross injustice of this. How come I never married a hot Spanish bird with loads of money? Answer – because I wasn't born with a silver spoon up my arse and didn't go to Westminster School and Cambridge, that's why.

Am distracted from reverie on the injustice of the educational system by sound of Clegg speaking. "The proposals from the Conservatives for tax breaks for marriage are patronising drivel that belong in the Edwardian age."

Am amazed – someone in British politics who speaks his mind at last and knows what he thinks! Someone who's not afraid to tell the truth! Decide then and there that definitely won't vote Respect. (Also, there isn't a Respect candidate for Brook Green area). But can I really vote for wishy-washy soggy-liberal not to say centrist politics of the sort that always makes me want to puke? The only answer to this is maybe. At least Clegg clearly detests Tories just as much as Labour and obviously isn't the sort to play second fiddle to anyone. If he continues to impress might well cast my vote for him.

(Note to self – remember to contact old-mate-from-The-Mirror Piers Morgan and ask how he got the brilliant "I've slept with no more than thirty women" confession from Clegg. And while he's preening himself about what a great interviewer he is, ask if he could put in a word with The Mail on Sunday suggesting I write an article entitled "I've slept with no more than sixty women").

(NB – Forgot to mention that my musing about voting intentions is purely hypothetical because always spoil my ballot paper as protest against pathetically undemocratic first-past-the-post voting system).

Sunday 11th April

12.20 a.m.

Go to bed but can't sleep because still resentful about missing out on marrying someone hot and rich and Spanish like Miriam. Is it really just the inequity of the educational system?

3.25 a.m.

Having 3rd pee of the night when remember that I've only ever married blondes, which explains it. Go back to bed feeling better but horny. Fall asleep before get round to doing anything about it.

4.50 a.m.

4th pee.

5.55 a.m.

5th pee.

7.20 a.m.

6th pee.

8.10 a.m.

7th pee. Ponder doing something about feeling horny but as I clearly have prostate cancer have rather gone off idea.

11.55 a.m.

Go to Galloping Gastro and seek oblivion via house Rioja and try not to think of hot Spanish women or prostate cancer.

1.00 p.m.

Change to Merlot in the hope that it will take mind off all things Spanish.

Doesn't work, so go to table where they keep free Sunday papers. As I'm about to pick up The Sunday Times a young tousle-haired guy slips in front of me and scoops up the iniquitous right-wing Murdoch rag and saunters over to a group of similarly tousle-haired guys and distributes its many sections around the table.

Try to read iniquitous right-wing Sunday Telegraph without paying for it but it isn't the same. Just don't get the same feeling of beating the system as when reading The Sunday Times without paying for it.

Watch tousle-haired oafs with growing resentment as they drink their beer and munch their bean and pancetta salads and laugh and chat and cast very occasional glances at their Sunday Times.

4.30 p.m.

Tousle-haired Tory oafs still "reading" my paper.

5.20 p.m.

Appallingly selfish and inconsiderate overpaid newspaper-hogging bastards finally leave. Rush to their table and scoop up all the bits of the bean-and beer-stained Sunday Times and return triumphantly to my table.

Feeling of routine and familiarity slowly re-asserts itself. Even a subversive and iconoclast like myself needs a little bit of ritual on Sunday. Sense of calm and well-being flows over me as glance contemptuously through aspirational right-wing Murdoch crap.

6.30 p.m.

Catch sight of smart-arse A A Gill review by mistake and am filled with fury and resentment. Obsessed all over again by the futility of believing one can ever beat this country's insidious system of privilege and public school and posh accents. Even reminding myself that he's nearly 56 and not a tenth as witty as me and almost certainly not writing his magnum opus doesn't help. Face up to the fact that maybe I'm a tiny bit jealous.

6.45 p.m.

Remember that Jeremy Clarkson and he are best friends and feel better. If I was jealous before, definitely not now.

Monday 12th April

Midnight – 8.15 a.m.

Pee 8 times.

8.30 a.m.

Ring GP to book emergency appointment.

"We have a window for emergencies at midday, sir."

"That's fine."

"But you might have to wait a little while because we have a lot of emergencies on a Monday."

"How long is a little while?"

"It depends on how many emergencies there are, sir."

"So is it an infinitely extendable window?"

"Not infinitely, no sir, we all go home at five o'clock."

"Is there a toilet in this window?"

"We do have a toilet, yes sir. So can you tell me what exactly the problem is?"

"I'd rather not."

"I'm sorry, but as it's an emergency I have to check. Perhaps you could tell me the general sort of area."

"Why don't you just put down that it's serious?"

"I'm sorry to be intrusive but –"

"So am I."

"– but are you really sure it's serious, sir?"

"Yes I'm really sure it's serious, in fact it's so serious I'd like to book the crematorium at the same time, would that be a problem?!"

"I'm sorry, sir?"

"I'll be there at twelve."

8.50 a.m.

Decide the totally impromptu crematorium remark is rather witty – in a black laughing-in-the-face-of-death sort of way. Pity there's no one to share it with.

9.10 a.m.

Am shaving in front of the bathroom mirror and try a revised version of the crematorium remark for possible public use later. "So I booked an emergency appointment at the doctor and they asked me if it was serious. I said yes extremely serious, in fact so serious I was wondering if could book the fucking crematorium too!"

My reflection laughs appreciatively. A biased audience, but better than nothing. Decide I'll definitely remember it for later use.

If of course there is a later.

9.45 a.m.

Decide to take mind off imminent death by checking emails.

To my surprise, *one of them is a proper one!* And I can hardly believe who it's from.

Dear Mr Appleforth,

Mr Lebedev has asked me to tell you that he would like to raise a glass of vodka to you (as we say in our country) to congratulate you on your highly accomplished article about David Niven's prick. He thought it was as witty as it was perceptive but unfortunately not quite right for his forthcoming (still top secret) lifestyle-cum-gossip magazine. But as a fellow ex-commie, he would like to express his solidarity by commissioning you to write a series about famous capitalist film stars for a little Russian newspaper he is in the process of buying called Pravda (please don't tell anyone because it's top secret). The idea would be to provide a searing socialist critique of the sick materialistic money-obsessed world of Hollywood stardom while dwelling as salaciously as possible on their sex lives, and he thinks you would be perfect for this.

Please drop me a line if you're interested and maybe we can have a vodka and a samovar together and discuss it.

Yours sincerely,

Vladimir Bitedikof (Assistant to Mr Lebedev, KGB retired)

I stare at it for some while. My emotions are all over the place. They're principally shock and hurt and bewilderment that my oldest and dearest friend in the world, Wills, should think it funny to mock me like this in my hour of need. (His email address at the top is a bit of a giveaway).

I phone him to express my shock and hurt and bewilderment. And get his answerphone. And leave a bitter message.

10.15 a.m.

Too distressed and upset to get dressed. Am still pondering the fickleness of friendship, indeed of all human relations, when I catch a whiff of something unpleasant. Try to ignore it but can't. Realize it's my shit-streaked dressing gown, which I haven't got round to washing.

Make toast and look for coffee but have run out of Gold Blend. Find very old half-bag of real coffee and make that.

Notice that the combined aromas of toast and coffee help counteract the shit smell.

Wonder if there's an article in this. "Helpful hints around the home". Maybe for Good Housekeeping. Or for Martha Stewart's Living Magazine? (Need to check if she's out of prison first or it'll only go to a minion). Or how about emphasising the bachelor angle and sending it to GQ?

(Note to self – remember to chase up Dylan Jones re Niven article. Maybe not quite yet because he'll only have received it half an hour ago assuming he gets into the office at ten o'clock. Give him till tomorrow).

While eating breakfast I notice other stains on dressing gown as well as the shit ones. Am amused to recall where the stains came from and think this is *definitely* potential GQ material! Decide it's washing day, so get dressed in jeans and "I love hot mums" T-shirt and put multi-stained dressing gown in the wash along with wine-stained "Dick Cheney – Before he Dicks You!" T-shirt. Then take them both out and spray the stained bits with Vanish and put them back in. At the last minute remember to chuck in three weeks' worth of socks and underpants, then add Persil Concentrated and apple blossom flavour conditioner and turn it on.

Feel pleasingly domesticated. Think how nice it will be not to have to fish out socks and underpants from dirty clothes bin (well, pile in corner, actually) to re-use them.

Odd how such small things can transform one's mood.

Am able to think more calmly now about Wills's betrayal. Wonder whether Wills is a worse best friend than Jeremy Clarkson would be. A few imponderables here, the main one being I don't know Jeremy Clarkson from Adam (not gay son's lover Adam – the made-up one). But the fact that my old mate from the Mirror Piers Morgan hates him surely counts for something. Also the fact that Clarkson, like A. A. Gill, writes for the iniquitous right-wing Sunday Times. Also that he likes cars, and that the guy with the stupid hair in Top Gear seems nicer than him.

Get distracted from Wills v Clarkson best friend debate by terror based on certainty that very soon the doctor is going to tell me I have weeks to live. It's at times like this I wish I was in a relationship with a warm, loving, understanding woman who'd put her arms round me and comfort me. Ideally one with blonde hair and big tits who'd insist we have sex right now on the sofa just to take my mind off things.

Decide I am profoundly alone, as are we all existentially speaking, but think I am even more so. Am tempted to pop in to the Galloping Gastro en route to the surgery and have a large dose or two of their house anti-depressant. But worry it might create a bad impression, specially as I realize I've run out of Trebor mints, so decide against it.

So spend the remaining hour making a list of all the positive things in my life.

1. *The prostate cancer might be the slow sort.*
2. *Beneath Daphne's shapeless brown cardie I'm sure I could make out the last lingering vestige of a vaguely curvacious female form.*
3. *Noticed yesterday in prominent Murdoch Sunday rag whose name I shan't mention that Sir Michael Caine spoke out in support of Tory crap about voluntary national service and screwed up his lines! (Question – why didn't the Cameronians get someone younger and*

more cutting edge to do it instead of him? E.g. Dixon of Dock Green possibly?)

4. *If I mention cancer to Daphne she'll definitely put out because deep down she's a caring, loving woman.*
5. *Have great hopes for future professional relationship with Anthea Greenspan, enthusiastic assistant editor of Saga magazine. Possibly personal relationship too if Daphne doesn't come across soon.*
6. *Must never forget that the source of greatest joy, which gives my whole life meaning, is my family – my three, possibly four, adorable children, all of whom I love deeply and unconditionally (though not sure about Quentin at the moment).*
7. *Very nearly have clean socks and underwear.*
8. *Also T-shirt and dressing gown.*
9. *On balance my best mate Wills is probably less of a prick than Jeremy Clarkson. Marginally.*

11.15 a.m.

Finish list (only takes half an hour unfortunately).

11.20 p.m.

Can't think what else to do.

11.30 a.m.

Remember something to do! Empty washing machine!

Am in middle of draping clothes over backs of chairs to dry them when phone rings. Decide to finish job in hand because it's oddly soothing, but also because am afraid voice might sound too shaky if try to talk on phone.

The answerphone clicks on. It's treacherous alleged friend

Wills. And he keeps pausing, as if he's struggling not to laugh.

"Hi there mate, how are you keeping? Your phone message didn't sound too happy! Sorry about that! But it's not very nice telling Lebedev I'd told you about his top secret new magazine – not quite how loyal friends for over thirty years are meant to behave, is it?! Mind you it never got to him of course. Someone in his office fielded it and sent it to me for a laugh. In fact, I've got it in front of me now."

There's a sudden burst of laughter, followed by snorts and choking.

"Sorry – sorry..."

A lot of throat clearing.

"But I've decided to forgive you, mate, because I get the feeling my epistle from the Gulags might have caught you at a sensitive moment. So I'd like to do something to make it up to you. What I'm thinking is you might reconsider my offer to contribute to Sudoku Weekly. Yes, I *know* it's not quite your thing – and yes before you say it, the fact that it's numbers not words makes it even less your thing! I can already hear you yelling at me, 'How can I be subversive when all I've got is fucking numbers?!' But you can, Arnie, I just know you can. OK you'll need a bit of ingenuity. But isn't that what being a professional is all about, accommodating your talents to a new form and still coming up with something great? Isn't it, mate?"

Have never heard such rubbish in my life and spend ten minutes working out scathingly idealistic reply, then realize am late for my death sentence and have to run.

11.55 a.m.

Somehow arrive five minutes early. Have a pee then tell the

woman at reception my name. Not sure if she's the one I talked to but she gives me a frosty look and tells me there'll be a wait. I smile and say thank you very much because am determined not to be antagonistic to the medical profession, all of whom do a wonderful job, because if I am they'll make me wait even longer.

Sit next to tatty pile of magazines and choose last December's Woman's Own and read it from cover to cover. Then read March 2008 edition of Country Living from cover to cover, then April 2007 edition of Build It Home Improvement magazine. Ponder on the fact that the NHS prides itself on catering for its customers nowadays, but as I'm not a woman and hate the countryside and have no intention of improving my flat it hasn't catered for a single one of my needs so far. Think I'll write to NHS complaints manager asking about magazine policy and suggesting modest compensation would be in order.

Have three more pees while waiting for my window within a window to open up.

2.25 p.m.

Am lying on my side on an extended piece of kitchen roll on top of an examining couch minus my trousers and underpants (not clean ones unfortunately because they're still drying) and with nether regions exposed to fat middle-aged male doctor and yummy female student doctor.

Cannot and do not want to move because yummy female student doctor has finger stuck up my arse. Time seems to have stopped, or maybe it's really been up there for some while. Anyway am in trance-like state and pondering the fact that many people would pay serious money for this. Then ponder the more serious fact that if Tories win the election free rectal examinations by yummy student doctors will doubtless become a thing of the past, and feel political rage coming on and think there's definitely an article in this. But who for? The New Statesman possibly. Or one of Richard Desmond's top shelf mags? The problem with the former is it preaches to the converted, while the latter might require photos.

Tune in to Dr Fatty, who's droning on to the yummy student doctor. "Can you feel a walnut in there? Something that feels like a walnut?"

"No I don't think so..."

"Move your finger round."

God that's good.

"I'm not sure..."

"Keep moving your finger. It's there, I just felt it myself."

The embarrassing thing is that *that* wasn't too bad either.

"Oh *yes*. Yes, I can feel it now! Yes, just like a walnut..."

Have to stop myself groaning. Reflect on the irony that this could be the nearest to sex I get for the rest of my life but am not allowed to make the proper noises.

"You can put your trousers back on now, Mr Appleforth."

"Right – thank you..."

I put on my underpants and struggle with my jeans while trying to catch the eye of the yummy student doctor but she pretends she doesn't notice. I wonder if suggesting a drink after work is out of order but the surely unnecessary vigorousness with which she scrubs her hands in the sink makes me think I might be wasting my time. (Another thing I've learned about women – they often give their true feelings away with these little unconscious actions).

"Well there's nothing wrong with your prostate, Mr

Appleforth," says Dr Fatty. "It's a perfectly normal size."

"Are you sure?" I'm delighted. But for the briefest of moments also a tiny bit sad, almost as if I've lost a friend. "So why do I keep peeing so much?"

"Could be all sorts of things. Have you had any urinary tract infections recently?"

"No."

"How about cystitis?"

"What are you trying to suggest? That's a girl's thing, isn't it?"

"It's more common in women than men, yes, but men certainly do get it, specially sexually active gay men..."

"I am *not* gay!"

"Are you sexually active?"

"No *not* with men."

"So are you sexually active at the moment with women?"

I try to say it quietly so the yummy student doctor won't hear.

"Sorry?"

I try a bit louder.

"I'm sorry I really can't hear you..."

The yummy student doctor seems to have forgotten about scrubbing her hands and is looking at me with a little smile. Which makes me glad I didn't ask her out for a drink after all.

"No I am *not* sexually active, not just at the moment!"

Dr Fatty chuckles.

"Did I say something funny, doctor?"

He stops chuckling, but seems to be trying to avoid the irritating student doctor's eye. "No not at all. Do you drink a lot of coffee?"

"Why?"

"How many cups a day would you say?"

"I don't know – three…"

"That's fine. And do you drink alcohol, Mr Appleforth?"

I stare at him. "Yes a bit."

"How much is a bit?"

"It varies, doesn't it?"

"So how much have you drunk over the last week?"

I carefully work it out. Then I divide it by seven, then halve it. Then I tell him.

"That's far too much. Your weekly quota shouldn't be more than twenty-one units. You need to seriously cut down your drinking, Mr Appleforth. Cut it down by three-quarters and you'll sleep properly without having to go to the toilet every five minutes. And you might still have a liver in five years' time!"

The weird thing is he obviously thinks I'm talking about weekly intake. Anyway, I nod dutifully and tune out. I've had this crap from doctors for years and I haven't died yet. Instead of listening to him I think about some of my drinking heroes, like David Niven (drank like a fish, died aged 73) and Peter Cook (drank like a fish, and died – no, cancel that one…) and Jeffrey Bernard (drank like a fish and had a leg amputated then died aged 65. Oh fuck).

3.30 p.m.

Sit in the Galloping Gastro drinking my first glass of Rioja, which has been delayed by several hours for medical reasons, and wonder how to cut down on the booze.

Don't get very far with this line of thinking, so ask myself a few fundamental questions instead.

First – why am I wasting time worrying about this politically correct nonsense? Is it the unfortunate combination of Dr Fatty's warning and sudden terror about having bits cut off?
Second – let's face it, amputation isn't very likely, is it? Wasn't it the fags that did for Jeffrey Barnard? If it was I'm OK, because haven't smoked since 22nd November 1990, when I gave up to celebrate Margaret Thatcher's downfall – a momentous day both personally and politically.
Third – so is there really any reason to cut down?
Fourth – doesn't sound like it, does it?
Fifth – OK, how about financial?

This is the hard one. The fact is that because of chronic lack of government subsidy I'm forced to spend too much on alcohol. Now I'm 61 I do get a few measly things free, eg travel and prescriptions – but only for certain drugs. The profoundly anti-working-class Labour government lets me have middle-class drugs like Prozac and Seroxat free so it can get the Middle-England Daily Mail vote, but refuses to prescribe the well-proven working man's mood-enhancer, alcohol. If Gordon Brown had any political nous at all he'd realize that free-alcohol-for-health-reasons-for-over-sixties-working-men could win the day for him even now. Much though I loathe him he'd certainly get my vote, and that of countless other working men in their sixties too.

But as he's a moany old puritanical son of the manse I daresay his finger will remain stuck firmly up his Presbyterian fundament and a great opportunity will be lost.

I sometimes wonder if he really *wants* to win this election.

4.40 p.m.

Ask Michelle for another small dose of the house antidepressant and find I'm down to my last fiver. Realize that the one and only reason to cut down on the booze is indeed financial.

As Michelle refills my glass I compliment her on her nice lacy blouse and ask her if she'll join me. She rather coolly says for what. I say for a drink. She says no, and hurries off. I sometimes think I'll never understand women.

Drink Rioja on own and realize I couldn't have paid for her anyway.

Go home depressed, even though am apparently not going to die.

11.20 p.m.

Have drunk nothing except Coke all evening in order to conserve alcohol supplies with the result that have had to sit through eleven hours of Heartbeat and twelve hours of Midsomer Murders on ITV3 without falling asleep once (NB – Not actually twenty-three hours but that's what it felt like).

But at least have proved Alice is wrong – even when awake I still don't understand the plot.

This nightmarish evening makes me face the fact that as I probably can't look to the Government for support I desperately need to earn money in order to buy enough booze so I can doze happily in front of ITV3.

Not a wildly ambitious dream, surely?

But how to achieve it? How, how, how?

Tuesday 13th April

12.05 a.m.

Decide nightmarish sleepless evening cannot be followed by nightmarish sleepless night so take three herbal sleeping pills made of lettuce.

12.30 a.m.

No effect. Take six more.

1.00 a.m.

Still no effect. In desperation decide to have glass of 3 for £10 Tesco reddo as sleep-inducing chaser. Am shocked to discover have run out completely, so decide to make do with glass of Grand Marnier. Reach for the bottle, which is on shelf over kitchen sink, but have pushed it too far back behind the Amaretto and the Cointreau and have to stand on chair to get it. Finally get hold of it, but in doing so slip off chair and knock Amaretto and Cointreau bottles into sink where they both smash.

Still have the Grand Marnier however, so carefully open the bottle and pour a glass.

Nothing comes out.

1.10 a.m. – 6.00 a.m.

Have nightmarish sleepless alcohol-free night.

6.05 a.m.

Realize there's only one answer. My guilt-free, opportunistic, unprincipled best friend Wills has won. Prostituting my talents to Sudoku Weekly is the only way forward.

This realization has a calming effect and sleep without peeing till eleven.

11.30 a.m.

While ironing now miraculously shit-free and other-stains-free dressing gown, I wonder if maybe Wills is right and maybe I wouldn't be prostituting my talents after all, but merely, as he put it, accommodating them to a new form. Decide that this is the case and that my earlier negative view came from a dark depressed 6 a.m. place to which I certainly do not want to return.

The more I think about it the more I realize this could be a real challenge as well as a money-earner. As Wills wisely put it, isn't accommodating your talents to a new form what being a professional is all about? Am so stunned by Wills being wise that burn a hole in dressing gown.

Try to get rid of burn with washing-up liquid and scrubbing brush, which makes it worse. While doing this make creative decision to start thinking of Sudoku like haiku or the iambic pentameter, and get very excited.

12.20 p.m.

Go to Galloping Gastro to have more creative thoughts. Michelle isn't there, just a young guy who stares at me angrily. As have no money I ask him for a glass of house Rioja and suggest he puts it on the slate. He denies they have a slate, so I ask for a glass of water, with ice, which seems to make him even angrier. I wait till he's given me the iced water then give him a coolly withering look and turn away. Go to table where they keep the newspapers and look for the Daily Mail (which of course is even worse than iniquitous right-wing Murdoch press). Find it and sit down and study Sudoku puzzles for half an hour.

Group of tousle-haired young guys come in who I think I recognise from Sunday (can't be entirely sure because all tousle-haired young guys look the same to me nowadays). They order lots of drinks and food and ask the angry young guy to put it on the slate, which he happily does.

Decide this favoured treatment is because they all went to the same public school and that this country's class system is as pernicious today as it ever was. Feel proud of my uncompromising radicalism and wonder how soon I can get money from Wills for contributions to his mag.

2.00 p.m.

Decide that the answer to the above is *never*. Can't understand sodding Sudoku puzzles so how can I accommodate my considerable talents to this stupid fucking form?

As I leave in disgust I pass the table that the tousle-haired young toffs have recently vacated and see a couple of half-drunk glasses of reddo. Pause to knock them back then catch sight of the angry young guy, who seems to reserve his anger just for me. Give him the coolly withering look again and leave.

As I walk back to my flat a miracle occurs (probably because of the half-glasses of reddo). I suddenly see how I can make a unique contribution to Sudoku Weekly after all.

I'll do it by convincing Wills he should have a quiz section at the back, written by me.

But how do I convince him?

The only way is by writing brilliant quizzes and giving

them to him at our weekly Joe Allen lunch (tomorrow).

(Note to self – make sure they're witty and characteristically subversive, but at the same time remember to accommodate my talents to the "popular" readership, perhaps by exploring the celebrity culture they're obsessed with. Interestingly enough, have often noticed on buses, in tubes and while dining in Burger King that a high proportion of the readers of such magazines belong to the older demographic. Which will of course play to my strengths).

2.45 p.m.

Am writing my first quiz when phone rings. Am so deep in creative throes that I don't answer it – even when I realize it's my future patron.

"Hi, Wills again. Worried that I haven't hear back from you! You're probably so insulted by my suggestion you're never going to talk to me again! Just to say I've booked our usual table at Joe's in the profound hope that I'm wrong, mate. If you do turn up I'll buy some really expensive wine, and even grovel apologetically if you insist!"

Fantastic. I'm starting from a position of strength!

Wednesday 14th April

1.30 p.m.

I stroll down the stairs to Joe Allen and see Wills at our usual table, looking twitchy and worried because I'm deliberately even later than usual and have ignored his increasingly anxious texts. He sees me approaching and beams and leaps up and we high-five in the middle of the room, like we always do. I notice there are two glasses of champagne on the table, and as I sit down he grins and asks, "So what have you been up to?"

"Apart from wanking, you mean?"

He roars with laughter, but overdoes it a bit by slapping his knee several times as if he'd never heard it before, even though, as I mentioned earlier, it's a joke we've been cracking weekly since 1974. Anyway we clink glasses and drink our champagne and he immediately orders more.

While we're waiting I decide to let him off the hook and tell him that as a personal favour I've decided I'm willing to work for Sudoku Weekly. He gushes for several minutes, then I tell him about my brilliant idea for a quiz section for the not-quite-so-young who are obsessed with celebrity.

"What about Sudoku? It's a Sudoku magazine, Arnold..."

I'd anticipated such negativity because Wills is nothing if not literal and unimaginative. "Yeah well I'm sure your mates Dawn and Jennifer would just love a witty quiz section that –"

"But Dawn and Jennifer love *Sudoku,* Arnold."

"So you keep saying. But I'm sure they'd welcome something a bit more mentally challenging too. They used to be radical fucking alternative comedians, didn't they?!"

"Sudoku *is* mentally challenging, that's the whole point of it!"

"Yeah, yeah but not *really.*"

"Yes *really.*"

He's starting to piss me off now. So I try another angle. "Think of it more as a sort of post-modern quiz section, Wills. A sort of anti-quiz quiz section. By which I mean you need to be a little bit sharp to get it – like Dawn and Jennifer. Do you understand what I'm saying?"

The problem with having a best friend like Wills is I'm so much cleverer than him it can get really embarrassing at times. Like now for instance. I watch pityingly as he screws up his eyes and squeezes the bridge of his nose like he always does when he's out of his depth and panicking but is too stupid to admit it.

"You mean you think this might attract some of the clued-up AB readers the advertisers are always so desperate for?"

"Do I *think* it will? I *know* it will! And not just a few, my old mucker!"

"I see. Well, that sounds...Well...Yes...Maybe...So have you got anything to show me?"

Before he can change what passes for his mind I unhitch from my chair my "Slime Minister Tony Bliar" hemp man-bag (which I bought half-price at Politicos Bookshop bag section a couple of years back when Gordon took over) and pull a folder out of it. And take out a piece of paper and pass it to him.

He reads very slowly, following the words with his fingers and saying them to himself like he always does:

Which well-known person of-a-certain-age do you most want to be like?

1. *Sir Trevor Nunn*
2. *Woody Allen*
3. *Your dad (for female readers – your mum)*
4. *Pat from EastEnders*
5. *Twiggy*

When he's finished he looks up thoughtfully (is this what blue sky thinking is? Not much sky in Joe Allen's mind you so perhaps not. Must google when get home). After some moments he empties his champagne glass and gazes across the restaurant. He does this for so long I start to wonder if he's looking for Dawn and Jen to check out their reactions.

"It's brilliant," he says finally. "Pithy, original, subversive but with a broad cultural reference that'll attract both the thicko demographic – ie the reference to Pat from East Enders – which let's face it is our core readership, but also the clued-up AB demographic – ie the references to my mate Trevor and Woody Allen. Twiggy will appeal to both because of her M and S ads. Mum and dad will appeal to everyone. And you've even achieved a perfect fifty-fifty gender split, which is specially amazing considering you've got a list of five." He pauses for breath after this astute off-the-cuff analysis, then smiles at me, and I swear he's looking misty-eyed. "You know, Arnie, in its way this is flawless. It's like you've been waiting to do this all your life, mate. It's like, what do you call it, those little Japanese poem thingies..."

"Haiku. And don't call me fucking Arnie or mate."

"Sorry. So have you got some more?"

"I might have," I smile.

"Please."

I toy with my empty champagne glass, just to make him wait for a bit, then casually take another piece of paper out of my folder and pass it to him. This one's even better.

He flexes his finger and starts to read, no longer suspiciously but with a smile of anticipation.

Which sex symbols of your youth and early middle-age do you still secretly lust after?

1. *Barbara Windsor*
2. *Diana Dors*
3. *June Whitfield*
4. *Lady Isabel Barnett*
5. *Pearl Carr and Teddy Johnson*
6. *Marianne Faithfull and Sandy Shaw doing it to each other in bed with the Singing Nun watching.*

After poring over it for some minutes he looks up at me. There are actual tears in his eyes now. "You know what I'm going to do for you, Arnold? I'm going to start a quiz section right now, well when I say right now I mean in the very next edition, and I'm going to publish both these quizzes exactly as they are."

You have to give it to Wills, he might be a craven arselicker and a lickspittle and an unprincipled lackey of the system but he's a brilliant editor. I don't know what it is, maybe it's that combination of quiet inner-confidence and an infallible instinct for quality.

"My one criticism is..." (Strike out "he's a brilliant editor

– etc. etc." He's an interfering cunt like all the others). "My one criticism is, it's such a great trip down memory lane, and such a fantastic little nostalgic vignette for the AB baby-boomers that I just want more of it..."

"No problem." (Strike out "Strike out 'he's a brilliant editor – etc. etc.'" And the gratuitously unpleasant sentence after that).

"And look I'm the last person to try to interfere with the creative process, but what about Kathy Kirby?! And Dusty Springfield?! And Alma Cogan?!"

"I thought they were lezzies?"

"Really? Well that could be *great! Fantastic!*"

"How interesting – I'd no idea your mag had a strong lezzie demographic."

"Maybe it doesn't. But it *could,* couldn't it? It certainly *could.* Personally I'm all for it. The broader the demographic the better, that's what I say!"

I'm beginning to get a bit worried now. "So you don't want to censor it in any way?"

"Certainly not!"

"Not even the mucky bit about Marianne Faithfull and Sandy Shaw and the Singing Nun? I mean I know how naturally craven and pusillanimous you are, Wills – I'm not *judging,* it's just part of your nature..."

"No I'm definitely going to stick my neck out on this one Arnold!"

"Yeah, great, of course, but look I wouldn't want to land you in the..."

"I've made up my mind! I'm going to stake my professional future on this. And if they don't like it they can go screw themselves!"

"Shit..."

He chuckles. "What's this? A tiny bit jealous, are you, that your cop-out friend is being brave and fearless for once, just like you, and finally standing up for what he believes in?"

"No, dickhead, I mean *shit* you'll be out of a job next month just when you could have been some use to me. So how about you pay me for the work so far?"

"You know, I do understand the system, Arnold," he smiles. "It's all to do with personal contacts, you see, and as I've spent a lifetime cultivating them I really have nothing to worry about."

"Money, Wills."

He smiles again and takes five twenties out of his wallet and puts them in front of me. I wait, and he adds another fifty. "That's all I've got, I'm afraid." He leans forward. "But let me say, it's worth every penny!"

The new glasses of champagne finally arrive and we raise our glasses.

"Can I be personal?" he smiles.

"No."

"I'm going to be anyway. It's so great to discover after all these years that there really is an area where we can work together."

"Yeah."

"I mean it!"

"So do I, Wills, so do I!"

This seems to make him happy, and we glance at the menu, and he orders something poncy as usual, while I order Caesar salad and cheeseburger well done and chips like I always do.

As I sit there gazing at him as he rabbits merrily on, I

wonder how he does it. Manages to be so happy about everything, I mean.

"Can I be personal, too, Wills?" I say.

"Absolutely. In fact, you know, I wish you were more often, Arnold."

"Right. There's something that's been bothering me about you for twenty-five years, Wills."

"What's that?" he asks eagerly.

"How come you're still only onto your second wife?"

"That's really easy. It's because we love each other."

"I'm being serious, Wills. Is it because you've got a very low sex drive, and you're so boring and suburban that you're not into pussy? I don't mean that offensively of course..."

"No, no, no offence taken! Well as for sex drive – well it's a difficult one, isn't it? Of course nothing's plain sailing, and we all have our ups and downs..."

"Oh *right,*" I laugh sympathetically. "You mean you're off up the East Croydon tennis club shagging anything that moves? Now I get it!"

"Actually I don't belong to the East Croydon tennis club, though I hear very good things about it..." He gives me a tolerant smile. "You see the thing you just don't get, Arnold, is that Mary and I really still love each other. We *really really* do. We often laugh about it – we always say it's a marriage made in heaven, even after nearly thirty years!"

"That's great," I say, managing to smile back, which is difficult when you're trying not to heave.

"Thank you! You know it's so great, the two of us having a proper personal conversation like this, about love and things. It's amazing, I mean we've never done it before have we, not in the God knows how many years we've known each other! I'm touched."

"Me too."

"No I am."

"So am I – I just said. So what do you do for sex if it's not the tennis club?"

"What?"

"Look I know you still love her deeply blah blah blah, but the novelty must have worn off, to put it mildly – so how do you manage? Have you got a webcam lady? Or a nice masseuse…?"

"You're perfectly right," he says with a little sigh. "After twenty-nine years it's not just about sex. It's much more complicated than that. No of course we don't have sex like we used to."

"I'm not trying to be intrusive, Wills, you know me better than that…"

"I know you're not. I know you're searching for something yourself, Arnold. I'm not stupid, I know that despite the brave front you're desperately trying to fill that emptiness, that gaping void that I imagine must get harder to cope with every year…"

"I'm not trying to fill any gaping fucking void, I'd just like to know why all my marriages went wrong and for some weird reason yours doesn't!"

"Yes of course. Sorry…"

"And don't smirk."

"*Sorry*… Perhaps it's just you need to learn to compromise a little more. Marriage-wise I mean, not professionally of course! Unfortunately, the initial excitement of a relationship does wear off, of course it does."

"Yeah well that's when I'm out the door, I never got past that stage."

"Exactly. That's where you've gone wrong, if I might say so. You have to accept you can't always have it all your own way. Like Mary and I. When I think back to the early days... well we used to have sex every day at least. Twice a day often, it was great! But as time went by I just had to accept that that couldn't continue. There were so many other things going on, the domestic chores, bringing up kids, not to mention just getting older and more tired. And now it's probably only half that, but I've come to terms with it..."

"Half what?"

"I'm sorry?"

"How many times is half that?"

"Look let's face it we're not just middle-aged now, Arnold, we're actually getting old," he smiles. "And the painful fact is that the old hormones just don't whizz round like they used to, which I suppose is why I don't mind nearly as much as I thought I would!"

"How many times do you do it if it's half what you used to do?!"

He frowns. "We're really not on the same wavelength, are we, Arnold? I'm sorry but I'm not entering into a sexual competition with you.

Whatever I might have been like in my youth, I certainly no longer regard sex as being about quantity, as far as I'm concerned it's about things like closeness and intimacy. Reducing it to mere numbers isn't just sordid, it feels like a betrayal of the connection Mary and I have –"

"How many times do you do it a week?!"

"Four or five! Now just shut up about it!"

I can't even look at him.

After a little while he calms down, and glances at me resentfully. "OK so what about you? You do it a lot I suppose, do you?"

2.30 p.m.

I'm so traumatised that I merely toy with the two bottles of St Emilion Grand Cru Wills eventually orders, and only have a single Armagnac instead of my usual double to go with the pecan pie and ice cream and as a result leave Joe Allen disturbingly sober.

On the tube home I try to focus on billionaire Lebedev's free Evening Standard to take my mind off my recent sexual humiliation. I read that it's Lib Dem manifesto day, and Nick Clegg has said the Lib Dems will "hardwire fairness into British society". I laugh hollowly at this, just as the train stops at Earls Court and a lumpen proletariat youth with a swastika on his forehead gets on and glares at me and asks what's funny. I say it's something Nick Clegg said. This doesn't seem to satisfy him so I read it out and laugh hollowly again, and drily say like hell they will! He says what the fuck are you talking about? I wearily explain that after years working to change society I've come to the reluctant conclusion that human existence is so unjust that no political party can litigate for fairness, and am about to tell him about how much pussy my boring best friend Wills gets, just by way of illustration, when he cuts in and tells me he's BNP and do I want to fucking make something of it?

Uncomfortable few minutes while he glares at me malevolently and I pretend not to notice. Get off at West

Kensington and run back to next carriage and get on again.

3.10 p.m.

Get off at Hammersmith. Unfortunately, lumpen proletariat youth with swastika is waiting for me. I smile in best affable manner and attempt to stroll casually past and he says, "What have you got written on your man-bag, eh, pooftah?" I smilingly explain that it's a satirical joke about Tony Blair and he says, "Well it's spelt wrong, cunt." Am getting a tiny bit stressed by now and explain that actually it's *meant* to be spelt like that – the misspelling of his name as Bliar is actually central to the joke – and he comes closer and says, "So are you taking the piss out of people who can't spell? Are you taking the piss out of my dyslexic fucking sister then? Are you, eh? Eh?" Before I can stop myself I hear myself satirically shouting, "Am I bovvered? Am I bovvered? Am I bovvered then?!" just like Catherine Tate on the DVD box set I bought at Kensington High Street Oxfam the other week. I'm astonished by the rapid change of expressions on the youth's pustule-packed face – amazement then disbelief, then rage, then even worse rage.

"It's *Catherine Tate,*" I hurriedly tell him. "That's who I was imitating. She's hilarious – you 'll love her! Look, I'll lend you the box set – she's more your generation than mine anyway. In fact, you know you can keep it if you want...!"

The youth is standing so close to me now that I can almost count the pustules, and I feel a numbness spreading through my body, like I imagine those Americans on death row five minutes after they've gone for the poison option. As I'm about to accept the inevitable, a young woman loaded down with designer purchases brushes past him with her Nicole Fahri bags and he turns his scowl on her and pours out an effortless stream of abuse. Appalled though I am, I'm afraid I put gallantry to one side and run like hell.

Thanks to my trusty freedom pass I get through the barrier in seconds, leaving the BNP retard way behind.

"Oy, come back!"

I walk briskly off. Then glance round and see him still stuck at the barrier, struggling furiously with his ticket.

I smile and raise a finger and shout "Fuck you, pooftah!" A group of people around me find this hilarious and applaud enthusiastically, which cheers me considerably. Then the BNP retard works out how to use his ticket and gets through the barrier and I run like hell again.

After five minutes have to stop running. Not to look at the pretty daffodils and crocuses on Brook Green and wonder at the delights of spring and nature etc etc but because have dreadful stitch and can't go an inch further. Try to touch toes to get rid of stitch but can't get anywhere near them. Even so, the stretching helps, and find I am able to walk again. Glance round and relieved to see the coast is clear, so resume journey home at normal pace, feeling a little smug about the fact that even though am possibly three times his age I managed to lose the BNP retard somewhere near Hammersmith roundabout.

"Oy, cunt, come 'ere!"

I resume running. The stitch returns and is soon unbelievably agonising, but am interested to discover, as many an athlete has before me, how easily one can get through the pain barrier when the motivation is there.

Before I know it am approaching the Galloping Gastro, but the BNP retard is gaining on me. Consider going into pub to seek sanctuary like they do in churches. Wonder if same rules apply. That Richard Burton movie flashes through my mind – the one where he plays that religious bloke, what's his name, Becket, who thought he was safe in his own church but King Peter O'Toole's thugs burst into the church and off him even so. Decide maybe better to err on the side of caution, specially as at this point the angry young guy comes out of the pub and sees me running towards him and I get the feeling that given the chance he'd behave just like Peter O'Toole's thugs.

My suspicion is confirmed when he shouts, "Go for it, Adolf, go for it!"

The BNP retard is so close now I begin to wonder if am going to make it safely home. If not, will the Catherine Tate box set be enough to appease him? Am not convinced.

Get key out as I approach my flat and see a pile of dog shit on doorstep that's so huge it makes previous offerings pale into insignificance. Neatly sidestep it and jam key in lock and open door. But BNP friend is too close and lunges at the door as I try to shut it. As he lunges he lands right in the bumper-sized offering of doggy-doo and skids spectacularly and falls arse over tip, head crashing really hard on the step. I try to shut the door again but can't because he's sprawled unconscious across the doorway. Then, like Arnold Schwarzenegger in Terminator, he staggers groggily to his feet, a very mean look on his face.

At which point Lizzie the Lezzie comes breezily out of her house, a picture postcard in one hand and her dogs on a lead in the other.

"Oh how *gross,*" she exclaims at the BNP retard as he sways unsteadily in my doorway, "you've got poo all over your shirt! For heaven's sake this is a desirable neighbourhood! Get out! Get out! Go on – before I let the dogs on you. I said *shooh!*" He looks more like Arnold Schwarzenegger by the second and his menacing glare scares the crap out of me but I'm astonished to see it has no effect on Lizzie – unless it's to make her even more annoyed. "I'm a local magistrate, young man, and if you don't disappear this instant I shall see you tomorrow, in court, and I guarantee that you *won't* like the consequences." All he's got to do is bop her and she'd crumble into a heap of old bones on the ground, but to my amazement he starts to back off, muttering resentfully. "And if you've got something to say," she shouts after him, "please come back here and say it clearly! One thing I can't bear is muttering!" This strikes me as wilfully perverse, but he doesn't take her up on it. "And if I see you in this neighbourhood ever again – and when I say ever I mean *ever* – you will seriously regret it!"

I watch him slope off down the street, broken and defeated, then look at Lizzie with new respect. "Are you really a magistrate?"

"Bollocks I am," she smiles triumphantly. "But it got rid of the ghastly little oik, didn't it?" She glances down at the dog shit, now covering my entire doorstep like a super-size serving of Nutella Hazelnut spread. "All I can say is, thank heaven for the phantom crapper. I'd say you owe him a vote of thanks, don't you agree? A cost-free security system, after all!"

At that moment it crosses my mind that if Lizzie wasn't a hundred and twenty-eight and a lezzie, I could almost fall in love with her. She's not just fearless, she's got a sense of humour too.

Then I notice she's holding something out to me. It's the picture postcard she came out of the house with. "I was about to pop this through your door. I do hope you can come."

I look at the picture. It's a photo of Lizzie standing between Margaret Thatcher and Norman Tebbit, and she's got her arms round them both and all three are smiling broadly at the camera.

"What the fuck's this?"

"I beg your pardon?" she smiles, very Lady Muck suddenly.

"Why are you giving me this disgusting picture of you with your arms round the two people I despise most in the world – well leaving aside Tony Blair and A A Gill? Do you think it's funny? Do you think I'm a closet fucking Tory or something? Is that what you're trying to tell me?!"

"Oh lovely – lovely! How priceless...!" She starts to snort, and her massive bosoms shake up and down really alarmingly.

"Are you OK? Are you having an eppy, Lizzie? Have you got your pills?"

"I'm fine! I'm fine! Really...!" Eventually the snorting subsides and her tits stop shaking and a little hankie magically appears from her sleeve and she blows her nose on it really loudly and she starts to calm down. "I'm afraid I Photoshopped it, Arnold, on my Apple."

"You what?"

"I thought it would be amusing to see your reaction. And it certainly was!"

She looks as if she's about to start off again but I glare at her and she stops. "So they're not your best mates?"

"Unfortunately, no. I'm sorry – it was terribly childish of me, I know. Oh dear – your face ... such a picture...!" The snorting resumes and she whips out her hankie again and snuffles helplessly into it.

"I'm glad you find it so amusing, Lizzie," I say stiffly, and it crosses my mind that if she hadn't saved my life three minutes ago I might be getting a little offended. And as for falling in love with the old bag, forget it.

"Anyway," she smiles brightly, "I do hope you can come."

"Come to what?"

She takes the postcard from me and shows me what it says on the back. "You are cordially invited to drinkies and dinner chez Lizzie. 7.30 for 8, Thursday 15th April. (That's tomorrow!) RSVP."

"I don't do dinner parties, sorry. Loathsome bourgeois rituals where the over-privileged stuff their faces and have solemn discussions about Serious Issues."

"Oh we never discuss anything serious at my parties, it's strictly forbidden. See you at 7.30."

"I just said, Lizzie, I don't do dinner parties."

She looks me up and down critically. "And a proper shirt might be in order, too."

She turns to go back into her house, but I'm starting to get annoyed. "And on the very rare occasions that I *do* go to dinner parties, I never wear proper shirts! Anyway, I'm busy tomorrow evening!"

"Don't be silly, Arnold," she smiles back, "you're never busy! I'd say you're the least busy person I've ever met in my life."

Before I can make a cutting reply she's gone, taking her yappy dogs with her. I'm tempted to bang on her door to defend my alleged inactivity because she clearly has no idea that creative people need more "leisure" time than normal ones so their unconsciouses can bubble away uninterrupted.

Then I realize I can't be arsed, and go back in, carefully avoiding the remains of The Biggest Dump In History.

3.50 p.m.

Realize that debacle with BNP retard has made me forget to buy Tesco 3 for £10 reddo on way home to celebrate possible career renaissance on Sudoku Weekly, so cannot have post-prandial tincture prior to lie-down on sofa, so am in appalling position again of being forced to watch TV totally sober (well not quite totally).

Turn on TV and Channel Four appears. Am baffled. Haven't watched Channel Four for nearly a year and a half. Can name the exact date – 12th December 2008, when Carol Vordeman got chucked off Countdown. Had been loyal to cutie Carol for 26 years and nearly 5000 episodes and felt impelled to boycott Channel Four as protest against pernicious epidemic of ageism in the media (also because there's sod-all else on Channel Four).

Sadly, my years of devotion to hottie Carol (age 49 – perfect!) were sorely tested when discovered recently she's a Tory. But it could be even worse, she could support class traitor Gordon Brown, so have decided to forgive her, and as a result my Channel Four boycott continues. Have to admit I briefly broke it to take a peek at the new girl. What a disappointment! She just hasn't got what Carol has – that disturbing mixture of Diane Keaton (in her Woody Allen days) and Stephanie Beacham (in her Dynasty days) and my arithmetic teacher with the lipstick and the come-on smile when I was eleven.

Realize am having minor erotic reverie – in front of Noel Edmonds on Deal or No Deal. Feel really embarrassed.

Trouble is I go way back with Noelie, just like with Carol. The big difference is I've loathed him even longer than I've loved her. To be precise, since '76 when was forced to watch him on "Multi-Coloured Swap Shop" with one of my kids. (Not sure which one. Quentin, was it? Yes, Quentin – have worked it out – definitely Quentin – maybe that's why he's gay!)

Seriously though, I sometimes feel am haunted by Noelie, because discovered years ago in Guardian birthdays column (which yet again I was not in!) that we're the same age. I mean *exactly the same age.* Also he's been married three times, just like me. And he disappeared for years and years, just like me, but now he's everywhere again (more like John Nettles than me, unfortunately).

So have sometimes wondered if Noelie is my doppelganger – my shadow, as the Jungians would call it. So is the fact that have had minor erotic reverie in front of his creepily cheery face significant? A little nudge-and-a-wink from the dark side? A warning maybe of the onset of middle-aged hormonal change or something equally dreadful? The sight of Noelie's gleaming slicked-back hair certainly gives me a pang. Not sexually I hasten to add, but nostalgically – for those halcyon radical Time Out days when the world was young and we all loved taking the piss out of old Noelie (except Wills, who really liked him).

Quickly switch channels before I become emotional.

ITV3. That's better. Good old ITV3.What's this? Richard Briers pottering about being ancient. Nothing to disturb the hormones there. Nice countryside. Hate the countryside of course but nice to see it on TV. Funny how everything on ITV3 has nice countryside – Marple, Midsomer Murders,

Heartbeat. Perhaps it's in their charter. Oh there's Susan Hampshire! Not as ancient as R Briers of course, but not quite the English rose she once was. (But then which of us is?) They're talking about ghillies. Sounds filthy. What are ghillies? Some sort of old people's sex aid? (Note to self – google "ghillies"). Oh no it's a Scottish programme. Monarch of the Glen – of course! It's something to do with fly fishing. Oh bugger. (Note to self – don't bother to google "ghillies").

Am about to switch channels again but it's the adverts. Must admit I do have a weakness for adverts. Not morally or philosophically of course because they're exploitative and offensive and in every way repugnant. But they do have some funny bits...

Think I'll switch channels after the adverts...

6.20 p.m.

Wake up and it's Midsomer Murders. *Again.* I swear it's the same one I saw last week...Or is it? Or are they just so similar that after half a dozen it's impossible to tell them apart? Think am onto something here...Or is there only one episode of Midsomer Murders, endlessly repeated?

Ruminations about popular TV drama suddenly abandoned when hear a suspicious noise over the sound of the television. It's a door shutting. It's obviously the BNP retard and he's broken in and he's hell-bent on revenge.

They say your whole life flashes before you when you're about to die. But all I can think of is what I *haven't* done in my life. Which is have sex – with someone else I mean – not for three months anyway. And then it was with the fifty-year-old binge-eating divorcee I befriended at Notting Hill Nando's. Which was great of course in its way. After all, any port in a storm, as she said herself! But it certainly had its limitations… *And it was only one and a half times – if that – which is nothing compared to deeply boring best friend Wills who manages four or five times a week!*

During this life-flashing-before-your-eyes bit I vow that if by some remote chance I survive my swastika-ed nemesis I shall do one of two things – contact the Nando's lady at once, or pursue some other sexual avenue *urgently*.

Hear movements and try to take mind off imminent death by weighing up the pros and cons of above. Advantage of approaching binge-eating Nando's lady – sex virtually guaranteed. Disadvantage – sex with peri-peri chicken and coleslaw fun at first but wears off. Advantage of pursuing other sexual avenue – novelty. Disadvantage – huge effort involved in pursuit, very possibly ending in failure.

Can now hear conversation over television sounds. Christ, he's brought his BNP mates to help. Try not to move a muscle and stare hard at John Nettles acting happily married with his smiley wife, and find myself wondering not for the first time why they never let her out of the kitchen, while at the same time hoping that if I remain motionless the BNP gang will think I've died and rigor mortis has already set in so there's no point kicking me to death.

Then get a whiff of dog shit and hear a familiar voice. "Oh for heaven's sake Jamel, you've got cack all over your shoes! Oh God no so have you, Tobias!"

"And so have you, mummy. We treaded in it on the doorstep – I sawed it happen!"

"For God's sake don't talk like a baby, Tobias, you know you're just doing it to annoy me, it pisses me off so much…"

"Oh look look there's grandad. Look, Jamel, look – he

looks like he's deaded!" Peals of laughter.

"Not *deaded*, Tobias. Do you know how much I spend on your sodding schooling? Why do I bother?! For Christ's sake you speak Latin better than you do English..."

I don't want to sound sentimental, but sometimes the joy of being a dad can overwhelm one completely unexpectedly. This is one of those times. OK, I know I'm not a perfect dad. Maybe because I'm human! But all I can say is the sight of my darling daughter and her two little boys walking dog cack through my flat brings tears to my eyes – even though they're wearing their hideous prep school uniforms in the middle of the Easter holidays.

"Alice! What a lovely surprise!"

"Oh so you are alive. You see, he is alive, Tobias!"

"Just about!" I get up and give her a kiss and a hug and she tries to wriggle out of it like she always does. Then I get down to give the boys a kiss and a hug and Tobias says "Ow pongy breath Grandad! Pongy pongy pongy!" I chuckle and wait – in vain as usual – for Alice to discipline the little tyke. Then turn and give Jamel a kiss and a hug, and he actually seems quite happy about it. For some reason Jamel hasn't (yet!) been turned into an unbearable little snot-rag by the snobby prep school my Labour-voting daughter insists on sending them to. I only wish I could say the same about Tobias.But I do sometime wonder if the fact that Jamel is so much nicer has something to do with the fact that he's half-Jamaican (Note to self – is this a politically correct or incorrect thought? No idea – must google to find out).

Talking of multi-racial families, Alice really is like me in so many ways, and this is just another example. Not that I'm a single mum of course, but if I was I know I'd be like her –

right at the cutting edge of multi-cultural single-parenting.

"So how did you get in?" I ask, as she wrenches off the children's shoes then takes off her own and lines them up in a neat cack-splattered row by the door.

"I've got a key."

"How did you get a key? I didn't give you a key, did I?"

"No, Dad, Quentin and Roger and I had a meeting and we decided we needed to have access in case you had a stroke or something and no one found you for three days."

"Why do people keep talking about me not being found for three days?!"

"Work it out for yourself. Anyway, we didn't want to get into a long argument with you about it so Roger took your key and had a copy taken last time you were at his place."

"How did he manage to do that?"

She doesn't answer because she's distracted by Tobias, who's whining on about being bored because he's forgotten his Latin primer so he can't do his prep. Then Jamel says Latin is crap (an opinion I totally agree with – not that I've ever studied it) and Tobias says no it's not, *you're* crap, and hits him. And Jamel gives him an impressive whack back (I do like Jamel more and more) and Alice grabs them both and tells them to go and sit on the sofa – on a *clean* bit of the sofa, *if* they can find one – and just be quiet and watch Midsomer Murders or whatever rubbish grandad has been dozing in front of.

"I was *not* dozing."

"Well you were at Roger's. He told me you had far too much to drink at lunch then fell asleep in front of a Foyle's War retrospective – the one you'd insisted several days before that you desperately wanted to see. That's when he took the key out of your pocket and drove off and had it copied."

"OK, OK, it was just a little zizz..."

"And on the way back he popped into the golf shop where he bumped into Brucie and Jimmy Tarbuck, and they had a few jokes then they played eight holes on the virtual golf simulator and when he came back you were *still* out cold. So what do you mean *just a little zizz?* You spend your whole life asleep, Dad!"

I decide to ignore this unwarranted attack. "So have you all got copies of my key?"

"Just me."

Harsh though Alice can sometimes sound, I get a rush of fond fatherly feelings on hearing she's so concerned. "Well that's great, I'm delighted."

"Why are you delighted?"

"Because you're my lovely daughter and I'd so much rather you had the key than the boys."

"We drew straws for it, Dad, and I lost."

"Oh, right."

I see her looking round the room critically and start to feel depressed. "So why have you come round, Alice? Great though it is to see you, of course!"

"You know, if you continue to live in utter squalor like this, Dad, we'll be forced to do something about it."

"I like it like this."

"No you don't, no one could like it like this."

"I do. It's homely."

"It's disgusting and unsanitary and you couldn't even be bothered to clean the dog cack off the doorstep, so what little remains of your carpet is now covered with it. And as for the *smell...*"

"Don't worry about it," I smile reassuringly, "it wears off eventually."

"You know that if you carry on like this you could end up in a home?"

"Sounds great! I know – how about your home? You've got four bedrooms after all!"

This shuts her up, like I knew it would. But not for long. "Why don't you have a cleaning lady?"

"I've had three cleaning ladies," I beam at her, "but they divorced me!"

Not a glimmer of a smile. Whatever happened to the great sense of humour we used to share? (Could it be her mum's fault? Answers on a postcard, as they say!)

"We worry about you rotting away in here, Dad," she says. "Rotting away and dying and not being found for weeks and weeks..."

"Oh it's weeks and weeks now? Thank you!"

"No *seriously* we do. All of us worry. Even Quentin – which is amazing considering your homophobia and your constant rudeness to Adam, who's actually a real sweetie..."

"How nice that you all worry so much!" I say, using the old irony again. "Why exactly is it again...?"

"Because you just *vegetate* in here, Dad. You don't *do* anything – you don't go anywhere except to the pub. You do *nothing at all* with your life!"

"That's not true!" I say indignantly. "Compared to Peter Cook I do enormous amounts..."

"Why are you comparing yourself to Peter Cook? He's dead! So what have you got in your diary at the moment then?"

"Lots of things. I'm going to a lesbian dinner party

tomorrow, and only today I went out for lunch with Wills…"

"Oh *Wills…!*"

"What do you mean 'Oh *Wills…!*'?"

"I mean Wills doesn't count."

"Why doesn't he count? He's only my oldest and dearest friend!"

"He's your *only* friend, Dad."

"Be that as it may, he certainly counts. Particularly because he's just commissioned me to write a series of think-pieces for his very impressive new magazine, as a result of which I'm now on the point of repositioning my career and –"

"Dad you don't *have* a career. *I* have a career – you don't."

I regard her icily. "That's what you think, is it?"

"I'm afraid I do. Anyway, you're too old for a career. They only want young people – young attractive women specially – which is why I'm surviving and you're… Look I really don't want to upset you, Dad, but let's face it you're a has-been, really, aren't you?"

I stare at her, my hurt and anger instantly vanishing. "That's it."

"What's it?"

"The title. For my magnum opus! *The Diary of a Has-been*. Brilliant!"

"What magnum opus?"

So I tell her all about it. And as I do I realize that she's the first person in the world I've even mentioned it to.

To my surprise she listens intently. She doesn't say a word till I've described the whole thing in detail (well the whole thing except for the bits about her and her mum, which I somehow forget to mention). When I've finished I look at her, moved by how gripped she's been. "So what do you think?"

"How can I put this?"

"Be completely honest. You know I respect your integrity, even though you work for the BBC and have to be a lackey of the establishment ... *I know!* Maybe we can work on the TV version together! No need to commit now, baby, but how about getting that depressed looking guy from Foyle's War to play me? Isn't that a great idea?! He's obviously got hidden depths and he's enigmatic, you know I've always thought there was a similarity..."

"There's no similarity at all, Dad."

"Of course there is! And he's only a month older than me – I googled him once! And the ladies love him of course, just like me..."

"Do you want to hear my opinion or not?"

"Yes of course I do, I just said I did!"

"Well to be brutally honest, Dad, no one's interested in the life of a geriatric loser, sorry."

I smile and nod thoughtfully, and wonder how quickly I can write her out of my will. Then I remember I haven't got a will, and even if I had one there isn't anything to leave to anyone. So I tune back in to what she's saying...

"And they're not interested in diaries, I'm afraid. Diaries are so last century. It's dramatised blogs and tweets now. But don't get me wrong – confessional stuff is all the rage, you're on the right track there. But it's got to be a blog or tweets and it's got to be written by a young woman, an attractive young woman..."

"Can I borrow your photo then?"

She laughs brittly. "I said *young,* Dad. I'm not young anymore! I'm thirty-two, I'm ancient! In fact, the BBC is already trying to push me off to Antiques Roadshow but I'm not going to go without a struggle…"

"But I thought you said you were surviving?"

"I am – *just.*"

"Oh baby, I didn't know, I'd no idea…" I hug her again and this time she doesn't resist, in fact she starts sobbing into my shoulder, and I hear Tobias saying pongy grandad's making mummy cry but I ignore the little crap-head.

A few minutes later, Alice is still sobbing and my shoulder's getting stiff and I realize I'm not sure what to do next, having carefully avoided this sort of tricky emotional stuff all my life. So I tell her to go and sit in the armchair and relax and I'll make a cup of tea. She sits down but she's incapable of relaxing and pretends it's because of the springs. I patiently explain that you just have to perch on the very front of it, it's easy. Then she's worried that the kids are watching too much TV, so I tell her I'll sort out the kids and get them something creative to do, so why doesn't she go into the kitchen and make the tea?

I find the crayons I bought for them to play with five years ago and grab some paper, and turn John Nettles off – to Jamel's fury, though Tobias says he finds the whole thing rather simplistic. (Whatever happened to the fucking baby-talk?) I get them to sit at the table and suggest they draw a funny picture of their headmaster. "Headteacher," says Tobias. "And no thanks I don't want to."

"Well who else is there you'd like to make fun of?"

"How about you?" says Jamel.

Clearly this isn't getting anywhere.

Then I have a brainwave and tell them I'll give them a fiver each if they wash the dog-shit off the carpet. Suddenly we're in business. I go into the kitchen and sort out scrubbing brushes and soapy water. I'm a little worried about what to tell Alice because her concept of creative play for children is so middle-class, but she's crouched over the kettle just staring at it as it boils and doesn't notice.

So I quickly sort out the boys and come back and make the tea, then sit companionably next to Alice while she sits hunched over her tea, staring at it without speaking.

Eventually she says something, still without looking at me. "There's another reason I came round."

"Not up the duff again, baby?" I ask sympathetically.

"No."

"You know you can trust me. You know I'm not judgmental and I'll be there for you, don't you, just like I've always been?"

She looks as if she's about to say something really nasty, but stops herself. "My therapist thinks my career problems aren't just to do with getting older. She thinks the psychic damage you've done me has made me take a negative glass-half-empty approach to everything in life, and she's trying to teach me how to take a more positive glass-half-full approach."

I really can't pass up such an opportunity. "Talking of glasses, why don't we leave the kiddies and pop out for a quick half to celebrate?"

"To celebrate *what?*"

"Well, us having this sort of deep and meaningful father-daughter chat for a start. It's great, isn't it?!"

She gives me one of her withering looks that I've often thought explain why she's never been able to keep a bloke for more than three and a half minutes. Then she frowns, as if she's remembered something, and carefully pats my hand, as if she's trying to be affectionate but doesn't quite know how to. "Let me give you an example, Dad."

"Great! An example of what?"

"Of the glass half-empty thing," she says patiently. "You see when Mum told me you'd persuaded her to come to the therapist too, so that it'd be the three of us, I was really suspicious about your motives." I try to look hurt and surprised but she's back frowning at her tea again. "But my therapist thinks it's just another example of my glass-half-empty attitude, and it's great that you're so concerned about me."

I smile forgivingly, but she doesn't see that either. "So your therapist doesn't think I'm an uncaring arsehole like certain other people whose names I won't mention?"

Alice reluctantly shakes her head.

"Well perhaps you'll thank her very much, and tell her she's quite right, I'd do anything for my little daughter. And yes OK I might have made a few mistakes in the past..."

"A few?" She does the brittle laugh but I ignore it.

"But that was a long time ago and you know I'm getting rather tired of being labelled in such a negative way. Because people *are* capable of change, Alice, and nothing is more important to me than my relationship with my children, specially you, you know that – my whole world revolves around you, baby..."

"Good. Because I've arranged we're all going to see her a week today, that's Wednesday."

"Can't do Wednesday, sorry."

"Why not?" She looks up at last.

"Because I see Wills on Wednesdays. We have lunch every Wednesday. We've had lunch together every Wednesday for nearly thirty years. Any day but Wednesday."

"You know how upset Mum'll be, don't you? She's already specially re-arranged her schedule, so if she hears you can't..."

I look at her and with a sinking heart I realize she's right. If I don't show a bit of flexibility all the hard work I've put in with her mum will be wasted, and my chance of doing a bit of horizontal bonding just for old times' sake will be reduced from not very good to zero.

"I was winding you up, baby," I smile teasingly. "You know me. Of course I'll come!" I get up. "You just tell your mum and your shrink I'll be there. Now how about popping out for that quick half to celebrate?"

"Why do you keep wanting to celebrate?! I'm a complete psychological mess, Dad, I haven't got anything at all to celebrate!"

"Oh no – of course – you're quite right..." I'm at the door now. "You don't mind if I have a little celebrate on my own then? Let yourself out, eh, baby?"

I hurry out through the living room and chuck Tobias and Jamel a tenner and get out before their mum sees what's been keeping them so unnaturally quiet. They're pretty pleased with the deal, the materialistic little bastards, but I suspect she might be less so.

7.40 p.m.

Am sitting in the Galloping Gastro, halfway through a celebratory bottle of the house Rioja, trying to work out what exactly it is I'm supposed to be celebrating.

Suddenly realize what it is. *What I should be celebrating is being alive! In three days I've escaped death twice!* First, from the big PC – prostate cancer. Second, from being kicked to death by the BNP retard.

I refill my glass and toast my good fortune, ignoring the look on the face of the angry young guy at the bar. As I do so a weird feeling comes over me. I wonder if it's a heart attack so I quickly empty my glass and pour another because red wine is really good for the heart. Then I work out it's probably not a heart attack, because it's a pleasant feeling. And by a process of deduction I finally work out that what I'm feeling must be happiness.

Because things are going well for a change. Not only am I still alive, but I've got £124 in my pocket (£150 from Wills minus £10 for the child labour minus £16 for the Rioja) and a career renaissance might be on the cards! What more could life have to offer?!

Then I remember the promise I made a couple of hours back when I thought the Nazis had come to get me. *If by some remote chance I survive I shall do one of two things – contact the Nando lady at once, or pursue some other sexual avenue urgently.*

I grab a soiled napkin (recently cast aside by loud-mouthed tousle-haired Tory oaf) and ignore the suspicious gaze of the angry young guy behind the bar and start to write.

List of sexual avenues

1. *Alice's mum (tricky but still worth a go)*
2. *Carol Vorderman (suspect I need to have got a bit further with career renaissance, on the other hand she's not doing too well either)*
3. *Anthea Greenspan (Saga mag bird – also lifelong fan! Really intriguing and with lots of potential but could look like a horse)*

4. *Nando lady (if all else fails)*
5. *www.quickshag.com (if all else fails including the Nando lady)*

I gaze at the list and wonder whether to add Michelle, but to be honest I didn't like the way she responded to my compliment about her nice lacy blouse. Surely women should be gracious about accepting compliments (I don't mean that in a sexist way). While still pondering, I look up and am taken aback to see Michelle has appeared from nowhere and is standing next to the angry young guy behind the bar. They've got their arms round each other and are gazing at me. I find this both unnerving and rude and decide to exclude her from the list. I'm about to return their impolite gaze with an icily superior smile but before I have a chance a huge Alsatian leaps over the bar and makes for me.

"*Benjie...*" says the young guy in an amused tone, and not surprisingly the hideous beast takes no notice and hurtles towards me and I wonder if I'm going to escape death a third time or not.

"*Benjie!*" says Michelle, a tiny bit more urgently, and the murderous creature skids to a halt within inches of my manhood.

Far from being apologetic, the angry young guy chuckles. Clearly he finds the idea of his customers having their bollocks chewed off hilarious. Then he strolls over and takes the growling, dribbling creature by the collar. "Sorry," he smiles briefly, "I don't usually bring him in." And turns and drags him back to the bar.

I'm so traumatised that I quickly swallow the last of the Rioja, and as I wait for the medicine to work I ponder the irony of nearly being de-bollocked while planning my sexual comeback. As I get up to leave I give Michelle a reproachful look, but she doesn't seem to notice.

I try to make a dignified exit but the angry young guy is now just outside the door smoking a fag while his canine friend feasts off a huge bowl of what looks like human remains and I'm forced to edge awkwardly past. As the young guy glares at me and the Alsatian growls threateningly I have a sudden blinding flash – I've found the phantom crapper and its owner!

But I decide not to do anything about it just yet.

Thursday 15th April

3.25 a.m.

Wake up and go for pee. Then remember have still forgotten to buy more 3-for-ten-quid Tesco reddo so can't go back to sleep because of anxiety about the lack of booze in the flat. Lie wide awake wondering how I could possibly have been so stupid as to feel happy last night. Career renaissance is a pathetic illusion, and still have no money really, and most depressing of all, *boring suburban cop-out best friend Wills is probably having sex at this very moment!*

Despair of ever having sex again. Am convinced that no one on my list will even look at me, not even the Nando lady. (Well perhaps the Nandy lady – let's be realistic). To make matters worse, suicidal despair makes me feel really horny. Then remember www.quickshag.com and get out of bed and turn on computer.

Almost don't bother to check emails first because feeling so horny, but am glad I do because there's a reply from GQ magazine. Maybe they like my David Niven article!

Dear Anthony Appleforth,

Dylan Jones asked me to get in touch with you because he's now read your article and hates it.

I'm terribly sorry about that.

But be of good cheer, because your name rang a faint bell with him. Are you by any chance the father of St Paul's School alumnus Quentin Appleforth? I ask because Dylan's mate Dave Cameron recently told him that Quentin is best mates with Dave's best mate Georgie Osborne. So if you fancy writing something "cool and quirky" (for the AB male demographic) about what it's like being the unsuccessful dad of the best mate of the future Chancellor of the Exchequer, Dylan promises he'll read it very sympathetically.

Yours faithfully,

Sebastian Youngbottom (GCSE work experience placement)

PS He also asked me to point out that, contrary to the inference in your letter, GQ is a highly tasteful men's magazine and we don't show "tits", as you offensively refer to them. We nearly show tits.

I immediately write an email back.

Dear Sebastian,

Please tell your poncy right-wing boss Dylan he's a tosser. And so are his snobby Bullingdon bugger mates Dave and Georgie. And tell him he can stick his condescending offer right up his overpaid Mail on Sunday arse.

Yours faithfully,

Arnold Appleforth

I go and make a cup of tea then come back, refreshed, and re-read it (an invaluable trick I picked up in those irreplaceable early years writing the nature column for the Market Harborough Gazette) and wonder if I've got the tone quite right. So I have a little think and make a few changes.

Dear Sebastian,

I'm so sorry Dylan Jones wasn't keen on my article. But his idea for a father-of-the-nearly-famous-at-one-remove article is really great. It really got the old creative juices going! So please tell him I'll get right down to it!

Thanks again, mate!

Anthony

PS It'll involve quite a bit of research, so how about a few grand up front? I leave the exact amount to Dylan!

4.30 a.m.

Lie in bed more wide awake than ever, wondering if am even more of a cop-out than Wills. Think I will never sleep again.

11.00 a.m.

Wake up and get down straightaway to writing GQ article. After all, have no choice. (Note to self – drop hint to Roger that miniscule monthly allowance he gives me allows me *no artistic freedom whatsoever* so am forced at 60-plus to take on disagreeable work that cannot be good for health. Don't forget to add pointedly, "Perhaps this is your unconscious intention!")

2.15 p.m.

Go to Oxford Street to buy T-shirt for this evening's dinner party. Lizzie wants me to wear a proper shirt but am not happy about such conformist attire so have decided on a compromise. As it happens I already own a proper conformist shirt, so intend to wear it over T-shirt (which I've noticed cool people do, eg Matt le Blanc on Friends on E4, to whom I think I bear a more than passing resemblance).

Have gone to Oxford Street instead of T-shirt section of Politicos Bookshop because reckon it might not be a good idea to embark on serious political discussions tonight. I go to scruffy shop called Metal Banana which is full of non-political T-shirts. Find a lot of them hilarious, and eventually choose one which reads "This T-shirt would look great on your bedroom floor!" Choose it for two reasons – one, it makes me piss myself laughing; two, hopefully it will relax Lizzie and her girlfriends and show them I'm really not anti-lesbian. Then maybe it'll encourage them to lose their inhibitions later! (NB – only joking of course!)

I take the T-shirt to the counter and the young girl puts it in a banana-shaped bag and asks if it's for my son. When I say no it's for me, she bends over and does a snorting noise (just like Julie Burchill did, oddly enough). Then she straightens up and stares at the counter instead of me and says that's ten pounds fifty. Then when I ask if she'll give me a reduction because I'm over sixty she bends over and does the snorting thing again.

I don't want to sound boring and clichéd and predictable, but have to say that sometimes nowadays I don't understand the younger generation.

1.20 pm.

Finish GQ article. Worry whether can ethically claim hefty research fee as have written it rather quickly. Then work out that as it's about father/son stuff it can reasonably be said my entire adult life has been research for it, so should clearly claim shitloads.

Plus, I reckon it's brilliant, just what Dylan Jones will be looking for to stick between the after-shave ads!

Cool fathers and not-so-cool sons

Let's face it, has there ever been such a cool magazine as GQ? Far be it from me to be sycophantic, but whenever my gay son lets me sneak a look at his latest much pored-over copy of GQ I instantly feel young again!

One thing I specially love (and so of course does my gay son!) is all that designer stubble. On a personal note, I myself happen to have stayed stubbornly stubbly since that glorious revolutionary hirsute summer of '67. So I was flattered and delighted when I first picked up my son's copy to see that GQ had at last caught up with me facial-hair-wise!

You might have noticed I just said that looking at GQ instantly made me feel young again. Well I was lying. Because despite having a 39-year-old gay son I already feel young, thank you very much!

So why exactly do I feel young?

After much reflection, I'd say it's because my 39-year-old gay Tory son seems years older than me.

And why is that?

Many answers spring to mind. Maybe because he's best mates with sober-suited wallpaper heir Georgie Osborne. And because they went to the same snobby public school which produces close-cropped shiny-faced prematurely aged Tories like there's no tomorrow. And maybe also because they both have boringly monogamous relationships and a caring, responsible attitude to life.

But I'm sure none of you cool GQ-reading guys are like boring old Georgie or Quentin – well are you?

But I bet half your mates are! In fact, I bet they already read the Daily Telegraph and are boringly faithful to their girlfriends. And who knows, maybe they're even planning to marry them! And you know what? Before you know it they'll be having babies too. And that's when the whole cycle starts again!

And mark my words, if you're not very careful you'll be joining it, and you too will end up a bitter, resentful dad wondering where his youth has suddenly gone and what's it all about Alfie?

Because just remember, the fear of death is about one thing and one thing only – the scary realization that your children are always going to be younger than you, despite how middle-aged or even old they might look!

But why do they have to look like that? Why are sons nowadays so often significantly older-looking than their dads?

It's because of jeans and footwear – simple as that!

Take Sir Trevor Nunn, celebrated director of Wicked and the complete works of William Shakespeare. Trev has been around for so long that many people believe he first directed Shakespeare's plays when they were hot off the quill. Whether or not this rumour is true is beside the point. What I will say is he wears a mean pair of jeans. And trainers, too. And you can bet your life his kids don't look half as young as he does!

Because if you're wearing the right clothes, age is an irrelevance nowadays.

Of course, you cool young GQ readers probably think

this is of little interest. But mark my words, one day you too will get older. And when your kids grow up the world will have moved on so logically they'll look not just a bit older but massively older than you. Hopefully this will help you get through that three-in-the-morning fear of death that by that time will undoubtedly obsess you and cause you sleepless nights and feelings of suicidal despair.

Another plus is that you'll be able to distract yourself from this existential terror by flirting with your son's girlfriend, like dads always do. And just remember – because you'll undoubtedly look far younger than him, you'll have an amazingly high chance of pulling!

Finally, here are a few suggestions to help you when that not-so-far-off-day arrives:

1. *Try wearing bright red leather shoes, which will make a refreshing change from trainers. An "elderly" acquaintance of mine once wore them and they looked great. (NB – he's dead now but I don't think there's a connection. But don't wear them for too long just in case).*
2. *Read Philip Larkin. However depressed you think you are you can bet your life he'll have felt 20 times worse! Oddly cheering somehow!*
3. *Read some more Philip Larkin.*
4. *Get very drunk (like Philip Larkin did a lot).*

(Note to readers – Please keep this article. In 30 years' time when you're really struggling with mortality you'll appreciate it, believe me).

6.30 p.m.

Re-read it and am bowled over by its lighthearted wisdom plus just the right amount of sophisticated sartorial stuff. Write brief email to Dylan Jones's 12-year-old arselicking jobsworth to accompany it.

Hi Sebastian,

Hope the work experience is going well! Bet you're off out tonight to snort a few lines, eh? Good for you, mate!

Meanwhile I attach the new article that I've been slaving over non-stop since 4 o'clock this morning. OK, I've not done exactly what Dylan asked for – I've done something much much better!

Btw, if the references to Philip Larkin and Shakespeare are too high-brow for the Armani-wearing illiterates who read your fantastic mag, I'll happily change them – though it'll cost you!

Talking of which, I'll send a detailed breakdown of the considerable research costs later.

Cheers mate.

Arnold (Anthony if you prefer!)

Email it off and feel creatively drained and have a quick relax in front of ITV3 before getting ready to go to Lizzie's.

Oh God it's Miss Marple. Lots of fucking countryside again. Try to pretend it's Midsomer Murders countryside then maybe I'll be able to get a kip, but the combination of G McEwan croaking away and the lack of Tesco 3 for

£10 reddo makes me stressed and am forced to change channels.

Oh no – a news item about tonight's leaders' debate! Apparently there's never been one on British TV before so it's a *really* big deal, blah blah blah... Well if it's such a big sodding deal why is it just Brown, Cameron and Clegg? Why not George Galloway too? Do we have a democracy or don't we? Needless to say, the pathetically biased BBC's so-called "political correspondent" doesn't even mention this.

Am even more stressed now, and search kitchen cupboards in hope of finding cooking sherry. There isn't any. Not surprising really because I don't cook.

Am tempted to pop along to the Galloping Gastro for pre-prandial snifter. But don't want to keep Lizzie waiting because secretly am rather scared of her, and have noticed odd fact that quick snifters in public houses have a bit of turning into long drawn-out ones without me noticing. Think this is because public houses exist in different time dimension from rest of the world. (Note to self – is there an article in this? Maybe for Science Today? Or SciFiNow? Or if written in matey way – that I'm really getting the hang of now! – could be lifestyle piece for Dylan Jones and his designer-stubbled GQ crowd).

Decide there's not enough time for snifter so quickly get changed into evening gear, and instead of arriving fashionably late at 7.35 as planned, arrive a really uncool twenty-five minutes early at 7.05. But at least I'll get a drink that way.

7.06 p.m.

As I sip my glass of very superior reddo, I'm pleased to see Lizzie and her lezzie guest laughing appreciatively at my "This

T-shirt would look great on your bedroom floor!" T-shirt. Good start to the evening!

7.20 p.m.

They're still laughing. Try to stop them laughing by pointing out that am wearing a boringly conventional M & S shirt over it but that just makes them worse.

7.30 p.m.

Lizzie gives a final chortle and fishes her hankie from her sleeve and blows her nose loudly, and her lezzie friend comes to a giggling halt too. Am of course delighted they're in such good spirits, but disappointed there's no sign so far of them taking the hint and dragging me off to bedroom to watch.

But the night is young!

Surprised that Lizzie hasn't introduced me to her guest yet. Is it a new laid-back David Cameron-type upper-class Tory thing? Or is Lizzie just embarrassed because she's only half her age? Anyway, Lizzie does one last deafening honk on her hankie and stuffs it back up her sleeve and says she's got to "do something with the asparagus" and totters off into the kitchen.

The mystery guest smiles at me. I smile back and wonder how old she is. Forty-ish? A bit spotty, and a bit flat up top, but maybe lezzies are all flat up top... No that's not true. Dusty Springfield wasn't flat up top. Nor Kathy Kirby. Nor is Lizzie of course! In fact, it's an unforgivably stereotypical sexist assumption on my part. Wonder how long it would take me to convert her to heterosexuality. Minutes? Hours? Be a bit of a challenge anyway.

I notice she's looking me up and down with, I have to report, more than a little interest.

"So what exercise do you take?" she says. "Do you go to the gym?"

"Certainly not," I say. "Taking exercise and going to the gym are narcissistic and extremely fucking decadent."

"*Yum yum* – I know!" She grins and licks her lips and I wonder if she heard what I said. "So has Lizzie told you who I am?"

"No."

"I'm Anthea."

"Oh yeah?"

"*Anthea.*"

"Who the hell's Anthea?" I smile.

"Anthea Greenspan! Your greatest fan!"

I frown. "What – you mean Saga magazine Anthea...?"

"That's the one! How brill to meet you, Arnold!" She kisses me on both cheeks and squeezes my hand, then covers it with her other hand and squeezes it even more, and I find myself wondering if she really needs converting.

Before I can ask her, Lizzie totters in with the asparagus and we sit down to eat. Meaningful conversation ceases as we spend the next five minutes stuffing our faces and drinking wine and Anthea and Lizzie burble about how lovely everything is.

"You know asparagus makes your pee go green," I say eventually. Just to shock them out of their complacency. Lizzie and Anthea fall about laughing again but I carry on. "You know you're only laughing as a defence mechanism because you can't deal with anything that's a threat to your prissy bourgeois middle-class fucking value system?"

Lizzie snorts and blows her nose again on her now very soggy hankie. "He's so gorgeous, isn't he?!" she says "It's like living next door to someone with Tourette's! He brings out all these lovely maternal feelings in me, Anthea!"

"I can imagine," says Anthea, and twinkles at me in a decidedly unmaternal way. I feel Mr Stiffie stirring and edge my chair closer to the table in case he's going to be embarrassing.

"Fancy meeting you here though," I say. "How long have you known each other?"

"A fortnight."

"A fortnight?!"

"Yes but we got on immediately," says Lizzie. "Then we got chatting about where we lived, and Anthea suddenly realized I lived next door to her lifelong hero! Which I was *totally* amazed to discover was you, Arnold!"

"It's true," beams Anthea.

"So I thought why not arrange a little evening *a trois?* It'd be such fun. And it *is*, isn't it?"

A trois? Christ, maybe it's really happening – a threesome with a couple of lezzies – or maybe one lezzie and one who's bi! I try to stay calm and chatty and manage another smile. "So where exactly did you meet?"

"Oh at a little do, you know," smiles Lizzie.

"What sort of do?"

"A little celebration, that's all..."

"What were you celebrating?"

"Well I don't want to name-drop, but it was to celebrate Mikey giving that marvellous speech of his."

"Mikey?"

"Mikey Caine. *Michael* Caine – sorry, Sir Michael now of

course! We go way back you see. You know the speech – the one about voluntary national service!"

"Oh yeah," I say, trying not to smirk. "The one where he screwed the fucking words up – yeah I know the one!"

Anthea cuts brightly in. "Yes Lizzie and I were there to cheer him on – he was fabbo!"

"Fabbo?"

"Yes really!"

"And might I ask what you were doing at a Tory rally, Anthea? I know Lizzie's a fucking Tory but –"

She beams. "What do you think?"

"You're not?!" I say, appalled. "How can *you* be a Tory?"

"Of course I am. All the best people are Tories, Arnold," she smiles.

"Don't be ridiculous. Name me one!"

"Peter Cook."

"OK – OK I'll give you Peter Cook, but name me another..."

"Ian Hislop..."

"OK – OK but that's only two...!"

"Keith Floyd."

"That's only three. Anyway what made you think of –?"

"Carol Vorderman."

"And what made you think of Carol Vorderman?"

"How about Barbara Windsor? How long do you want me to go on?"

This is freaky. Maybe she's been a fan so long she can read my mind. Or maybe she's been secretly reading my diary...

"Have you been secretly reading my diary?!"

"What?"

"Nothing."

"Anyway, I think I've proved my point," she says, and sits back and smiles.

"What point?"

"That all the best people are Tories. That's why I assumed you were."

I ignore her twinkly-eyed attempt at flattery. "Bollocks. What about Arthur Scargill? And Tony Benn? And Ken Livingstone?!"

"They're Tories too," she smiles. "They're all Tories – everyone is!"

Lizzie and I exchange looks. "I've got a chickeny stewy thing for mains," she says hurriedly. "When everyone's ready..."

"Shut up, Lizzie," I say, and turn to my greatest fan. "Do you have any idea who Arthur Scargill and Tony Benn and Ken Livingstone are, Anthea?" I ask.

"Not really," she smiles. "I never read the papers."

"But you're a magazine editor, you're meant to have your finger on the pulse and your ear to the ground!"

"But I only like the funny bits."

Lizzie pipes up again, clearly trying to keep things on a lighthearted note. "Wasn't Arthur Scargill that ghastly northern thug who Margaret Thatcher gave a pasting to?"

"I said shut up, Lizzie."

"Rightio," she beams. "Goodness, this is fun, isn't it?"

I ignore her and turn back to Anthea. "I fail to see how you can have thought *I* was a Tory when you were – so you told me! – such a fan of my hard-hitting Private Eye pieces in the 80s!"

"But I thought they were ironic."

"What?"

"*Weren't* they?" she smiles. And leans across the table and squeezes my hand again. "Are you *sure* they weren't? Just a weeny bit?" And she gives me the twinkly look again but I ignore it. I've never had sex with a Tory on principle (well not knowingly) and I'm certainly not going to start now.

Unfortunately, Mr Stiffie thinks otherwise. And once he's drawn my attention to it I can't help wondering what it'd be like. Really dirty, I bet. But I'm not going to think about it anymore...

Then I remember Anthea hasn't emailed me back yet about the lighthearted think piece I sent her for Saga magazine. Not that stuff like that matters of course, not compared to my political principles, which are far more important than worldly success *or* Tory pussy. On the other hand, why screw up your chances?

"Yeah, well I suppose there might be an ironic element in there too, just possibly..." I say thoughtfully.

"Of course there is! By the way I loved the new think piece you sent me," she says, reading my mind again. "Lots of irony there too of course!"

"Yeah – absolutely – loads of it!"

"Which think piece is this?" says Lizzie. "I hope you're paying him well, Anthea. I feel very protective towards little Arnie..."

"Don't keep calling me..."

"Well I would pay him well, Lizzie – *you know* I would. But you know how things are..."

"Oh golly yes. *Sorry*. Shouldn't have spoken!"

"What's all this? What's going on?"

Anthea coughs apologetically. "There's been a tiny change in my work situation," she smiles. "Nothing mega, so no need to get in a tizz, but I'm afraid I'm no longer at Saga magazine."

I force a smile back – I'm getting really good at this – and stick in a little laugh for good measure. "Really? Yeah well never mind. That's how the cookie crumbles, isn't it? No problem. C'est la vie, eh?" Bloody great. Bloody typical of my luck.

I empty the rest of the reddo into my glass and wave the bottle at Lizzie. She smiles understandingly (that's what I love about her!) and picks up the bottle then gathers the plates and totters off to the kitchen.

I empty my glass and stare bleakly into it. There's some sediment in the bottom and I scoop it out with a spoon and eat it. While I'm trying to deal with the disgusting taste I become aware that Anthea is wittering on. "… But I'm finalising plans to start up an online magazine and I'd really love you to contribute to it…"

"Oh yeah?" I muster a smile. "So what's it going to be about?"

"It's really high concept, you'll love it. It's a post-Saga online mag for oldies who won't admit they are! Isn't that great? It's got your name all over it. You're just perfect for it."

"Do you reckon? Really?" I ask modestly and accidentally dribble some of the red wine sediment down my T-shirt and my M & S shirt too but she doesn't seem to notice.

"Yes of course! And I've got lots of other great oldie celebs promising they'll contribute too. Melvyn, Brucie, Des O'Connor…"

"But I'm not a celeb," I say as I try to wipe off the sediment, which makes it worse.

"You are to me, Arnold. You always have been, you know

that! And even if you weren't, the main thing is I need people who are over seventy but in denial about it." I open my mouth to protest but she's on a roll and doesn't give me a chance. "To be honest, some of the famous oldies don't quite measure up. Some of them even play *golf*. I mean what use is that to me?! That's what you're *meant* to do when you're a wrinkly, isn't it – it's entirely age-appropriate!"

"Yeah but fair's fair, they probably make up for the golf bit by being married to brain-dead dolly birds who are half their age..."

"That's sweet of you defending them, Arnie, but it's not the point. I need oldies who are *a hundred per cent* in denial, not just fifty per cent! And at the moment the only person I know who *really and truly* fits the bill is you!"

I sense I'm in a seller's market for once in my life, so I smile across the table. "Well, it's just possible I might be able to come up with something for you..."

She gives me a twinkly look. "What do you mean *something?*"

"What I'm saying is, I might be able to come up with something that you like, babe."

She casually undoes the top button of her blouse and leans forward and I realize maybe she's not as flat up top as I thought. "I'm sure you can, Arnold – I've no doubt about that at all!"

I get the feeling I'm being sent mixed messages here. Before I can ask her if I'm right she pouts and gives me a little slap on the wrist. "But I was talking about the *magazine* – naughty!"

Lizzie totters back in with the chickeny stewy thing. As she serves up I glance across at Anthea and wonder if I'm misinterpreting the situation. But she catches my gaze and grins and her eyebrows go up and down like Frankie Howerd's, and I'm forced to conclude I'm not. No girl-on-girl action perhaps, but the good news is I have the strong suspicion I won't be needing www.quickshag.com after all. Not for a while, anyway.

"So what happened about the dog poo?" Lizzie asks conversationally as we tuck in. She clearly hasn't noticed the sexual tension, which I'm pleased about.

I fill Anthea in about the phantom dog shitter, and she gazes at me as I speak, mouth part open, hanging on my every word. Which I must admit is really hot. Mr Stiffie thinks so too, and becomes such an embarrassment I have to pull my chair in even further, which hurts Mr Stiffie as much as me. I try to ignore the pain and tell Lizzie the latest, about the angry young guy and Benjie the homicidal Alsatian. She's gratifyingly indignant, like I knew she'd be. In fact, she's all for abandoning her chickeny stewy thing there and then and storming off to the Galloping Gastro and confronting man and beast in the name of good old-fashioned libertarian Tory values.

"Yeah, maybe – but..."

"What do you mean *maybe – but?*"

"It's all very well for you but I still want to be able to drink in there. And talking about drink, where is it?"

"Oh golly yes – *sorry...*"

Etiquette wins the day, like I knew it would, and she totters off to find another bottle. The moment she's gone Anthea leans across the table and tells me I'm naughty. *Very very naughty*. And if I'm interested she's got an emergency ration of reddo in the car for later...

Mr Stiffie is now on full alert and itching for action so to speak. And nothing I do puts him off. Not several more glasses of Lizzie's reddo, not the sticky toffee pudding plus dessert wine, not even having to listen to Lizzie gushing on about how scrumptious David Cameron is – almost as scrumptious as Boris! – and how it's high time we had a proper old-Etonian running the country again and you wait, he'll really trounce those dreary lefties in the leaders' debate tonight!

11.05 p.m.

Unfortunately, Mr Stiffie lets the side down seventy minutes later, just when I really need him.

At least I think he does. All I can say with absolute certainty is that I wake to find myself sprawled on my bed in my sediment-stained "This T-shirt would look great on your bedroom floor!" T-shirt and nothing else. There's a painful throbbing in my temple that's reassuringly familiar. Then I feel a sudden weight on my chest and I think I'm having a heart attack and I lie there, too terrified to move. Then eventually I look gingerly down and see an arm lying on my chest – and I follow the arm and see it's attached to Anthea, who's dead to the world next to me, snoring gently, naked except for a grey bra and brown socks.

She opens her eyes and sees me staring and smiles. "Well, you're a bit of a stallion, aren't you?"

"There's no need to take the piss."

"Who said I was taking the piss?!"

Maybe she means it.

But it doesn't *feel* like we've done it. I have a surreptitious peer inside the duvet just in case I can see any evidence.

"What are you looking for, my little petal, mmm?"

"Nothing. Go back to sleep."

I wait till she turns away then wait a bit longer then have a feel in the bollock region. No tell-tale signs there either. Weird. So what do I believe?

She turns back and gazes at me with that contented smile you often see in women who've just had an amazing sexual encounter. Well I often see it. (Well I used to, till three months ago). And it makes me realize it's perfectly possible that I did it without noticing. A sort of Pavlovian response, possibly in my sleep.

She snuggles up, and I feel a woolly sock stroking my leg. "Shall we do it again?" she murmurs.

"Yeah OK. Cool by me!"

I half-expect her to laugh scornfully and say we didn't do it really you tosser, you were so pissed you fell asleep. But she just smiles that adoring smile and I realize that my greatest fan has been fantasising about me sexually for years and years and now she really expects me to live up to it.

So we get down to it.

No problem. I mean it's been three months and I'm really horny... And even if we've done it half an hour ago I can do it again – surely...

Maybe it's the responsibility...

Or maybe it's the reddo then the dessert wine then the emergency rations from her car...

Or maybe it's because I'm sixty-one...

But I'm really doing my best. Because I'm desperate not to let my number one fan down.

And I'm desperate that this time *I* remember doing it, too – because with my luck it'll be another three months before I get another chance and even then the list of alternatives isn't great...

But I try to excite myself by fantasising about them...

1. *The Nando lady (definitely)*
2. *Daphne (???!!!)*
3. *www.quickshag.com (endless possibilities!)*
4. *Carol Vorderman (out of my league but great for fantasising – like now!)*

Nearly there.

Nearly but not quite.

Keep trying. Mustn't stop now! The last thing I want is to stop now!

Anthea looks up at me, frowning. "You're not going to have a heart attack, are you?"

"Stop talking, I'm having to put a bit of effort in that's all..."

"You do look rather sweaty."

"*Stop talking...*"

"If you say so." Mr Stiffie has come back from the dead and we're in the final straight, we're really working together here. If I close my eyes I can help him over the last hurdle, I can get him to the finishing line by fantasising she's not Anthea she's... "Can you hear something?"

"*Shush!*"

"*Sorry.*"

Even though Mr Stiffie and I are struggling we've been here before. We've been round the block a few times and I get back to where I was fantasy-wise and Mr Stiffie is really appreciative....

"I'm sure I can hear something..."

"Look babe," I gasp, "I might be sixty-one – sorry *seventy-one* – but even so I'll give you the best orgasm you've ever had in your underprivileged life but only if you stop fucking distracting me..."

"Arnie I really think..."

"*Shit* I give up."

There's a neanderthal yell and a massive whack on my jaw. Everything goes dark. In the distance I hear hysterical yapping...

Maybe Anthea was right. Have I had a heart attack and gone to heaven (not that I believe in heaven)? If so, why are the dogs yapping? Dogs don't go to heaven, do they? Try to get up to see but can't.

Try again and there's yapping and yelling and another whack and everything goes black.

Monday 26th April

The Guardian Obituary
Arnold Appleforth

Fun-loving leftie hack, fondly known as "Arnold The Antichrist" by The Daily Mail and mates.

My dear departed friend and colleague Arnold Appleforth was one of the old school. Self-taught, self-loathing and incorrigibly self-destructive, Arnold was a born hack. His journalistic career began in the depths of Leicestershire and progressed to riot-torn Brixton, where he enthusiastically wrote anything their local rag would let him, thence to the exhilaratingly glamorous freelance life of El Vino's and the various bars of the BBC – in those far-off halcyon days when the BBC allowed alcohol on the premises.

As I raise a metaphorical glass to his talent, I find the tears well up as I recall what is lost. The past is another country, but how grand it was to be alive then and to know Arnold Appleforth! What innocent fun we had in those golden days!

Let's not get sentimental. Arnold hated sentimentality. I still smile as I recall his oft-repeated words, "Sentimental fucking wanker" – invariably hissed at me as the tears sprang to my eyes as I took in the latest disastrous news about his roller-coaster personal life.

Fortunately, there was always the work. Speaking personally, I'm immensely privileged to have commissioned the very last pieces he wrote – two brilliant quizzes, haiku-like in their simplicity, that sparkle gem-like on the back page of this very week's "Sudoku Weekly".

Writing quizzes was an entirely new venture for Arnold,

but he bravely overcame his famous night-time fears and approached it with his customary integrity and discipline and determination to transform a traditionally rather limited genre into his own unique statement.

Let's make no bones about it, the work was Arnold's salvation. When the world was young and we first became bosom buddies he would enthusiastically turn his hand to anything – from second-string theatre reviews in The Guardian (always his favourite paper!) to drily witty op-ed pieces about the broken society for The Daily Telegraph, to his famously controversial episode of All Creatures Great And Small in which Peter Davison (or was it Christopher Timothy?) toys with becoming a Marxist.

Because, let's face it, there was always a touch of the leftie in Arnold.

It's there in his journalism, and there too in his all-too-rare, invariably heavily censored contributions to popular TV drama after the All Creatures Great And Small debacle made him for too many years persona non grata at the BBC. I remember with special fondness an episode of Miss Marple he wrote in the 80s, in the first draft of which Joan Hickson railed against the vicar's decision to send his son to private school and fingered him as the murderer purely for that reason. When I subsequently agreed to rewrite it for the BBC with the correct murderer and the correct motive back in place, just as Miss Christie had intended, he attacked me furiously for being a craven lickspittle and lacking all integrity.

Which was fair comment, of course. I never had his fire.

All the same, I was never entirely sure if it was really politics that motivated him or just a perverse desire to get up people's noses.

Many were the liquid lunch we shared at our regular Covent Garden eaterie where we argued fiercely about this very point. I fondly remember how Arnold would get ruder by the glass until by the second bottle he was hurling abuse at me, my family, his family and of course the great and the good who were stopping him reaching the creative heights where he instinctively knew he belonged.

Talking of family, Arnold was a great dad too. Perhaps too much of a rebel to be a conventional stay-at-home dad – as his several divorces suggest – but as he often said to me, "You do enough responsible shit to make up for both of us, don't you, mate?" Which was undoubtedly true. But despite his absence from their lives he was in his own unique way an enormous influence on all three (possibly four) children, if only by giving them so much to rebel against.

Arnold's gift for the telling phrase never deserted him, even at the most difficult times. I recall a poignant occasion only months before his death. What, he asked me as we lunched in our favourite Covent Garden eaterie, is the point? Where is my fucking raison d'etre if I can no longer get up in the morning and meet you for lunch and look at you pityingly over the vino reddo and think to myself, well at least I'm not a total fucking cop-out like him?

Goodness, how I miss him. The dry subversive humour. The starkly unsentimental ability to see right through the phoneyness, even his own. "I'm not just a hack," he'd say to me, "I'm a pseudo-intellectual fucking hack, and don't you forget it!"

He was – and I don't.

But I can't help secretly wondering if beneath that unselfpitying Wildean façade there lay something else entirely.

The heart of a truly sensitive man perhaps?

"Fuck off," I hear him wittily retort.

Because that was Arnold. Insightful, epigrammatic, ever ready with the smart one-liner and the acidly accurate put-down. Rest in peace, Arnie, closet sudoku fan and quiz fiend – literary Jack of all trades – and master of quite a lot of them, too.

Wills Gradley, East Croydon, 2010

Arnold Appleforth, leftie hack, born
22 December 1948; died 15 April 2010

11.40 a.m.

Am lying in bed with breakfast on tray in one of Roger's many spare rooms when am rather surprised to read the above.

Took me a while to get to it because was catching up on lots of other things that have been happening in the last ten days. For example, there's been a volcanic cloud coming from Iceland and creating havoc. Actually Roger's never very welcoming wife Kelly told me about it when she was moaning about bringing me breakfast – apparently their little girl Angelina's play-school assistant can't get back from her break in Barbados with Simon Cowell so Kelly's even more knackered than usual because she's been forced to look after her for five minutes. (Why do some people have children, I ask myself?!) And there have been two more TV leaders' debates while I was *hors de combat,* and Nick Clegg has demolished Brown and Cameron and been voted the most popular leader since Churchill. Brilliant! Good for him!

11.50 a.m.

Re-read obituary to make sure am not hallucinating.

Midday

Re-read it again.

Then re-read it several more times. (Seven in fact). Decide to phone Wills to congratulate him, but can't find mobile. Then remember that the BNP retard trod on it after repeatedly bashing me with fist and while trying to escape Lizzie's dogs. Also remember that when I regained consciousness Roger lovingly promised to get me a new one but still hasn't got round to it. (Cheapskate). Go downstairs to phone on the landline – after making sure no one is in. Not exactly trying to deceive them, but they seem to have got the impression I'm still bedridden and incapacitated and wouldn't want to shock them.

"Hi, Wills!" I say cheerily into the phone.

"Who is this?" he says in a shocked voice.

"Who do you think, Cuntface?!"

It's great to hear him getting angry. "Look whoever you are, I regard it as deeply offensive that you should go round pretending to be my dear departed best friend Arnie, and using his catchphrase is tasteless beyond belief!"

"It *is* Arnie – I mean Arnold!"

"Clearly you haven't read today's Guardian or you would realize that's not the case."

"You've been misinformed about my death, Wills. I don't know who did it. There are a lot of malicious people out there, most likely some Daily Mail fucker or one of my ex-wives..."

"Goodness... you do *sound* like Arnold ..."

"Of course I do!"

"Is it really you?"

"Just tell me which dickwad told you I'd snuffed it, Wills."

"It's so great to hear you, mate! Did you like the obit?"

"I want to know who's got in in for me, Wills. I mean who especially."

"Look I understand you're upset, but I hope you realize this is pretty difficult for me me too…"

"No one's said you're dead, Wills! *So why is it difficult for you?!"*

"Look I'm over the moon you're alive, mate, of course I am – but frankly it's really embarrassing because my credibility will be in shreds."

"You don't *have* any fucking credibility, Wills."

There's a pause, then a contented sigh. "God, I didn't realize how much I'd missed you."

"Yeah yeah…"

"So did you like all the stuff about your wit and integrity? I hope you'd write as flatteringly about me when I pop off!"

"You must be joking. So who did the dirty on me, Wills?"

"You know, thinking about it… perhaps I misinterpreted something…You see I phoned last Monday to confirm Wednesday lunch and when you didn't get back I got worried. So I rang your lovely daughter at the Beeb and she said you'd been attacked. And I said, 'Is he dead?' and she said, 'What do *you* think?' You know, in that voice she always uses – well to me anyway… And I remembering thinking that given the constant abuse you've given your body over the years, and your age too of course, well the slightest attack would be more than enough to finish you off."

"So you didn't bother to find out any more details?"

No reply.

"Wills?!"

"Well...I had a lot on my plate... I mean I needed to find someone to take over the new quiz page! I mean your contribution was great, mate, but life moves on. And I remembered how much Dawn loves Sudoku and she doesn't seem so busy nowadays and –"

"Dawn French is *not* taking over my quiz page!"

"It's a bit late now, I've offered it and she leapt at it – sorry!"

I cannot believe I'm hearing this. Treachery, thy name is Wills.

"Look I've got to go in a tick. It's great that you're alive and congratulations and all that but Dawn and I are off to train for the London Marathon, so I'd better say bye bye..."

"You're not interested in hearing what *really* happened then?"

There's a silence. "Yes of course..."

"You don't sound very sure about it."

"No I am...No – great...! Love to hear it!"

So I tell him in considerable detail. "... So after Anthea had had two or three orgasms she was begging me for a break. And I said, look babe, I can't go on forever either nowadays so how about I just give you a couple more then we're finished? Now while we'd been on the job, Lizzie had been busy clearing up next door then she'd taken her doggies to the Green for a crap, and she was tottering back to her house when she saw my front door was open. So she pops her head in and hears bloodcurdling yells, and she and her doggies follow the noise and it's coming from the bedroom. And it'll surprise you to know it's not Anthea, it's this BNP retard trying to kill me... Are you there, Wills?"

"Yes – yes of course..."

"Now one of the things about my neighbour Lizzie is she's a hundred and ninety-three but she's completely fearless, so she and her doggies leap on the guy and he hasn't got a chance. And she and the doggies keep guard till the filth come and take him away. Meanwhile Anthea has got her knickers on at record speed and driven me to the hospital. I'm on the critical list for some days, then one day I regain consciousness, and one of the first things I think is I really can't keep using valuable NHS resources when there are far needier people around. So I check out and take a cab and go and stay with my son Roger and his wife, who I'm sad to say really don't appreciate how lucky they are I'm still alive. But let's face it, I'm used to rejection and treachery, Wills. I find it everywhere I look – specially professionally – know what I mean?!"

I wait for his mealy-mouthed, self-justifying response. There's no reply.

"Wills?"

Still nothing.

"Wills, there's no point sulking, why don't you just admit you're in the wrong? OK, we'll talk about it Wednesday ... Are you OK for Joe Allen on Wednesday, Wills?" I laugh bitterly. "Of course you've probably been so busy pounding the pavements with your new mate Dawn you didn't notice I missed last week, even though you wrote my sodding obituary..."

A woman's voice cuts in. "Please hang up and try again."

"Sod off Dawn, I know it's you. It's not even a good impression."

"Please hang up and try again."

"Dawn? What have you done with Wills, Dawn? Please put him back on at once."

"Please hang up and try again."

"Well, fuck you too, and by the way The Vicar Of Dibley was shit."

1.40 p.m.

Snack on pathetic provisions from Roger and Kelly's Smeg fridge and sip glass of reddo from a bottle from Roger's "wine cellar" that he doesn't think I know about because it's under the rug at the back of the living room. The label says "Petrus Pomerol 2007". Seem to recall that Petrus is posh. Not impressed because am not a wine snob and have to say I prefer the house Rioja at the Galloping Gastro.

Mind you, the second glass tastes better, and while sipping the third I wonder if just possibly it wasn't Dawn French on the phone after all. Hope it wasn't because would hate her to think I was rude about The Vicar Of Dibley simply because am resentful about her getting my job on Sudoku Weekly. Even though it's true.

Go back to bed. Am nodding off while pondering friendship and betrayal and the loss of trust and decency in modern life when am disturbed by a ring on the doorbell. Go to the window and peer through the curtains, in case it's suspicious-minded Kelly trying to catch me out of bed.

See it's Quentin and can't be arsed to talk to him, even though he's my own flesh-and-blood and love him dearly, but just as I'm putting the curtain down he waves up at me, grinning like a loony. So am forced to go down and let him in, but make him come upstairs and talk to me while I'm in my sickbed just in case Kelly turns up.

"But won't she wonder how I got in?"

"Good question, Quentin...How about I say I somehow

struggled to the window and threw the key down?"

"So you've got a key?"

"No I haven't. The bastards wouldn't let me have one."

He looks appalled. "Why wouldn't they? What possible reason could they have for that?"

"When I was lying here the other day having a brief period of consciousness they said that if they lent me a key I'd only go off and copy it, then they'd never see the back of me because I'd let myself in any time without asking."

"How callous! You wouldn't do something like that, would you?"

"Of course I would."

"Oh, right."

"I mean, we're family, aren't we? And families are meant to be there for each other. That's the whole point of them, isn't it – they're meant to look after each other!"

"You're absolutely right, Dad, they are!"

"So can you give me fifty quid? I've lost a job to Dawn fucking French and I was depending on it..."

"Of course – I'd be delighted." He eagerly gets out his wallet and gives me sixty and says he's sorry but he hasn't got any tens.

"No problem, I'll keep the change."

"Please do," he smiles warmly. I carefully put it in my pyjama pocket and stuff my hankie over it so Kelly won't see it. I glance up and he's still smiling warmly. "You know, Dad, I've been thinking about that awful attack on you. I've been thinking about it such a lot the last few days. And I have to say, I've come to the conclusion that I'm glad you're not dead after all."

"Well thank you, Quentin. So am I."

"No I really mean it. And, you know, it's made me feel I need to get to know you better before you die."

"Please don't talk about death, Quentin."

"No but it has. It's really shaken me up and made me think about stuff. About fathers and sons, you know, and inherited characteristics and things like that. And the extraordinary thing is, it's made me realize that even though you were as uninvolved in my upbringing as you could possibly get away with, I've still turned out amazingly like you in all sorts of ways!"

"No you haven't."

"Yes I have. I mean really, deep down. And the great thing is, I think maybe I can cope with that."

"You haven't turned out like me, Quentin. You're a fag and you haven't dipped your wick anywhere else for sixteen years, how could you be more different from me?!"

I'm disturbed to see he isn't at all offended. He just smiles. "You remember when I saw you last, with Adam, at Priscilla Queen Of The Desert."

"Yeah of course. How was the second half? I got chatting to the barmaid you see and…"

"The second half doesn't matter, Dad. But you remember the interval? You know, when we were chatting and you insulted Adam like you always do, and you said terrible things about our civil ceremony and George Osborne, but in the middle of your foul alcoholic diatribe –"

"I thought you said you were glad I wasn't dead? Doesn't sound like it."

He smiles forgivingly. "Just because I'm glad you're not dead, Dad, doesn't mean you're not a disgusting pig most of the time."

"No, I suppose it doesn't."

"But while you were being disgusting you said something I've not been able to forget. You said there's no point being gay if you're not promiscuous. At the time I was as offended as Adam by your monstrous homophobia..."

"I am not homophobic! Why are you telling me all this crap when I'm just back from death's door?"

"Because it stuck with me. It resonated in some way I couldn't understand. But over the last few days I've realized why. Naturally enough I've defined myself throughout my life so far by being everything that you're not, but I realize now that I've been in denial. The truth is, Dad, *I* want to be promiscuous and play the field too, just like you've always done! And it's nothing to do with the gay thing, it's simply because I got it in my DNA from you!"

I gaze at him, and put my arm round him and hug him. He struggles to get away (just like Alice always does – odd, this DNA thing). But I've got hold of him and I'm not going to let go till I've dealt with my emotions and have pumped him for a few answers too.

"So how does little Adam fit into all this?"

"It's been painful, I must admit. I've had to tell him I can't go through with the civil ceremony and I think we should take a break from each other for a few months."

"Great – well done!"

"Adam doesn't think so, he's devastated."

"Yeah well he'll get over it. I mean plenty more fish in the sea, eh?"

He laughs briefly. "That's exactly what he said you'd say."

"Did he really?!"

"Yes. And I said, well if that's what my father tells me then

I think I'm duty-bound to take it seriously."

"I'm impressed, Quentin. I never thought I'd be able to say that about you but I am. So one last question. How's it going?"

"How's what going, Dad?"

"The promiscuity – after all those wasted years?"

"Well… it's early days… very early days…"

"Come on, you can tell your Dad. Is it as good as you thought it'd be? Or is it even better?!"

I smile at him and at first he's too embarrassed to meet my gaze. Then he manages to and smiles sheepishly. "It's great, Dad. I don't know why I didn't follow your example years ago!"

You know, parents sometimes talk about the satisfaction they get from seeing their kids following in their footsteps. Frankly it's not something I've experienced much before. There were a few moments with Alice when I felt she showed some of the same creative flair and sparky rebelliousness as her old Dad, then she'd ruin it by moaning about my drinking or swearing or the school fees or some other bourgeois bollocks. So the satisfaction and pride I feel now for Quentin is a first. I hug him again, and this time he only struggles in a token sort of way, and I say, "Can I give you a bit of advice, son?"

He struggles harder now, but soon gives up. I smile fondly. "Look, I'm the first to admit I don't know much about relationships, and even less about arse-bandits, but what I want to say is this. The thing to realize is we're all human really, and the same laws of human behaviour apply to us all. And over the years I've learned that one of the most basic laws is that everyone needs a bit of spare from time to time. That's a fact of life, Quentin…Well that's it – that's all I've got to say. Except, go out there and enjoy! And if you're ever riddled with doubt and full of self-recrimination and all that crap, just remember what your old Dad said – all that matters is that you're getting some!"

2.30 p.m.

I stand on the doorstep and wave Quentin an emotional goodbye. He waves fondly back, then turns away and crosses the road and makes a beeline for a young black traffic warden, obviously thinking I've gone in. I hear him ask when the free parking starts, which is odd because he doesn't drive. The traffic warden says six-thirty and walks off but Quentin follows and expresses surprise that it's so late. The parking warden grunts and keeps walking and Quentin keeps following and asks if that means he's free at six-thirty, in which case how about a margarita at the Lord Nelson because it's two for one till seven o'clock?

I'm determined not to be over-protective so I force myself not to intervene as the traffic warden turns on him. This is what's called tough love, I tell myself, teaching your kids you won't be there forever and they've got to learn to fight their battles on their own one day.

As I go back into the house Roger's wife Kelly screeches to a halt in her vulgarly ostentatious Range Rover, and tells me I'm a lying bastard because I've been pretending to be bedridden and helpless, no wonder I'm all alone and no one likes me because I'm a selfish opportunistic blah blah blah – "And thank God you're not *my* father!"

"I agree wholeheartedly, Kelly," I smile coolly. But she doesn't seem to find it funny.

2.50 p.m.

She does, however, find it funny when I suggest that since she's chucking me out the least that she can do is drive me back to my flat.

3.10 p.m.

Wait in rain for twenty minutes for bus. Kelly's Gucci carrier bag disintegrates and have to stuff underpants, hankies, socks and "Che Guevara wears David Cameron T-shirts" T-shirt into various pockets. While doing this, drop all six copies of my Guardian obituary into puddle. Am in the middle of retrieving them when see turd floating in puddle and am reluctantly forced to abandon them.

3.55 p.m.

Great to get home!

Not so great to find there has been no post in the ten days I've been away except bills and circulars, and a scrawled note from Lizzie, which says, "Hiya! Did you know I saved your life?! That's twice now, so you owe me one!!" Blench at what sort of repayment she might have in mind. Decide best not to think about it and focus on finances instead. Put bills in "pending" pile, and wonder yet again why Roger refuses to increase my miniscule monthly allowance despite earning a trillion pounds a second. While languishing on sickbed I did my best to convince him that the attack might have done permanent damage to my brain, but he laughed and said – *very* predictably! – "would anyone notice?" Finally managed to get £100 from him after observing I'd been unable to work for over a week while hovering between life and death, but only after enduring pathetic "did anyone notice?!" joke again.

Bored with finances and realize am feeling horny. Far too little privacy in bedroom in Roger's house, so have been unable to take remedial action since having coitus violently interrupted by the BNP retard ten days ago.

Thank God for the internet. Turn computer on and am about to go to www.quickshag.com when see there are emails. Lots of them!

Forty-eight are for Viagra, Cialis, Dobies Garden Seeds, jury service, Russell Grant's Psychic Readings, Crazy Offers On Replica Watches, Ryanair and Carol Vorderman saying she's heard about my amazing sexual reputation and is desperate for a quickie. (Made up the last one).

The forty-ninth is from devoted daughter Alice, sent two days ago.

Hi Dad,

What's all this rubbish about being too ill to go home and having to convalesce at poor old Roger's house? I know you've been stringing it out so you could get out of seeing the therapist, but it hasn't worked because we've rearranged it for this Wednesday. AND NO EXCUSES OR MUM WILL WANT TO KNOW WHY.

I've had an odd couple of phone calls from your chum Wills. I think maybe there was some sort of misunderstanding in the first one, not sure what. Then he phoned telling me about your obit in Monday's Guardian and said he hoped I thought it was a fitting tribute and he thought there was a great sitcom in it, starring David Jason.

Love, Alice

P.S. I'm not sure about David Jason. I thought John Nettles would be better.

Stare at my daughter's email and wonder why the fates are so determined to screw up Wednesday lunch with Wills, because this makes it two weeks running I'll have missed it. Am about to email the two-faced bastard suggesting tomorrow instead when there's a ping and another email arrives.

To the estate of my dear mate Anthony Appleforth.

Dear Estate,

I've no idea who you are, but I do so hope this gets to you. You might or might not have heard of me, depending on whether you're cool or a suburban prole, but my name's Dylan Jones and I edit a fab little men's mag called GQ.

I write to you in a state of shock and grief because I've just read Anthony's obit in today's Guardian. (I'm more of a Daily Mail man myself, but some leftie dumped it in my retro men's barbers in Jermyn Street so I had a quick gander).

While I was grieving and having my hair cut, it struck me that his death is a great hook for the article he emailed me on the very day he kicked off.

After I'd moseyed back to the office I told my work experience guy Sebastian about my brill idea. By an amazing coincidence he was about to turn Ant's article down because it was self-indulgent crap. Of course I usually take Seb's opinions seriously because he's the voice of youth and really knows what's going on in the street (specially if the street is in Eton) but this time I overruled the little jerk. I reminded him that his isn't the only demographic. GQ has to appeal to old farts like me too, and the article might be crap but it's got lots of father-son stuff and intimations of mortality stuff too (which I'll have to edit, mind you – we don't want to get too doomy, do we?!)

I hope you're as thrilled as I am by this chance to give dear old Ant the sort of send-off he so richly deserves.

I attach a contract and if you could sign it and return it PDQ that would be great. The sooner the better, because ever since Diana snuffed it we've found death is a big seller. Btw, I thought white type on a tasteful charcoal background would be cool. Less depressing than black, and there's a new series of ads it would go brilliantly with. What do you think?

Ciao for now.

Dylan

I glance at the contract then write an email back.

Dear Mr Jones,

As sister and sole surviving relative of Arnold Appleforth, I am lost for words. Your manner is condescending and your terms are derisory. There is probably little you can do about the manner but you can certainly do a lot about the fee. (Hint – anything less than a multiple of three will not be given serious consideration).

I would appreciate a swift response because the Guardian is already experiencing huge interest in Arnold's back catalogue as their readership is full of the lefties you mention and they are proving more than happy to cough up big time for anything they can get hold of by my beloved brother.

Yours disgustedly,

Alison Hamilton-Parker (Lady)

PS The Lady bit doesn't mean I'm not a leftie, by the way. Have you heard of Antonia Fraser???

Re-read email and feel have got the tone just right and send it off.

There's a ring at the door and I open it to find a messenger wearing a puffer jacket with the slogan "Happy Hedge Funds Inc Plc" on it. He hands me a package and asks me to sign for it.

"Why?"

"Because I can't give it to you otherwise."

"How do I know what it is?"

"You don't till you open it. It's a calculated risk."

"And how do I know that signing your handheld computer won't put me on the government's database forever so they can encroach on my personal liberty even more than they already do?"

He sighs and points at the "Happy Hedge Funds Inc Plc" slogan on his jacket.

"What's that?"

"I work for them."

I laugh mockingly. "Look anyone can buy a puffer jacket and have a slogan printed on it. Do you think I'm that stupid?!"

"OK forget it I'll take it back..."

"No wait! Wait! OK, tell me who runs it."

"You won't know him."

"Try me."

"You'll never have heard of him."

"Why are you being so evasive? What are you, MI5?"

"For Christ's sake. OK. It's some golf-playing dipstick called Roger Appleforth ... Shit, that's your name, isn't it? Maybe you have heard of him then. What is he, your grandson or something?"

I don't deign to give this an answer, just take the package and sign for it and slam the door in the rude bastard's face.

I open it. There's a new mobile phone inside, with a typed message from darling son Roger.

Hi Dad, Sorry I wasn't there to say goodbye. Will really miss you! Got a minion to buy this to replace your broken one so you can phone or text any time – easier for you than popping over! He put your old simcard in it too so you won't even need me to come and sort it. See you soon. (Kelly says how about on your 65th? She does make me laugh!)

From the desk of Roger Appleforth, signed in his absence

I turn on the mobile and it works first go. Amazing.

Lots of texts from Anthea...

Tuesday – hope ur ok and hole in head is better

Later Tuesday – did u get my text?

Wednesday – hello?

Thursday – forgot to say – hope u enjoyed other evening as much as i did! Am still tiny bit sore but worth it! What a stallion u are!

Friday – doctor has told me soreness is due to vaginal dryness and given me prescription for Premarin Vaginal Cream. But ur still a stallion, sweetie!

Saturday – vaginal cream is brilliant and am raring for action again

Sunday – did u get last text about raring for action?

Today – just read ur obit in guardian. Deeply shocked. Why no mention of ur sexual stamina, sweetie? Typical politically-correct man-hating polly toynbee guardian rubbish.

Christ – we did have sex then.
No we didn't. We *couldn't* have done.
Or perhaps we did and I've forgotten again.
Why does this keep happening with me and Anthea? Or *does* it?!
I text her back at once –

hole in head a lot better thanks still alive need to see u

Can't fail to notice the irony that it's not just the BNP retard who has been doing things to my head, Anthea has, too! More subtly maybe, but just as disturbingly.

Decide that if she's off on some weird fantasy and, as I suspect, we haven't really done it then we must, and soon. For three reasons (at least):

1. *Want to have knowingly had sex with a fan before I die*
2. *It'll be preferable to www.quickshag.com (despite*

possible commitment problems that wouldn't exist with www.quickshag.com)

3. *If we fit it in today or tomorrow then won't be sexually needy when meet Daphne again at the shrink's on Wednesday, which will turn her on far more than me coming on hard, so to speak.*

Get a text back immediately from Anthea – how about tonight?

I wait for thirty seconds so as not to seem over-eager then text her back.

5.20 p.m.

Have just had half an hour's sexting with Anthea! *Sexting*, not texting! It was her idea and am ashamed to say I didn't know what she meant. But she's a great teacher. So dirty! Am knackered!

5.25 p.m.

Am having quiet lie down trying to play it back in my mind without letting on to Mr Stiffie when the phone rings.

It's Wills again. "Hi, You OK for Wednesday lunch? Hope so!"

"Sorry Wills," I say coolly, "I tried to arrange Wednesday with you earlier but failed and since then other things have come up. And by the way would you tell Dawn that her recorded-telephone-voice imitation is not just unconvincing but about as funny as Cannon and Ball?"

"What are you talking about?"

"While we're talking show biz, mate, what's all this shit about David Jason playing me? I have problems with this on so many levels. First and foremost, why wasn't I consulted?"

"Look I thought you were dead, mate, and –"

"Picky picky picky. Second, I want a fifty-fifty split. Not that money's important for such a profoundly personal project but it's the principle. And third, I don't want David Jason *or* John Nettles..."

"Look this is yesterday's news, it's not going to happen! Alice just phoned and she's thought really hard about it but with you being alive there's no hook, it's not sexy any more. On the plus side she's really keen that when you snuff it I come straight back to her."

"Oh *is* she?"

"Yes she is! Isn't that great?"

"Yes brilliant! Absolutely extraordinary!"

"Yeah, thank you, I'm really pleased you feel that way!"

I wearily contemplate trying to explain to Wills the concept of irony but realize I'd be wasting my time.

"So why can't you do Wednesday?" he asks.

"Mind your own business."

"Oh I see! Pussy, is it?"

"God I hate it when you're crude, Wills."

"What do you mean you hate it? You're crude all the time!"

"Yes but when I do it it's natural, when you do it's like Richard Briers, it really shocks me. Anyway I can do tomorrow."

"Right. Fine."

"See you at Joe Allen's at one."

"No hang on, wait. I was going to say, why don't we go somewhere else for a change?"

"What do you mean go somewhere else?"

"It's just that I thought it might be nice to go somewhere else for a change."

"Why?"

"I just did."

"But we go to Joe Allen's, Wills."

"Yes, I know, but I thought it might make a change to go somewhere else."

"But we go there every week, Wills – we've been going there every week for twenty-seven years!"

"Exactly," he says. "That's why I thought it'd make a change to go somewhere else just for once."

"But why?" I can feel myself getting stressed.

"Well because we've made one change already by not making it a Wednesday, so why not –?"

"No, Wills, we've made *two* changes. We've already made *two* changes. Not meeting last week was the first one, and now not meeting this Wednesday is a second one!"

"OK so why not live really dangerously and make it three?!"

"Because two is more than enough!"

"OK fine. Forget it."

"Thank you."

Silence.

"Only Dawn and I have been going to Joe Allen's so often recently that I thought I wouldn't mind going somewhere else."

"You and Dawn?!"

"Yeah. So I thought why don't I take my best mate to my new club? You didn't know I'd got a new club, did you? You'll really like it."

"But I like Joe Allen's!"

"I *know* you do, Arnold. But my thinking was, maybe you'd like my new club, too." I breathe in and out really slowly because I can feel a full-scale panic attack coming on.

"Has Dawn been there yet?" I ask suspiciously.

"No of course not."

"Honestly?"

He chuckles over the phone. "You know me, I wouldn't take Dawn anywhere before I've taken my best mate there, now would I?"

I've been so bruised and buffeted by life recently that frankly I wonder if this is true. I'm not sure I can trust anyone any more. Then I remember that Kingsley Amis had to have lunch at his club every day without fail, and I think I don't want to end up an inflexible and irascible old misanthrope like him. So I struggle to control the panicky feeling. "OK, we'll go to your club," I say quickly.

"Great, you won't regret it! We'll have a lovely time celebrating you being alive again…"

"But the week after it's got to be Joe Allen's."

"Yeah, yeah, yeah…"

"And on a Wednesday!"

"Yeah, yeah, yeah, yeah…"

"I mean it, Wills!"

I hear the dialling tone. At least I think it's the dialling tone. Unless it's his famous friend doing her stupid imitations again.

"I know it's you, Dawn, so fuck off!" I yell just in case, and put the phone down.

6.00 p.m.

Take a brisk walk round my leafy corner of village London. Need to have clear head and fully operational loins and other bits for promised shagathon later. So I cross the road to avoid the Galloping Gastro and am nearly attacked by the homicidal Alsatian while the angry young guy, who's taking him for a walk, watches and gurgles with laughter and at the very last second yanks him away from my bollocks.

Am so stressed that don't notice where I'm going and after half an hour realize I'm in a different hood entirely.

The panic attack I struggled with earlier returns at double strength and have to pop into unknown hostelry for medicinal glass of reddo to calm nerves. On returning to alien street outside realize that unfamiliar hostile hood is Kensington.

As I start back to my own more familiar hood I see a familiar face approaching. It's my old mucker from the Mirror – Piers Morgan!

"Hi, mate," I beam affably. "How are you doing? Been up to anything since they sacked you for those phoney photos?"

He looks me up and down in that amusing way he has, like he's got a smell under his nose. "Who the hell are you?"

"I'm Arnold Appleforth, remember? I was one of the 3am girls when you were on the Mirror, and I did that hilarious Wicked Whisper, you remember the one, about Sarah Brown liking to stick her fingers in Gordon's till? He was Chancellor at the time, it was really satirical!"

The smell-under-the-nose look changes to the pursed little smile that makes you think he's desperate for a pee. "Yes I remember it all too well. It wasn't satirical it was pathetically puerile."

"No, no it was *Swiftian,* Piers, I remember explaining to you..."

"And it nearly jeopardised my growing friendship with Gordon."

"Yeah," I laugh, "I remember you used to like him! What

a wanker he is as PM though, eh?!"

The pursed little smile gets even tighter. "On the contrary, Gordon Brown is the most brilliant Prime Minister we've had for years, and mark my words he'll win a huge majority on May 6th and will carry on running this country very successfully for a very long time to come."

I laugh appreciatively, but he hasn't finished. "And when he's won his landslide victory he's promised to reward all his chums – that's me and Alan Sugar. Don't tell anyone but he's making me Director General of the BBC and Alan's going to be Chancellor." He beams at the prospect of having a job again, then frowns and looks at me as if I was the one who'd cacked my pants, not him. "So how much money do you want?"

"Why do you think I want money, Piers? It's just great to see you!"

"Look, I'm disgustingly rich, mate, and you're obviously on your uppers, so no worries. After all I'm a lifelong Labour supporter and I really believe in redistribution of wealth…" He digs in his pockets and brings out a few coins and looks at them. "How about a fiver?" He examines them more closely. "Sorry – it'll have to be four pounds fifty." He counts out the money then gives me a slap on the back. "Great to see you Arnold. Got to go now, my limo's waiting to take me to meet famous people at the Ivy for my Mail on Sunday column. So bloody tedious, mate."

He's already on his way but I call after him. "Hey, that reminds me! You know that interview you did with Cleggy when he said he'd slept with no more than thirty women? I wanted to say – really fantastic! Proper journalism of the old school!"

He turns back, beaming again. "Well, that's very kind of

you, Arnold. Yes, I was pretty pleased with it myself. So what other things of mine have you seen? Did you enjoy my TV interviews where I made famous people cry a lot? They were bloody good too, didn't you think?"

"Oh yeah brilliant – real integrity there too."

He seems to have forgotten about the limo. "Thank you – thank you... *Integrity* – yes – I must remember that. By the way, just between you and me your Wicked Whispers thing about Gordon and Sarah was pretty good. Quite hilarious in fact. Don't tell either of them I said so of course!"

"No names no pack drill. Now back to Cleggy. How about if I did an *homage* to your great article by writing one called "I've slept with no more than sixty women"?

"An *homage?*"

"Yeah that means –"

"I know what *homage* means, Arnold – just because I'm a man of the people doesn't mean I don't understand French words! Yes of course you can! Anything to help a chap when he's destitute. In fact, look, I'll go one better than that. I'll put in a word for you with my mate Dylan Jones at GQ – he's the guy who published the Clegg interview!"

I stare at him. "I thought it was The Mail on Sunday?"

"No, no, no, good heavens no..."

"Look why don't you just put in a word for me with The Mail on Sunday?"

"But GQ is much classier, Arnold! It's the most popular men's mag in the country! What's the matter with you? I'm trying to do you a favour, mate!"

"Just I've got a bit of a problem there... A bit difficult to explain ... Don't think I'd better take you up on your kind offer, thanks all the same..."

"Fine. Up to you." He shrugs. "But tell me something – what's it like being such a loser, Arnold? Hope you don't mind me asking."

"No, not at all, Piers."

"Nothing personal – but why aren't you a huge success like me? Funny thing is, I often find myself wondering that about people. Probably because I'm a bit of a secret leftie and want everyone to have the same advantages as me, and you know stay at the Beverley Wilshire and hang out with Sly Stallone and exchange hilarious text messages with Lord Sugar. Christ is that the time? Got to go, sorry mate, I'm late for Amanda Holden. Fantastic to see you again though!"

He vanishes into the black limo that has magically appeared next to him. As I watch it glide off I smile to myself as I realize that despite his boasting Piers is a busted flush and his career is going nowhere. He probably keeps on the limo just to impress people like me!

I stroll contentedly home and am made even happier by the thought that Piers is trapped in the dead old worlds of print and TV, while I'm about to embrace the revolutionary new world of the internet, thanks to my number one fan Anthea.

I start to run as I realize I need to chuck together some brilliant ideas for her before she arrives at nine.

9.30 p.m.

Anthea very sensitively arrives half an hour late, as she thought I needed time to recover from my first experience of sexting. So have had loads of time to write brilliant new stuff for her online mag for oldies who won't admit they are, which I hope we can get out of the way quickly before getting down to business, so to speak!

9.35 p.m.

Am disappointed to discover that Anthea intended the sexting to be an end in itself, not just a taster. "So now we can have the whole evening free for work, sweetie, instead of hours and hours of shaggy shaggy!"

10.00 p.m.

Sit in kitchen drinking last of emergency ration of reddo that Anthea brought ten days ago. Feel confused. The pleasure of hearing her snorting and gurgling in the living room as she reads my brilliant new stuff is lessened by nagging doubt about whether we've ever really had proper sex and growing concern about whether she's a mad fantasist.

She trots in, enthusiastically brandishing my new pages.

"You're right, it's great, Arnold, it's all great! I'd say it's as great as all those ironically hard-hitting Private Eye pieces you did in the 80s…"

"They weren't ironic – how many times…?"

"They were to me, sweetie, and it's all in the eye of the beholder, isn't that what they say? You're amazing, just like Picasso really, still pumping it out at ninety, still as productive as ever!"

"I'm not fucking ninety, Anthea, I'm sixty-one, sorry seventy-one…"

"What does age matter anyway?! It's only a number, isn't it? On the other hand, I do think that for publicity purposes it might be helpful to pretend you're a little bit older than you are. You know, just to encourage the older demographic…"

"I am not going to pretend I'm ninety!"

"Why are you being so difficult, sweetie? I don't know what you're worried about, after a few drinks you could easily pass for ninety!" She slides an arm round me and nuzzles my ear. "The important thing is we both know you've got the sexual stamina of a thirty-year-old really. But let's keep it to ourselves, hmmm?" She sticks her tongue in my ear and wiggles it about and I try to stay aloof but Mr Stiffie has other ideas.

"I suppose I could pretend I'm seventy-five at a pinch," I say eventually.

"Eighty-five," she whispers.

"Eighty."

"You've got yourself a deal, my little geriatric stallion," she breathes, then resumes her work on my ear.

Wonder if I might be in with a chance after all. Try to unzip her jeans and ignore her spit as it trickles down my aural canal. Then realize it's buttons not a zip and try again.

10.20 p.m.

Have got one button undone. *Result!*

But still struggling with second button. Have almost got it undone when she pulls away and says, "Hang on a tick, sweetie, I almost forgot". And takes some papers from her pocket and asks me to sign them.

"What's that?"

"It's a contract of course!"

"What, *now?*"

"Please, please, please."

I give her a hurt look, but she sticks her tongue back in my ear and wiggles it about again. The spit is getting really tickly and the buttons are impossible, so doing what she wants seems the best way to keep the show on the road so to speak. But Mr Stiffie doesn't understand tactics and keeps distracting me and makes my handwriting wobbly. Anthea looks at my signature and frowns. "Are you *sure* you're not ninety?"

"For Christ's sake..."

"Of course not!" she smiles. And puts the contract in her pocket and jumps up and picks up her donkey jacket.

"Where are you going?" I ask.

"Some of us have got work to do, Arnold."

"What, *now?*"

She looks at me indignantly. "The World Wide Web doesn't stop at five-thirty and weekends, Arnold, it's twenty-four seven! I've never been so busy! The website's still under construction but I'll bung up your brilliant articles *tout de suite* and see if there's any response." She does up her donkey jacket and smiles. "By the way, you realize you won't get paid?"

I laugh heartily.

"No I mean it. There's no money in online mags, everyone knows that."

"So why did you make me sign a contract?"

"Oh well, things can get picked up, you know, like that Belle de Jour sex-blog thing."

I've no idea what she's talking about.

"So here's hoping for a great future together, Arnold!"

She moves to kiss me goodbye and I try for a bit of tonguing, but she aims a chaste peck at my cheek and I'm left looking like the homicidal bloody Alsatian when it was slavering after my gonads. Of course she finds this amusing. When she's stopped sniggering she pats me on the arm and insists on letting herself out. "We don't want you over-tiring yourself. It'd be terrible if you popped off just yet, wouldn't it?"

10.50 p.m.

Decide death by homicidal Alsatian is a risk worth taking, in fact might be a welcome relief, so dash to the Galloping Gastro. To my surprise the beast isn't there nor is its psycho owner. Buy a bottle of house Rioja and dash back home so I can ponder the ruins of my career and sex life over a glass or three.

After some pondering and drinking am forced to conclude sex life is too desperate to bear examination and even alcohol offers no consolation. Also realize that career-wise cannot rely solely on possible one-off-never-to-be-repeated payment from Dylan Jones (Note to self – make sure he doesn't make cheque out to Lady Hamilton-Thingy, because if he does am screwed).

So what to do?

Answer – write more quizzes for Wills. Fast. But have got to get him to ditch Dawn first. Celebrate this decisive thinking with couple of glasses. Then go for pee and come back refreshed and with more room for celebratory Rioja and am dismayed to discover have finished it.

Find there is no alcohol anywhere. But am determined not to be a victim so get sheet of A4 and red crayon and sellotape and print in large letters GET CASE OF 3 FOR £10 TESCO REDDO and stick it on front door.

Go to bed feeling cheered because have done something decisive.

Tuesday 27th April

12.55 a.m.

Can't sleep.

1.40 a.m.

Dream about Nick Clegg's Spanish wife Miriam doing steamy Flamenco dance. She snaps her castanets and whispers I'm so much hotter than pathetic public school politicos, even ones who are more popular than Churchill. She gets closer and closer and dances faster and faster till I see the beads of sweat on her sexy Spanish brow. But as the dancing reaches its climax I notice a half-glass of Rioja on the table behind her and have no choice but to push past her heaving breasts to get it and when I turn back she's gone.

1.45 a.m.

Go for pee. Then lie awake wondering if relocating to Spain might solve problems.

Decide it probably won't, so get up and turn on computer and go to www.oldies-who-won't-admit-they-are.co.uk.

Yes, my articles are up there! Nothing else, mind you, except for an inspiring welcome from Anthea.

"Hello, silver surfers! As you can see (if you can still see) this website is still under construction but I thought you might enjoy a taster of what's to come.

I'd like to introduce you to my new best friend and lead writer Arnold Appleforth. Arnold was ninety last week and is hale and healthy and insists he still shags like a rabbit. (And he certainly didn't die last week, though a well-known joyless leftie rag would have us believe otherwise!)

Personally, I think Arnold's insistence on behaving as immaturely as possible is a great example for us all, and I believe you'll find his pathological refusal to accept the ageing process in any way at all a genuine inspiration. So just sit back (or get someone else to help you sit back!) and enjoy Arnold's first ever online articles, the first of which is wittily entitled "Some do's and don'ts".

(Note to potential advertisers: all the articles on this website will be aimed at a wide and really selfish AB readership who have loads of disposable income because they no longer have snivelly kids or aged parents to drain their resources. Also, they're going to die really soon so they're desperate to spend as much as they can before their ungrateful offspring get their greedy mitts on it).

Some do's and don'ts

By

Arnold Appleforth

Here are some handy hints for the no-longer-quite-so-young to help them find their way along life's increasingly stumbling path. ("Stumbling" in the sense of needing to pause occasionally to sniff the roses and enjoy the riches life has to offer, not "stumbling" in the nasty sense of getting a bit gaga obviously).

1. Do keep using bad language

People often say that swearing is a sign of a limited

vocabulary. This is bollocks. They also say swearing is specially undignified in those-who-are-not-quite-so-young. This is not just bollocks but ageist fucking bollocks.

So don't give up your casually offensive use of bad language. Whether you are fifty-three or eighty-three the shock value of saying "fuck" in inappropriate circumstances is always gratifying. Far more fun than when you were "younger"!

Here are some particularly good occasions where you can shock people with gratuitous bad language –

a) *christenings – specially the bit in church*
b) *funerals – ditto*
c) *Christmas – specially Boxing Day morning when everyone's liverish and sick of each other and really stressed and edgy*
d) *posh very quiet restaurants. To get the best result here it's advisable not only to swear really loudly but throw in lots of raucous laughter.*

An interesting thought. Some people say there is too much swearing on TV. Not true! The problem is that most of the swearing comes from young TV chefs, leaving other much-loved but not-quite-so-young TV stars feeling resentful and left out. An obvious solution is for some of Gordon Ramsay's and Jamie Oliver's "fucks" to be confiscated and redistributed to the aforementioned much-loved but not-quite-so-young stars, e.g. John Nettles and David Jason. As a result, their shows will instantly become more cutting-edge and their example will help TV become a fairer, less ageist place. And who knows, Angela Rippon might one day end up back where she belongs, high-kicking and reading the news again!

2. Don't think that being bad-tempered and grumpy all the time is hilarious

Men often get bad-tempered as they get "older" but women are increasingly getting in on the act. This is because of endless shows in which programme makers desperate to come up with cheap TV let a load of self-regarding old crocks list in tedious detail all the things they hate about modern life. (Why aren't the Grumpy Old Men and Grumpy Old Women programmes ever on their own hate lists?!)

The danger is that watching these shows makes you believe that your growing intolerance makes you hilarious too, like the grumpy old crocks think it does them! Just remember – when Victor Meldrew does curmudgeonly it's funny. When you do it it's not. When the grumpy old men and women do it it's a boring pain in the arse.

But –

3. Do feel free to hate The Daily Mail

Every rule needs an exception, and this is it! If you've always hated The Daily Mail – fantastic, just keep hating. If you're one of those weird types who for some reason think they like it – have another think. And if you still haven't changed your mind have another *think.*

Because you can't really like it – it's so full of hatred for everything in the world that it makes the grumpy old men and women seem positively cheery in their view of life! And The Mail on Sunday is even worse! (Please note: I say this even though they have been known to pay me to write my own hate-filled pieces – which just goes to show how objective I am!)

But the one thing they don't hate is the past. They love the past and everything about it! Which brings me to –

4. *Don't get nostalgic: the past was mainly shit*

Contrary to what the Daily Mail says, life is far better now.

Here is an interesting fact: the often fondly remembered 1950s were like death warmed up.

Perhaps you think that John Major was right when he talked fondly of the traditional England he loved. And maybe in the 1950s people really did drink warm beer on the village green watching the cricket then stroll back to their Midsomer Murders houses and have tea and crumpets and do a bit of thatching before bed.

But if they did, it's only because there was nothing to watch on the BBC except the potter's wheel and Muffin the sodding Mule, and ITV wasn't even around to liven things up either, well not till 1955.

And all the shops were shut too – can you believe it?! In fact, there weren't any shops really, specially not on Sundays, and the pubs were shut all afternoon and you couldn't drink beer, warm or not, till you were eighteen.

Which means that people were so bored they even went to church! Can you believe that?

5. *Do use the internet indiscriminately*

   And encourage your grandchildren to as well. If they still say they want to play outside in the fresh air, tell them about the boredom and frustration you had to endure when you were their age – then turn off the Parental Controls and see how quickly their attitude changes!

6. *Don't feel guilty about not playing golf*

   Just because you're not-quite-as-young-as-you-were it doesn't mean you have to eat through a straw or dribble your dinner down your shirt or wear clothes made of polyester. And you don't have to play golf, either.

   So why not try something that's a bit less of a cliché for your age-bracket? How about giving paragliding or heroin a go?

7. *Do feel free to avoid garden centres*

   See the bit about paragliding and heroin above.

Am so excited to see my article up there for all the world to read that decide I won't send Anthea scathing email for saying I'm ninety after all.

Feel need to celebrate, so conduct yet another intensive search of kitchen cupboards. At back of third shelf down in second cupboard along find dusty can of tomato juice and even dustier bottle of Worcestershire sauce. Mix them together and add ice and take a swig and it feels like the back of my throat is on fire. Almost like drinking proper drink! *Result!*

Finish it off and return, miraculously refreshed, to peruse my second brilliant article.

Random thoughts to avoid now you're not-quite-so-young
By
Arnold Appleforth

1. *Why does everyone mumble in movies nowadays?*

   They just do. Get used to it.

2. *I hate multi-storey car parks*

   So what are you going to do, stick at home all day because you're terrified of going out because you can never find the fucking car afterwards? You've got to get out of the house sometimes. You can't watch re-runs of Murder She Wrote all day you know!

3. *I can do anything I want now I'm not-quite-so-young and no one can stop me*

   Remember that our prisons are overcrowded and full of frustrated cons of all sexual persuasions. So unless you want to spend your sentence being buggered senseless by those of a gerontophile persuasion, you might want to think again.

But if that's your secret fantasy, well go for it, lucky old you! In your case you really can do exactly what you want now, can't you?!

4. *I can say anything I want now I'm not-quite-so-young and no one can stop me*

   On the face of it this sounds a lot more reasonable, doesn't it? But ask yourself this – what exactly are you so desperate to say once you've thrown off the shackles of polite society?

   I'll tell you what. Nothing at all. You're just going to end up being another tedious windbag ranting on like all those hideous grumpy old men.

5. *I know I shouldn't, but I do find I like the Daily Mail more and more nowadays*

   Just fuck off.

6. *And I can't help agreeing with them a bit about the bad language thing too*

   And die.

7. *I've really started to miss my old house/ex-wife/dog recently*

   Why? You were happy enough abandoning them for that busty forty-year-old divorcee on that hot, sticky, summer afternoon six years ago – remember? So don't start whingeing now that her pneumatic appeal is wearing off.

That's life, mate!
Alternatively, have you thought about the internet? Why not try www.quickshag.com?

8. *I find I'm just not interested in sex like I used to be*

   You've been brainwashed by propaganda pumped out by so-called scientific research bodies funded by our ageist government to make us think we don't want it any more – e.g. life-denying bollocks about testosterone levels plunging as you get "older". All they're interested in is the youth vote. Well don't give them the satisfaction. You know what you've got to do – just pull yourself together and get in there!

9. *I find I'm just not interested in alcohol like I used to be*

   Not sex or alcohol? God you boring tosser – get a life.

Gaze admiringly at the effortlessly pithy prose I knocked off earlier, and not for the first time ponder the elusive nature of talent.

Go back to bed, still pondering. Decide the originality of even my most hasty scribblings suggests a mind at peak of creative powers. Not happy, mind you, that Anthea has casually cut ninety percent of the bad language, but on reflection decide that distinctive style survives even so and am so used to ruthless censorship that can't be arsed to make a thing of it.

Am so inspired by my own creative example that scribble a couple of brilliant haiku-like quizzes for Wills before going back to sleep.

11.25 a.m.

Wake up with just right amount of time to get to lunch with Wills without hurrying. Have leisurely wash and crap and get dressed, then have pleasant breakfast of now stale pitta bread and raspberry jam and "fresh" coffee that's not at all fresh, and the last of condensed milk, while catching a few minutes of Sixties fun with Heartbeat on ITV3. As I half-listen to their bucolic prattling I realize that I have that all-too-rare feeling of being at peace and in control of life. Get up and leave breakfast things on floor and set off happily to meet the day.

Then see red-crayoned reminder on front door – GET CASE OF 3 FOR £10 TESCO REDDO – and realize don't have enough time to get it before lunch and will forget to get it later and will probably never organise life enough to have supply of Tesco reddo in the flat ever again and have terrible panic attack.

12.20 p.m.

Am standing in hall whimpering and unable to move when the letter-box flap opens and a familiar voice calls out "Coo-eee! Are you all right?! What are you making that horrid noise for?" I struggle to pull myself together and manage to get to the door and open it and Lizzie breezes in with her doggies close behind. "You're not being attacked *again,* I hope? Saving your life three times would be embarrassing, dear – people might start to talk..." She peers around for intruders and seems disappointed not to find any. "So what happened?"

I try to tell her, but the only words I can get out are "lunch" and "best mate" and "drink". I point at the red-crayoned reminder on the front door and she tears it down and squints at it then smiles her crinkly smile, understanding at once. "Don't worry – I'll get it for you."

I manage to stammer my thanks. "How did I live without you? You're my guardian angel, Lizzie!"

"Actually I'm more of a Waitrose person, but I don't mind going downmarket for you, dear. Anyway I won't hold you up!" Suddenly her face is looming towards me and she's trying to give me a floury kiss goodbye – the exact opposite of the sort Anthea gave me, because she makes straight for the mouth and I have to move really fast so that it ends up just a cheek job. She purses her wrinkly lips and gives me a twinkly look. "*Naughty* boy," she says, and smacks my bottom really hard and leaves, taking her doggies with her.

1.10 p.m.

So taken aback by sexual behaviour of hundred and eighty-three-year-old definitely-not-lesbian neighbour that can't think straight, and as a result arrive at Joe Allen's only ten minutes late instead of my customary twenty-five. Then see Wills isn't at usual table and start to have another panic attack.

Then remember we're meeting at his club and feel better.

Get hopelessly lost trying to find his new club and hail taxi I can't afford and text Wills while enduring very expensive traffic jam.

Me – what sort of club is the garlic? Like soho house?
Him – no its a gentlemen's club
Me – like spearmint rhino?
Him – ha ha.
Me – what do u mean ha ha?

Him – like the savile and brooks and the in and out club
Me – what's the in and out a knocking shop?
Him – ha ha. Anyway hope u r wearing a tie
Me – ha ha
Him – what do u mean ha ha?

When I get to the really old looking Garlic Club (a satisfying forty minutes late) Wills is standing anxiously on its steps dressed like a dog's dinner.

We look each other up and down disapprovingly.

"I thought we were having lunch, not a fucking funeral," I say wittily.

He's looking at my "Dick Cheney – Before He Dicks You!" T-shirt, which I chose because it's the only one that's cleanish. "Are you deliberately hoping to embarrass me in front of some of the most influential movers and shakers in the media world?" he asks.

"I thought only retired colonels and other Tory wankers belonged to gentlemen's clubs?"

"Nonsense. I've just been chatting to Melvyn in the bar, and Andrew Neil's there with Boris, and Richard Desmond's there – *everybody's* there."

"Richard Desmond?! I've got a great idea for an article for – "

"You're not allowed to talk about work in the Garlic, Arnold."

"But he'll love it, it's about rectal examinations for the over sixties by yummy young student doctors. Maybe he could get some of his Asian Babes or Horny Housewives to do the pictures!"

"*Shush* – he doesn't do stuff like that anymore, Arnold,

he's very respectable now. He publishes OK! for heaven's sake."

I chuckle appreciatively then realize he's being serious. "Don't worry, I'll have a chat with him," I say as I make for the entrance.

"No you won't, and they won't let you into the Garlic dressed like that!" he says. And before I can stop him he's dragging me down the street. "You need a whole new outfit," he says and drags me into Paul Smith. Then sees the prices and drags me out and drags me into Next instead.

"You're such a pathetic reactionary," I say to him as I admire myself in the Next mirror in my new suit and tie and shirt and shoes. I can't help thinking the women in the Garlic will be falling over themselves to get at me.

2.30 p.m.

Dear Diary, let me tell you something you're not going to believe. *There aren't any women in the Garlic!* Which century are we in, for God's sake? Don't know which annoys me more, the lack of women or the way Wills keeps "joking" about me paying him back for the suit when I'm earning real money again.

Decide to ignore him and concentrate on the menu, which he says I'll love.

"It looks just like what I had at primary school!" I say, by which I mean it looks like shit.

"Yes exactly," he enthuses. "I recommend the brown soup, shepherd's pie and semolina pudding, it'll take you right back!"

"I'm not sure I want to be taken right back."

He pours me more wine, then grins and waves at Melvyn

at the next table, who ignores him.

"So why were you so keen to bring me to this sexist right-wing shithole, Wills?" I ask affably.

He laughs condescendingly. "It's not *sexist,* you're so politically correct, Arnold! This is the *Garlic Club!* Just because the Garlic Club doesn't allow women members doesn't mean it's sexist or right-wing, it means it happens to be a unique and much loved institution that goes its own charmingly idiosyncratic way!"

"Right."

"Why else do you think all these famous left-wing people would be eating here?!"

"Right."

He smiles, evidently pleased he's been able to explain something so complicated in a way that I can really understand. Then he leans forward and whispers, "Before I forget, there's been a great response to your quizzes in the mag. Specially after everyone thought you'd died!"

"Why are you whispering?"

"*I told you,* because you're not allowed to talk about work at the Garlic!"

"Oh yeah..." I start to whisper too. "So when are you going to tell them I haven't died?"

He avoids my gaze. "I'm not sure."

"What do you mean you're not sure?"

"I'm not sure it's strictly necessary..."

"Why isn't it necessary?!"

"*Ssshhh.*"

"*Why isn't it strictly necessary, Wills?* I *think it's strictly necessary!*"

He looks around shiftily. "There's no need to take

everything so personally, Arnold. It's just I'm not sure how relevant it is, now that you're no longer working for us. And, well, I'm worried about what Dawn will think…"

I'm not sure what their views on physical violence are at the Garlic so I force a smile and make an effort to respond tactically instead of with a more direct form of address. "So what about the older demographic, Wills? Will an alternative comedian like Dawn really appeal to them like I do? Have you stopped to ask yourself that? I thought you wanted to expand your readership beyond the under-thirties!"

He frowns, trying to work out what's wrong with my argument. "I'm not sure you're entirely right about the age-range she appeals to," he says eventually. "I mean don't get me wrong, the last thing I want is to be disrespectful about Dawn, but I'd have thought she might agree herself that she's no spring chicken…"

I smile because I can see I've got him on the run. "So why don't you phone and ask her?"

He laughs nervously and tries to hide his Blackberry under his napkin but I grab his wrist.

"You know, Wills, I've got online magazines who are desperate for my services. Magazines for the not-quite-so-young who realize what an invaluable asset I am. And you know why? Because I'm *flexible.*" He thinks I'm joking and starts to laugh but I silence him with a withering look. "You see I've been able to move with the times, mate. I'm looking to the future now while you and Dawn and your pathetic old-fashioned printed Sudoku rag are clinging to the past. But if your head's stuck so far up her arse that you can't see that, well, there's nothing I can do to help, is there? But if that's not the case, then as we're best mates I might just be willing to come to your rescue. If you ask nicely of course."

He looks really worried. "So what do you think I should do, Arnold?"

"Well for starters, I've written a couple of new quizzes for you. They'll get a great response, believe me."

"But I thought you were saying I needed to go online!"

"Look – one step at a time, OK? Let's just try to improve the content first, shall we?"

"Oh yes – yes of course..."

"This is the first quiz." I pass a sheet of paper across the table. "It's bang up to date but with a *soupçon* of nostalgia. It'll go down a bomb, believe me."

He reads it slowly, following the words with his fingers and muttering like he always does:

Which not-quite-so-young celebrity didn't really die last week?

1. *Nick Clegg*
2. *The Pope*
3. *Barbara Windsor*
4. *David Niven*
5. *Arnold Appleforth*

He stares at it for some moments. "Don't think I'm being critical," he says eventually, "but how can you be a celebrity when no one in the whole world has heard of you?"

"They've all heard of me now you've written my obituary, Wills."

His simple face lights up. "Yes of course they have, you're

quite right! Brilliant! So you're a celebrity now all because of me!"

"Exactly."

He leans back, really happy now, then glances at the quiz and frowns again. "One more tiny thing. Barbara Windsor."

"What about her?"

He glances round nervously, then leans forward again. "Just between you and me – the word on the street is she's leaving EastEnders."

"Which street?"

"Well the Radio Times actually – the word in The Radio Times is she's leaving EastEnders. *Very soon.* So will it still be OK to say she's a celebrity?"

I smile at him. "You know, she's not leaving EastEnders really, Wills."

"Well I don't want to argue with you, but I think she is."

"No she isn't. Not as far as the British public is concerned. Because in their hearts Babs will always be in EastEnders. I'd go so far as to say she'll always be right up there in the pantheon alongside Dirty Den and Angie."

He gazes at me admiringly, then squeezes my hand. "You know, Arnold, most of the time I think you're totally selfish and immature and a complete monster, but occasionally – just occasionally – you say something that makes me realize why we've been such great buddies for so many years."

"Thank you, mate."

He pours more wine. "Well you've certainly answered all my pernickety little points! And as for the quiz itself, needless to say it's witty, irreverent, and presses the nostalgia button just like you said. In fact, I'd say you've surpassed even your own immensely high standards."

"What about Dawn?"

He tries to look tough and ruthless. Then empties his glass and tries again.

"Just show me your other quiz and leave me to deal with Dawn."

"OK. This one's a little more cultural."

He looks at me warily. *Cultural?* This is Sudoku Weekly, Arnold, not The London Review Of Books."

"Yeah but I thought you might fancy trying for a more aspirational readership as well as the Asda types you normally go for. The Sunday Times market, you know – glossy gossipy shit with arty bits for the AB readership."

"Oh right, yes of course – now you're talking!" he says enthusiastically, and I pass him the second quiz and this time his finger really whizzes over the words and he's muttering away like a mad thing.

The not-quite-so-young drinkers' quiz

What do the following people have in common – F Scott Fitzgerald, Ernest Hemingway, Tennessee Williams, W C Fields?

1. *They're all dead*
2. *They're all pissheads*
3. *Three of them didn't win the Nobel Prize*
4. *Three of them don't have first names that sound like a toilet*

(Clue – Ernest Hemingway was the one who won the Nobel Prize)

He looks up, his eyes gleaming excitedly. "Hey, you didn't tell me you were targeting the American market too. Fantastic. You should die more often, mate, it's obviously good for the brain cells!"

"So how much are you going to pay me?"

"Let's not talk about money just yet..."

"OK just give me two hundred and I won't talk about it at all."

"Two hundred?! It was only a hundred and fifty last time!"

"Yeah but like you said you've got the American angle this time..."

"Look, sorry, I haven't got two hundred on me."

"OK a hundred and ninety."

"I haven't got a hundred and ninety either, Arnold," he smiles patiently. And empties his pockets onto the table. "I've got two pound fifty and my credit cards."

For the second time in less than an hour I have a great desire to smack my dear old best mate in the mouth, but I restrain myself and sit back and give him my Tony Soprano smiling-but-threatening look instead, and wait.

"I tell you what," he says eventually, "take the two pound fifty and you don't have to pay me back for the new outfit!"

Before I can tell him I wasn't planning to fucking pay him back for it, a waiter appears and slaps down our main courses, and I look from Wills' plate of nursery food to mine and try to work out what we ordered and fail.

Wills digs into his plate of slop enthusiastically while I examine mine more closely and still can't work out what it is. Then I see Wills abandon his fork and start to spoon his food up, and watching him is so unpleasant yet oddly riveting that I forget about trying to eat too.

Five minutes later he beams across the table and asks if he can have mine. Another five minutes, then he sighs and dabs his face dry with his napkin. “Lovely scoff,” he says contentedly.

“Right. Let’s get back to money.”

“Yes all right, OK,” he sighs, not sounding as keen as I would have liked. “So buying you a new outfit so you’re fit to be seen in grown-up society doesn’t strike you as the potentially life-changing act of generosity it actually is?” I shake my head. “Right. Then how about this? When you get back to your hovel, why don’t you flog it on eBay? That should keep you in industrial alcohol for a few days at least.”

He laughs but I ignore his juvenile attempt at humour and weigh up the pros and cons. The pros are that I’ll get some money from it and I won’t be allowed into poncy dumps like the Garlic again. I can’t think of any cons. “Yeah all right, it’s a deal, you cheapskate bastard,” I say finally.

“Goodo. I do hate discussing money, don’t you? Let’s celebrate!” And he waves a hand to order another bottle, which as usual with Wills arrives almost before he’s asked for it.

“To us,” he says, and we clink glasses and drink, and maybe it’s the spring sun shining through the stained-glass windows of the Garlic, dappling the walls with its faint rays, or maybe it’s the realization that I’m twenty years younger than everyone here except for Richard Desmond and Wills, but I suddenly feel really warm and generous towards the world and especially my dear old mate.

“So how are you doing, Wills?” I ask fondly, hoping he won’t take long with his answer.

“Actually, that’s one of the reasons I suggested meeting

here," he says. "I need to have a private conversation with you."

"Why couldn't we do that at Joe Allen's?!" He gives me a look, and I understand. "Oh I *see*, you didn't want Dawn to –?"

"Ssshhh!" He looks nervously round. "It just crossed my mind she might be a little you know jealous, if she overheard. Very arrogant of me to think so I'm sure but –"

"Jealous of what?"

"No I'm probably completely wrong – she probably really loves practising for the Marathon every day with me, and all that pounding the pavements together and working up a sweat has no subtext whatsoever..."

"What's she got to be jealous of, Wills?"

He clears his throat. "You remember me saying how much I loved my wife? And how much I still fancied her even after all these years?"

"Yeah I vaguely remember something about still shagging four or five times a week, some sort of fucking record I reckon..."

He looks really relieved. "Do you really think so? That's so kind!"

"Well not compared to me, but then I'm footloose and fancy-free..."

"Well exactly, I've always regarded you as the expert, which is why I wanted your advice."

"Whatever I can do to help." I smile supportively. "So what's the problem? Down to two or three times a week is it?"

"No certainly not." He laughs. "Quite the opposite!" Then he suddenly goes solemn. "The thing is, I'm having an affair, you see."

"Beg your pardon?"

"I said I'm having an affair, Arnold."

I look at my best mate across the table and I no longer want to smack him in the mouth, which would be a futile, immature gesture. I want him to have a heart attack and die.

Wills is still speaking but I can't focus. I find myself wondering if the God I don't believe in exists after all and he's punishing me again. Yeah, really good one, God. Great sense of humour – highly fucking ironic...

"I'm not going to leave Mary, of course..."

"No of course not..." I gaze at the little bastard and wonder where on earth he finds the time. Not to mention the energy.

"So what do you think I should do?"

"What do you mean *do?*"

"What would you do in my position?"

"In your position...?"

"I'm getting desperate, I'm open to any suggestions. I mean *any*. I really need your input!"

I manage a magnanimous smile. "Yeah of course. So let me summarise the situation. Basically you've got this bit on the side..."

"I wouldn't call her a –"

"Shut up. Basically you've got this bit on the side. But your problem is that now she wants to get serious and you don't..."

"No that's not –"

"Will you let me finish? You see it's all par for the course, Wills. You just happen to have led a very sheltered life, otherwise you'd realize it happens all the time. Unfortunately, the extra problem you're facing is that you're Mr Nice Guy so you haven't got the heart to chuck her, which is why you want Mr Experienced here to come along and take her off your hands."

"No that's not it at all."

"You don't have to be coy with me!" I chuckle. "And you can stop worrying right now. Anything to help my best mate. What's her phone number?"

"No I don't want you to take her off my hands, Arnold," he says, sounding surprisingly irritable. "That's not what I want at all. Penelope and I love each other very much and we've no intention of splitting up."

"Hang on hang on, you just said you loved what's-her-name..."

"My wife."

"Yeah her."

"She's not a *her,* she's Mary."

"Yeah whatever."

"I do love Mary. I love Mary and Penelope. I love them both. *That's* the problem."

I smile indulgently. "Don't be stupid, you can't love two people, Wills. For one thing it's greedy, for another it's not fucking possible."

"Just because you've never been capable of even loving *one* person, Arnold, because you're completely self-obsessed and solipsistic and have no understanding of the human heart whatsoever..."

"Sticks and stones, Wills..." I smile, which seems to make him even angrier. Then he sighs and pours himself more wine and drinks it. I clear my throat and he glances at me and finally pours me some too, the bad-mannered bastard.

"Sorry," he frowns. "Very sorry. You can't help being like that, after all."

"Thank you," I smile again.

"It's just that things are really difficult and painful, you see..."

"They sound fantastic to me!"

"No, they're not fantastic you see because Mary's found out. And she's deeply hurt of course, and she's talking about divorce, even though I keep telling her how much I love her and as a result –"

"As a result you're not getting any – well not on the marital front anyway," I say sympathetically. "What do you expect, Wills? Like you say, she's hurt – really *hurt*. Not that you've got that much to complain about as far as I can see because you're presumably still getting plenty from the bit on the side..."

"Please don't call her the *bit on the side!* She's a Professor of Philosophy and she specialises in logic and scientific methodology!"

"Sounds really hot," I say supportively.

He shuts his eyes tightly as if he's got a headache. "But yes I am still *getting plenty,* as you crudely put it... And not just from Penelope, actually... You see Mary's so horribly unhappy she needs constant reassurance..."

I'm dumbstruck again. But I force myself to speak. "So how many times a week are you getting it now, Wills?"

"Will you please not talk like that, it's so cheap and reductive. Why do you have to reduce everything to the purely animal? Don't you understand, the point is I'm in great pain because I'm in love with two women...?"

"How many times?"

"What does it matter? The point is I have deep emotional and spiritual connections with both of them, which is far more important than -!"

"How many fucking times?"

"Nine or ten, now will you please stop talking about it?" He glares at me. "I was hoping for your support, Arnold, that's why I told you all this, but apparently that's too much to ask!"

I try not to feel bitter. *He* wants *my* support – when so far as I can tell I've not even managed to go all the way with Anthea Greenspan and now I very much doubt I ever will! But I'm not going to reveal my vulnerable side to him. I do have my pride. I force another smile.

"Of course you've got my support, Wills. Anything I can do."

"Thank you. Thank you. I just want you to tell me what I can do to stop myself going insane, Arnold."

I've no idea at all. Then I remember something I once read in the advice column of Grazia. Or was it Cosmopolitan? Or it might have been Hello come to think of it. When I was reading one of them for research purposes, obviously.

So I trot it out. "I think you need some space, Wills."

"Space?"

"Yeah space." Then I remember another bit. "While you try to get your head together."

"You mean space away from both of them? That's an excellent idea. Really excellent." And before I can stop him he jumps up and hurries round the table and is hugging me. "So can I come and stay with you?"

"No way."

But he's still hugging me and doesn't seem to hear. "Will

Saturday be OK? I won't forget this, Arnold!"

I see my life spiralling into a nightmare. An embarrassingly clichéd nightmare at that. We're going to end up like the Odd Couple and he'll be Jack Lemmon and I'll be Walter Matthau. After even more hugging he lets go and I realize I've got to knock this on the head rightaway.

"Yeah, well, Saturday'd be great. Fantastic!" Then I frown, "Oh no, I've just remembered, I'm really busy this weekend."

"No you're not," he laughs, "you're never busy."

"What do you mean I'm never busy? Why do people keep saying that?! As it happens I've got a couple of major sexual encounters lined up."

"No problem, I'll bring earplugs. OK see you Saturday."

He's about to go back to his side of the table, then pauses. And I realize from the look in his eyes that he's going to embarrass me even more. "You know what?" he says. "You're the best, Arnold. No you are!" And I have a premonition of what he's going to do next. Before I can stop him he pulls me to him and plants his wet dribbly lips on my cheek and I can see all the fat old Garlic Club poofs beaming sentimentally at us, wishing they were in his shoes probably, and I realize this is the most embarrassing moment in my whole life and definitely the end of a very long friendship.

5.40 p.m.

Get home and steel myself not to turn on TV. Instead go straight to computer to flog suit etc. on eBay. After three hours have worked out that in order to sell suit, shirt, tie, shoes and socks have to flog each one separately, using weird online auctioning process, then wrap each one up and address it and go to Third World post office to send it off. Wonder how come millions of people far less intelligent than me can apparently use eBay without any trouble.

9.15 p.m.

Still haven't sorted it and am so stressed that turn on TV and try to have recuperative zizz in front of A Touch Of Frost. Drift off wondering how Wills could possibly have thought David Jason could play me. No similarity at all. Am at least three inches taller and haven't got a moustache.

Wonder which woman in my life Barbara Windsor could play once she's left the Queen Vic. Darling daughter Alice? No, Babs far too old. Lizzie then? No, Babs far too young, about a hundred years too young in fact. How about my number one fan Anthea? No. Then how about ex-wife Daphne? Ah yes! Right chest size and can really imagine Babs could have been a sexy bubbly waitress spilling all over my table just like Daphne...

Doorbell rings and wakes me from exciting casting dreams... Oh Christ, is it the BNP retard? Has he escaped from custody and come back to finish the job...?

"Coo-eee! I know you're there! Don't think you can hide from me, you naughty boy..."

Have no choice but to open front door, and there is Lizzie tottering triumphantly beneath a case of Tesco 3 for £10 reddo and gasping under the weight.

"Fuck me, it's my guardian angel."

"Oh how lovely!" she gurgles. "I just love it when you talk like an oik. Do it some more!"

I take the case from her withered grasp but ignore her request. "I'll just get you the forty quid," I say.

"No, no I wouldn't dream of it, it's my treat!" she insists.

"Isn't that nice of me?" And before I can stop her she's slipped into the flat and shut the door behind her.

I smile uneasily but I can hardly throw her out so I tear the box of reddo open just to make sure it's what it says it is. I gaze down at the dark shiny bottles, and it's quite an emotional moment really. "You know, you've saved my life three times now, Lizzie? Twice from the BNP retard and now with this."

"So I have – yes!" She beams and looks me up and down as if she's just been given me for Christmas and is wondering what to do with me. She brushes the lapels of my suit and straightens them then flicks off a stray bit of nursery food. "I love the new look, Arnold. Perhaps not as laugh-out-loud hilarious as your usual outfits but such a refreshing change."

"Yeah well I'm trying to flog it."

"Flog it?"

"Do you know about eBay?"

"Yes I know lots about eBay but I absolutely forbid you to flog it. Now that you've got a suit you can be my walker!"

"Your what?"

"It's what single ladies *d'un certain age* have to accompany them to smart social events, Arnold. And the minute the election's over and there's a proper Tory government again there are going to be *lots* of lovely smart events to go to…"

"I certainly hope not," I say indignantly. "The country's nearly bankrupt and we're all supposed to be tightening our belts!"

She looks at me blankly for a moment. "Oh you mean the recession thingy? Oh no you mustn't worry about that, dear, that's only for the proles. Davey and Georgie just love a party, specially Georgie – though he's not allowed to admit it of course nowadays. In fact, *entre nous,* he's promised me there'll be *lots* of shampers and foie gras and really expensive things the second he's got the keys to the Treasury – but it's all got to be hush-hush and behind closed doors in case the peasants start revolting."

I'm so shocked by this all-too-typical example of double standards in the corridors of power that I can't think what to say.

I notice she's smiling at me expectantly. "What are you being all quiet for, dear?! Aren't you going to eff and blind and tell me we should all be like Che Guevara and things? I just love it when you do that!"

I look at her sternly. "I've got to go to bed, Lizzie."

She flutters a pair of ancient heavily mascaraed eyelids and gurgles, "Is that an invitation?"

"On my own," I say. "I've got to be bright and fresh tomorrow to deal with my daughter's shrink."

This stops her in her tracks of course, and she frowns and puts on a serious look like women always do when you talk about your kids. "Oh it's marvellous that you're such a caring father, Arnold," she says earnestly. "It's one of the things I've come to respect about you, one of the very many things." She totters off to the front door. Then looks back and gives me a wink. "We'll just have to arrange another time then, won't we?"

Wednesday 28th April

12.40 p.m.

Go to Kensington public library and look through psychology section and take out Freud For Dummies and surreptitiously slip it in my man-bag, because don't belong to library because don't want personal liberty encroached on by being on London Borough of Kensington and Chelsea database. Read Freud book on bus to Kilburn.

1.50 p.m.

Put book away before going into therapist's "consulting room" (a converted garage next to hideous Kilburn semi). Reckon I understand psychoanalysis pretty well now.

2.30 p.m.

So far am very disappointed by therapy session. Not what I had hoped for at all. Therapist is about Daphne's age but no tits and no smiles and could do with washing her hair. Certainly not a part for Barbara Windsor. Nor would Babs want to play Daphne, I'm afraid to say. She's wearing the same beret and shapeless cardie as when I saw her last and in no way exudes the cheeky sexuality for which the Carry On star is even now famous.

Am worried that I no longer fancy Daphne because was rather banking on her. Is it because I'm sober? Or does it mean I'm impotent? Wonder if I could ask the therapist for sexual therapy but don't feel should ask just yet because when I tune in she's droning on about negative family patterns that made Alice feel unloved and led to her promiscuous lifestyle blah blah blah.

"Or perhaps she just fancies men a lot," I hear myself saying jocularly.

The three women stare at me. Not in a warm and loving way, but I'm all too used to that.

Eventually the shrink cracks a mirthless smile (the first smile from her of any sort in forty minutes I reckon). "So tell me, Arnold, what exactly was it about my description of the tense, unloving atmosphere Alice grew up in that you found so threatening that you felt the need to make an inappropriate joke about it?"

"What atmosphere, sorry, must have missed that?" I smile back. "Could you do a recap?"

For some reason this makes Alice angry. Now as I understand it from my recent reading the whole point of therapy is *you're meant to be honest.* But the way the therapist happily lets Daphne join Alice in slagging me off just because I've said what I thought makes me wonder if I've got it wrong. (Of course, coming from the unself-pitying self-educated hard-knocks school of life as I do, I've never been to a shrink myself. I can just imagine how the hacks in El Vino's would have reacted if I had!).

Finally, Alice and her mum pause for breath, and the therapist turns the mirthless smile on me again. "You know, I find your T-shirt really interesting, Arnold," she says.

This is more like it. Flattery I can deal with. "Yeah, thanks," I say, "I got it in the T-shirt section of Politicos Bookshop. I can give you the address if you want. Or I could take you there if you fancy – you know, any time you've got fifty minutes free!" Looking at her more closely, she's not that bad really. If she washed her hair and put on some make-up she'd look less like Popeye's girlfriend Olive Oyl and a bit more like Diane Keaton. Anyway, she ignores my invitation. But I'm used to women playing hard to get so I decide I'll wait till we've finished then ask her out for a Chinky. After all, a couple of glasses of rice wine and who knows?

"So why did you buy a T-shirt with the slogan 'I love hot mums' on it?" she asks. And why did you decide to wear it here today?"

This is easy. "*Why today?* Because despite what my lovely but troubled daughter might have told you, I have a deep belief in family. And Mum is at the heart of every family, isn't she?" I smile round at all three of them, and I'm so impressed by the bullshit I've come up with that I'm taken aback to see Alice glaring at me even more fiercely than before.

"Don't you believe your father, Alice?" asks the shrink. "Don't you think what he says is true?"

Alice opens her mouth but she's too slow. I smile at the shrink. "Don't worry, I don't take her anger personally because children have every right to be angry at their parents' failure. The way I see it, we're all only human and we're all flawed, and so we all fail occasionally, don't we, even when we start out with the very best of intentions. I mean I'm the first to admit I'm not perfect!"

"That's a very useful thought, Arnold, let's hold onto it. Don't you think it's a useful thought, Alice? Daphne...?"

I listen with an understanding frown as they tell her why it's not at all useful and why I'm an untrustworthy tosser (I paraphrase). When they've run out of insults I smile forgivingly and say, "Look, you'll probably think this is a real cliché, but as far as I can see every family needs its black sheep, someone they can blame for everything. And if that's the role the family dynamic requires me to take in order to ensure the mental health of certain other members of the family, well, that's OK by me."

"That's very generous of you," the shrink says. Then looks, rather less approvingly now, I'm delighted to see, at Alice and Daphne. "I see this constantly – Arnold is so right – members of families are so easily labelled and given absurdly over-rigid roles, and then expectations become so fixed that it's really hard to break the pattern..."

"Yeah," I nod thoughtfully. "It's like kids growing up expecting their dads to be there for them all the time. Great for a while of course, but maybe later on they need to know their dads have their own problems too – maybe they even need a bit of parenting themselves!"

"You're right again, Arnold," she nods vigorously. I'm really teacher's favourite now. "Parenting isn't just one way, or it shouldn't be." She looks at Alice and Daphne almost accusingly. "Don't you agree?"

They just sit there, lost for words. As my recent reading has taught me, therapists love silence, and she drinks it in, happily waiting for one of them to crack. After what feels like several hours they shiftily exchange looks and mutter something resentful. The shrink beams at me. "I think we'll take that as a yes, don't you? Well, this is a very helpful fresh perspective. So tell me, Arnold, in an ideal world what sort of parenting would you be asking for from Alice?"

"Me? Nothing, nothing at all. I was talking purely hypothetically; I'd hate anyone to think I meant it personally..."

"Yes I understand, of course," she nods even more vigorously. "Even so it'd be really useful if you could think of some small way in which, in an ideal world, the now adult Alice might be able to parent you."

I frown and look as if I'm struggling to think of something. "No, I can't think of anything really. Nothing at all... Oh yes – hang on ...Yes, I suppose – well now that my career is a little shaky and Alice is doing so well – maybe a little 'parenting' in that area..."

The shrink turns her gaze on Alice. "How do you react to that? The idea of trying to reconfigure the family dynamic by helping your Dad in some small way with his career?" Alice opens her mouth again but the shrink is glancing at her watch. "I'm afraid time's up. Well, we've done some extremely useful work today, laid some really useful foundations. Don't you agree, Alice?"

3.05 p.m.

The shrink turfs us out of her garage so quickly I don't have a chance to ask her out for a Chinky. On the plus side, I catch sight of a hostelry a few doors down and guide my reluctant ex-wife and daughter through its doors and order three Bloody Marys and ignore Alice saying she only drinks Diet Coke.

"What a lovely family get-together!" I say and raise my glass to both of them.

But Daphne is busy rearranging her beret and says "I'm not staying" in a tight little voice, and Alice is already crouched over her Blackberry tapping away.

"Time for a couple of jars and a chat about the session, surely?! Do you think your shrink likes Chinese, Alice?"

"I've got to go too," she says coldly, not looking up from her phone.

"No need to rush," I chuckle, and wonder whether to try hugging her but realize it's a waste of time.

"I'm needed urgently at the office. Gordon Brown has just called a sixty-five- year old Labour voting woman in Rochdale a bigot and everyone's gone ballistic."

"I thought you were on the Antiques Roadshow?"

"You don't listen to *anything*, do you, Dad?"

"Yes I do. But I don't understand what Gordon Brown calling a sixty-five- year old woman a bigot has got to do with you, Alice, you're not in news or current affairs!"

She sighs, as if it's so obvious it doesn't need spelling out. "They want me to help to persuade Caroline Quentin to do a drama-documentary about it."

"But Caroline Quentin's not sixty-five..."

She smiles condescendingly. "Of course she's not, Dad. You don't seriously think the BBC are going to have a woman of sixty-five playing a woman of sixty-five, do you? Actually they don't employ old actresses at all any more – and thank God for that."

"What do you mean thank God for that? You were moaning the other day about suffering from ageism at the BBC yourself!"

"Yes but a woman of sixty-five playing a woman of sixty-five!" She shudders in disgust. "Even I can see that's gross! Except in Cranford of course. It's different in Cranford, it's the only place where they still employ old actresses..."

"What about Barbara Windsor in EastEnders?" chirps Daphne.

"Between you and me," I say confidentially, "the word on the street is that Babs is leaving EastEnders."

This gets her excited, like I knew it would. “Is she going to Cranford then?”

We turn to Alice because she knows about these things, but she just smiles enigmatically, and kisses her mum goodbye and neatly avoids kissing me.

“How about I pop round tomorrow evening?” I smile.

“What for?”

“For a bit of father-daughter bonding, of course!” I wonder how I could have fathered someone who’s so appallingly suspicious about everything. “And maybe if we’ve got a few minutes left we could have a little chat about how you can help me with my career.”

“I’m busy tomorrow evening,” she says.

“Friday evening then.”

“I’m busy Friday evening, too,” she says with that hunted look I know too well.

“So what does *busy* mean?” I smile knowingly. “A new man, is it?”

“It means busy.”

I laugh fondly. “I’m sorry but as your father I insist on knowing what you’re doing on Friday evening. And if you refuse to tell me I’ll know it’s something deeply unsuitable and I might have to forbid you from doing it!”

Even Daphne has a little snigger at this.

But not Alice. “I’ve got a do at the BBC,” she says curtly. “Satisfied?”

“What sort of do?”

“Just a party, nothing important.”

She grabs her Blackberry and starts to go but I get my arm round her before she can get away. “Then I insist on coming with you, sweetie.”

"Don't be ridiculous."

"Look you heard your therapist, didn't you? She reckons it's really important for your mental well-being that you help out your old man – just think how good it'll make you feel about yourself!"

She's still trying to get away when her Blackberry rings and she answers it. "Yes I'm coming... Yes rightaway ...Yes *now!*" She turns it off and glares at me but I've still got my arm around her in fond paternal fashion. "All right Friday," she says resentfully. "I'll text you."

Her mum and I watch proudly as she dashes neurotically off, briefly brought together by our shared love.

I glance at Daphne and she avoids my gaze and rapidly buttons up her cardie. "By the way," I say with dignity, "I forgot to mention that I don't want to have sex with you anymore. Sorry, but you've missed your chance."

"Yippee," she says.

"Don't you want to know why?" I ask as she sets off briskly. "It's because I've got another woman in my life!"

This stops her in her tracks, like I knew it would. "*Really?* I'm so happy for you, Arnie, that's lovely. You must both come round for dinner then!"

Which isn't the reaction I'd been expecting. Then I realize she's just playing psychological games, like women always do.

"Yeah – that'd be great," I smile. "Did I tell you she's twenty-eight and a PhD and she just can't get enough of me?"

Two can play at psychological games.

6.10 p.m.

Get home and feel out of sorts. Wonder if it's because the

family therapy has brought out painful feelings that I've been forced to repress for too long. Decide that's crap and it's because the sun's nearly over the yard-arm and want to go to the Galloping Gastro but terrified in case I get my bollocks chewed off. The only solution is to open a bottle of yesterday's generous gift from my geriatric guardian angel.

8.40 p.m.

Woken from Doc Martin retrospective on ITV3 by doorbell ringing. A voice trills out that she knows I'm there and can she come in. Turn up TV and open second bottle.

9.40 p.m.

Wake up to find Martin Clunes has disappeared and been replaced by Reg Varney. Wonder if he's making a guest appearance in the idyllic Cornish countryside of Doc Martin, then realize he's dressed as a London bus conductor so probably not. Work out that it's the much-loved iconic sitcom On The Buses from the golden age of British TV. The subtlety of both Reg's performance and the script make me think I might have been over-harsh about John Nettles and Midsomer Murders.

Am trying to get back to sleep when the doorbell rings again and the all-too-familiar voice trills out, "Coo-eee – I know you're there – come on Mr Grumpy…!" There's no way I can go back to sleep now so I turn the TV up even more and look for the bottle and wonder if the price for a free case of reddo is too high after all.

Thursday 29th April

8.45 a.m.

Hear phone ringing through Tesco reddo haze and think it might be Lizzie so go back to sleep.

11.30 a.m.

Decide a glass of house Rioja at the Galloping Gastro might have a beneficial effect on inexplicable hangover, and surely have over-estimated the danger from Benjie and his psycho owner so set fearlessly off.

Benjie's psycho owner stands behind the bar, grinning to himself while serving me, while Benjie stands inches from my trousers, gazing hungrily at my crotch and dribbling. Buy a packet of crisps and sprinkle them in front of Benjie and escape to other end of bar with knackers intact.

12.45 p.m.

Managed to place myself in safe position next to big table of young tousle-haired guys. They have long upper-class legs that sprawl across the floor as if they own the place which means that for Benjie to get to me he'd have to run a little doggie Grand National first. The disadvantage is I can't get to the bar or have a pee or get a paper to read the latest gossip about Gordon Brown and the Rochdale bigot without having to speak nicely to the over-privileged turds. Wave to get Michelle's attention but she ignores me, as she's been doing for the last hour, so distract myself by staring at my new mobile phone and wondering why no one ever gets in touch with me on it.

1.25 p.m.

What do they say about watched pots never boiling? Have just received a text message from my darling daughter! Which leads to a lively exchange.

Her – c quentin not sure about playing bigot so big crisis at beeb will have 2 cancel friday sorry
Me – dont believe u am v hurt
Her – ok was lying sorry
Me – why?
Her – because dont want u to come with me
Me – why? r u ashamed of me?
Her – yes
Me – why? do I embarrass u?
Her – yes
Me – so dont u want to help me with my career?
Her – dont mind but ive no desire 2 ruin mine
Me – ok i understand baby
Her – do u? great! love u love u love u dad!! so ur definitely not coming?
Me – yes of course im bloody coming

Am about to turn off mobile when get *another* text. Brilliant that I'm suddenly so popular! Unfortunately, it's from former best friend Wills.

> *hi mate where r u? Phoned and left a message first thing and been ringing non-stop the last two hours. Have u died again?*

Don't think that's funny so turn off mobile. Get up and ask

the tousle-haired Tory tossers if they'd kindly move their legs, and they smirk and chortle and refuse. So plunge furiously through their arrogant, inbred, designer-trousered limbs while they kick and yell and whoop happily, obviously in their element. Realize the Eton Wall Game is probably like this.

Leave rapidly and slam pub door shut. Good news is think I got Benjie right in his slavering jaws.

1.50 p.m.

Get home. Time to work! Turn on computer and check emails. There's one from Dylan Jones. *Result!*

Dear Lady HP...

For a moment I wonder if he's been partying too hard, then remember it's my fictitious sister Lady Alison Hamilton-Parker and carry on reading.

Dear Lady HP,

So sorry for the absurdly low figure we mistakenly offered for your dear departed bro's last article. It was entirely the fault of my work experience guy Sebastian, so I've just sacked the little dickwad.

Here's a new contract, which I trust will be more to your ladyship's liking.

Ciao for now.

Dylan

PS It'd be great to meet up one day. How about Sunday brunch with our mutual mate Lady Antonia? There's a Caffe

Uno in her hood – how about that? (Btw I've got some two-for-one vouchers – economising is so cool at pres!)

I look at the contract, which is much better, and email him back.

Dear Dylan,

The revised fee is now just about acceptable so I'm returning the contract. As you will see, I've put down the details of Arnold's Co-op account and would be pleased if you could pay the money into it tout de suite, so it will then be part of his estate and no one will accuse me of half-inching it for myself.

Toodle-pip.

Lady HP

PS Lady Antonia and I are having a little aristocratic tiff just at pres so not keen to be in her hood pour le moment. Anyway prefer Strada – do you have two-for-one vouchers for that?

Re-read it and feel it has the right mixture of formality and friendliness so send it off. Then print out and sign contract as Lady Alison Hamilton-Parker and find envelope, and by chance also find very dusty but just about usable stamp (so don't have to disturb Lizzie!) Address envelope and pop out and post it.

Return feeling deeply satisfied with afternoon's work. Am about to turn off computer and have well-deserved glass of reddo when find an email from Wills.

Hi mate!

Getting worried because you're not phoning or texting back. So if you haven't died, just to say I won't be coming to stay on Saturday after all. (Christ I'd forgotten all about it! Thank God for that!) The thing is, Mary is hysterical and won't let me stay in the house a minute longer so I'm coming straightaway. Hope that's OK. (Sent from my Blackberry)

My horror at the prospect of Wills' imminent arrival is mixed with irritation that he's got a Blackberry. Why have both he and Alice got one and I haven't? Why didn't cheapskate son Roger buy me one instead of a crappy bog-standard mobile? Not that I'm into keeping up with the technological Joneses, but *why*? (Note to self – find right moment to bring this up with Roger, also tactfully suggest maybe an iPhone would be better than a Blackberry because am creative type and everyone knows creative types always use Apples).

Get out my pathetic little Nokia and text Wills so he won't think I'm at home at my computer.

sorry am away 4 next week hope u find nice hotel

Quickly get my coat and wonder where I can hang out till the coast is clear. Don't think the Galloping Gastro is a good idea. I know – Westfield! Gross temple to materialism is only ten minutes away and knowing how much I detest its false values Wills will never in a million years guess I'm there. (Also there's a nice Costa Coffee).

Hurry out and shut front door and bump into Wills, who's

standing on the doorstep surrounded by luggage and looking at his Blackberry and chuckling. He grins at me.

"You've got such a great sense of humour! *You – going away for a week! Brilliant!* Anyway it's good of you to let me stay, mate, I'm really touched." Before I can stop him he grabs me and plants his slobbery mouth on my cheek.

"Stop bloody doing that!"

"Doing what? Oh – you mean the kissing?" he smiles. "Yes it's belonging to the Garlic, we do a lot of kissing at the Garlic. It's a theatrical thing, you know..."

Yeah I saw all the fat old queens leering at us."

"It's perfectly innocent, Arnold..."

I give him a look. "That's what they all say."

"I'm sorry you have such a problem with spontaneous physical contact, but personally I find it rather liberating..."

"So how long have you had these feelings?"

"What feelings?"

"Look you're moving into my flat, Wills, don't start getting all coy with me. And don't get me wrong, I've got nothing against arse-bandits, nothing at all, it's just I'm not sure about sharing my flat with one."

He comes right up to me, and for a moment I'm not sure if he's going to kiss me again or hit me. He smiles sadly. "You know, Arnold, for some masochistic reason I value our friendship deeply, even after thirty-four years. But I'm afraid I've always found you seriously physically repulsive, so in the unlikely event that I do turn gay, I promise you you're well down the list."

This makes me feel a little better, so I let him in.

3.00 p.m.

I don't want to sound selfish, but he just sits and talk about his problems! I mean *endlessly*. And he gets iffy if I turn on the TV and gets even worse if I suggest he carries on talking while I doze.

So I'm forced to sit opposite him drinking tea for hours (I'm rationing the Tesco reddo – and btw why hasn't he brought a few bloody bottles?!) while he witters on about loving both Mary and Penelope, and why can't Mary realize that the penis is a glorious god-given thing that should be celebrated and shared and passed around amongst mates? And he doesn't mind if she celebrates and shares her vagina, in fact he doesn't care if she passes it round the whole of Croydon, so why should she get so upset when he just wants to share his cock with one other person?

He continues with variations on this theme for so long that in the end I'm so desperate I get up and stretch and say it's been a really long and emotional day so maybe time for bed. Wills looks surprised and says it's a quarter past seven. But I pretend I haven't heard and start clearing away yesterday's breakfast things and insist that sleep is the best cure for love's torments. "To sleep, perchance to dream, ay, there's the rub!" I add helpfully.

The only bit of Shakespeare I know casts its usual spell, and Wills's upper lip starts to wobble and he thanks me for being a caring and sensitive friend, and so thoughtful, he's so lucky having such an amazing best mate and he's really sorry he finds me physically repulsive.

When he's stopped gushing I offer him my bed and say I'll sleep on the sofa, and he starts all over again. "No I wouldn't dream of it. Absolutely not! I'm putting you out quite enough as it is..."

"I insist."

A few more tears then he gets up – and just in case he's thinking of kissing me again I tell him to keep his disgusting dribbly mouth to himself. He smiles warmly. "OK. But I'll never forget this, mate," And he picks up all his luggage and staggers off with it into the bedroom.

7.25 p.m.

Quickly settle down in front of ITV3 with a glass of reddo and am happily catching up with the latest developments on Heartbeat when Wills returns. I stare at the TV, trying to pretend he's not there, but he clears his throat. I try to ignore the throat-clearing too but he does it again.

"Look as I said I'm really grateful for your help and support, Arnold..."

"Yeah, yeah."

"No I am, I really am, and I hope you don't think I'm being personal..."

"No probs."

"Well that's great, because I was just wondering when you changed the sheets last."

I take my eyes off the actor who used to have his hand up Basil Brush and make a quick calculation. "That'd be about the time of the Nando lady, so that's about three months." I laugh fondly at the memory. "She made such a mess with her red pepper dip, Wills, I just *had* to change the sheets. Then she came back a second time – and this time there was coleslaw too, would you believe it?!"

"Actually, yes I would."

"Well, all I can say is, you should have seen it before I got the kitchen roll out!"

"Really?"

"Yeah really!" I laugh again and turn back to the Basil Brush man in the hope that Wills will take the hint and leave me alone. After a while I get the feeling he's gone, but I'm not going to look round and check. Then I notice that the Basil Brush man has gone too, which is a pity because I like him. I find myself wondering why they don't get the Sooty man on Heartbeat too. And what about Lenny the Lion while they're about it? I feel my eyelids flickering … And Keith Harris and Orville too? They're really heavy now…and I'm floating in that delicious pre-zizz moment…

Am wakened by heavy objects being dropped very close to me and leap to my feet convinced it's the BNP retard chucking his items of torture on the floor to torment me with.

It's Wills, surrounded by luggage. "You know, if you don't mind, I think I'll find a nice little hotel after all," he says apologetically. "But only if you're sure it's OK with you?"

"OK with me?" I gaze at him. "It's what's OK with *you*, Wills – that's all that matters to me."

7.45 p.m.

Wills leaves! Am so happy and will never complain about anything in my life ever again!!!

7.50 p.m.

Worry about whether I've been living on my own for so long that am in danger of becoming inflexible and unwelcoming and unappealingly set in my ways. Wonder if I should embrace humanity more (figuratively speaking) and try harder not to retreat into my shell.

The doorbell rings and I hear Lizzie's croaky tones floating through the letter-box. Turn up the TV and finish my glass, and fall asleep in front of Foyle's War before I can work out the answer.

Friday 30th April

Spend the day worrying again. Is it time for a major change in my life? Am I less honest with myself than I like to think I am? Have I become a bit of a monster without realizing it? How many years have I got left on this planet and how can I fill them most meaningfully? Should I take up charity work or get an allotment?

And do I want to go to the BBC do this evening? Do I *really?* Aren't I just deluding myself in thinking I have a place any longer in the superficial, bitterly competitive worlds of journalism and the media? Isn't it time to do something calmer and saner and more meaningful before it's too late?

If I had an allotment I could spend the evening pickling things. Which would be really satisfying.

Have made up my mind that I can't go on like I have been and am about to email the council about allotments when my mobile beeps. It's my darling daughter texting me.

Her – ur not serious about coming tonight?
Me – yes I am get over it

5.30 p.m.

Don't know why I got all whingey earlier! Just read through what I wrote – what a wanker! Really looking forward to the Beeb party now!

Go through wardrobe and wonder what to wear to meet twelve-year-old producers who Alice consorts with. Decide against suit because far too establishment, and finally decide on "Che Guevara wears David Cameron T-shirts" T-shirt because it shows I have cutting-edge sense of humour and it has contemporary relevance too, which apparently the Beeb are really hot on, though it is a bit whiffy.

Have wash and crap and get changed but it's still too early to leave, so have no choice but to open a bottle of reddo.

8.00 p.m.

BBC party is in a characterless little office with wine in plastic cups because everyone's terrified of David Cameron sacking them, but even so it's great! What is most gratifying is that whenever I mention my name all the twelve-year-old producers instantly recognise it and look astonished! I work out it's because when their baby boomer mums and dads dandled them on their knees and talked about the influences in their lives they told them all about my ground-breaking work in Time Out in '74, and my famous Private Eye tirades in the '80s, and maybe even my Daily Mail hate pieces (not to mention various other highlights I haven't mentioned!).

As I sip the licence-fee funded wine and enjoy the far-too-rare experience of being the centre of attention, Alice whispers in my ear that I'm drunk and disgusting and she's not going to have anything to do with me and stalks off. Sad though I am about our continuing father/daughter rift, I'm pretty relieved because I can now carry on networking without having her dragging me down like the deadweight she's become.

Faced with all these doting producers, I wonder which idea to pitch first. In the end I decide to go for the sitcom based on my magnum opus because I haven't got any other ideas, not new ones anyway. I've already worked out that the big problem is casting and not, as Alice callously suggested, that I've got to peg out first. David Jason and John Nettles are crap ideas so I pitch it to an attractive passing female and suggest hulkily handsome Matt le Blanc from Friends as me.

She listens and nods and frowns, then when I've stopped says, "So what's your mission statement?"

"My what?"

"You've got to have a mission statement. You can't do anything at the BBC without a mission statement."

"What's a mission statement?"

She smiles happily – she loves this. "I don't believe it! Well if you don't know the mission statement for the sitcom about your life, what about for your life itself? You must know the mission statement for your life!"

"Yeah of course I do," I chuckle. "What do you take me for?!" And I think about it really hard, trying to work it out, because I want to be honest here even though I don't know what the fuck she's talking about. "I guess it's to fill in the time between getting up and going to the pub, then fill in the bit between sleeping it off and getting back there at six-thirty. So I suppose that's the mission statement for the sitcom too!"

Then I quickly add that I'm not telling her any more without money on the table (it's always best leaving them wanting more!) and move off to the drinks table and refill my plastic glass with more plastic wine, which tastes so unpleasant I almost wonder if I've had enough. But I catch sight of Alice gazing at me judgmentally so I force it down and refill my glass again.

Just as I'm wondering why I feel a bit queasy a couple more twelve-year-olds approach.

"Hi!" they say, and we all shake hands and introduce ourselves.

Then one of them smiles knowingly at me. "But you're not

really Arnold Appleforth, are you?"

Before I can say anything the other one chuckles and says, "Look, we're all Guardian readers at the BBC, we all read the obituary..."

"It was a mistake," I say affably. "I'm not bloody dead. Ask my daughter Alice..."

I look round but she's disappeared.

"We *have* asked Alice. You see, we saw you lurch in after her and we saw her trying to ignore you, so we asked who you were and she said she'd never seen you before, you were just a boozed-up old tramp who'd followed her in. So why don't you just bugger off back to Shepherds Bush with all the other winos, and leave us to enjoy our soirée?"

"Because I've come here to pitch ideas," I smile.

"Well tough, it's Friday fucking night, we're not here to work."

"How about this for an idea?" I continue smoothly. "It's a Miss Marple story with a twist..."

One of them rudely groans and hurries off before I can stop him, but I get the other one in a fatherly grip and carry on. "You see, you start with an hour of the usual snobby Agatha Christie bollocks, then just when everyone's bored stupid with the fucking frocks and countryside, Miss Marple turns up at the church and rails against the vicar for sending his son to public school and fingers him for the murder for that reason!"

The twelve-year-old looks at me indignantly and says, "You pinched that from the Guardian obituary."

"No I didn't, *they* pinched it from *me.*"

"Anyway it's rubbish and Miss Marple's on ITV now."

"Well just bring back Joan Hickson and it can be on the

BBC too! Where's the problem? Don't you young people have any commercial nous at all?"

"You really are an extremely stupid old man."

"Don't *stupid old man* me, mate. What's wrong with bringing back a much-loved actress in a role she made her own?"

"She died eleven years ago."

"Nitpicking crap. This is the trouble, you just want to keep changing everything for the sake of it. I'm all for changing society, but why have you got to change the telly programmes too?!" I'm not feeling at all well now but I'm on a roll so I press on. "You know I even read the other day that the BBC's thinking of doing an updated Sherlock Holmes. Can you believe it?! What a stupid idea, he needs a fucking pipe and a violin and lots of smog! Why not leave it as it is?! It's like Doctor Who, it was never as good once William Hartnell left, you ask anyone!" I tighten my fatherly grip on the twelve-year-old because I'm suddenly having a little difficulty standing up. "The last thing I want is to sound condescending, sonny, but I am a bit of an expert here. I think it's safe to say no one in the world has slept through more hours of so-called television drama than I have. So why not listen and learn just for once?"

I see someone passing with a plate of vols au vents and realize I'm starving so I grab one and eat it, and vomit the vol au vent and a large amount of BBC wine mixed with 3 for £10 Tesco reddo over the uppity twelve-year-old.

11.45 p.m.

Am lying in bed trying to remember when I last felt so unwell when receive text from darling daughter.

Her – thank u for puking over my boss
Me – hes not ur boss his voice hasnt broken
Her – hes 38 and hes livid
Me – dont know why could have happened 2 anyone
Her – not at the BBC, no one drinks any more
Me – obviously why all their programmes are shit
Her – ur sad and pathetic
Me – dont u have anything nice 2 say then 2 ur poor sick dad?
Her – yes ur life is out of control and u live in squalor and ur a wreck. See u tomorrow at rogers

Oh fuck, Roger's, forgotten about that. Shit.

Saturday 1st May

12.25 p.m.

Get darling son Quentin to pick me up in a taxi *chez moi* en route to Roger's for long-threatened family lunch. This is not because have gone off mixing with the proletariat on public transport but because might throw up again if jolting about in close proximity to one of them.

Not quite ready when he arrives, and leave him in the living room while quickly work out what to wear. Think the Che Guevara T-shirt would be perfect for May Day so put it on then realize it's spattered with sick and take it off again. Settle in the end for "Dick Cheney – Before He Dicks You!" which will hopefully offend both Roger and upwardly-mobile wife Kelly and provoke lively discussion across the lunch table.

Come out of my bedroom and can't see Quentin, but find him in the kitchen with his head in the oven. Assume he's committing suicide because of his unfortunate sexual proclivities and drag him out, only to find he's clutching a grease-clogged dishcloth which he's been trying to clean the oven with.

Reflect that in some ways I wish I was gay because then I'd enjoy doing domestic tasks as much as Quentin does. As we leave, I ask if he's noticed any changes in the flat in the five or six years since he last visited, and he says "Unfortunately not, except for five or six years' more dirt". I imagine that in the house-proud homosexual community this counts as a joke.

As the taxi takes us across the Thames to the wilderness known as South Of the River, Quentin regales me with stories about his amazing new promiscuous lifestyle. He shares his experiences with me in eye-watering detail, clearly wanting his dad to be proud of him, and I try to listen in a caring, involved sort of way. But after the seventh identically sordid bunk-up in the public lavs of Holloway I have to politely tell him to shut up because I'm not feeling very well.

"But I can't talk to anyone else about it, you're the only person I know who understands the joys of anonymous, uncaring sex!"

"Not anonymous, Quentin. I always made a point of finding out their names."

"Aren't you proud of me then? Is that what you're saying?"

"Of course I'm proud of you," I say loyally, "you're a real chip off the old block!"

"Thanks, Dad," he beams gratefully.

"A bent chip admittedly but..."

My harmless quip provokes what I can only call a stereotypically hysterical gay response. "At least I don't drink like a fish and publicly disgrace myself – nor do I lie to and sponge off my nearest and dearest!"

I suddenly realize that he and Alice and Roger have been ganging up together and talking about me. I don't like the idea at all, which is odd, because the thought of the rest of the world doing it gives me an instant hard-on.

As we approach Barnes on the way to Roger's ostentatiously expensive house I gaze out at the suburban streets and think, as I always do when I come here, that Barnes is like Surrey but squashed into a very small space. And I ponder the bitter irony of spending May Day, the one day in the year where radical politics are still celebrated, in a hideously Tory environment with my hideously Tory family (except for Alice, who's voting Labour, which is even worse).

2.40 p.m.

Seated round the brand new dining table are Quentin, Alice, Roger, Roger's wife Kelly, Alice's sons Tobias and Jamel, and Roger and Kelly's three-year-old daughter Angelina. I try to ignore Roger going on about his great mate Fred the Shred being treated so unfairly, and Kelly going on about how amazingly cheap their new extendable oiled oak dining table was (£1295 from Heals!). But I find it harder to ignore the fact that whenever I reach for the wine Roger or Alice or Quentin "casually" grabs the bottle before I can get to it and pours just a tiny bit into my glass. More proof that they've been ganging up and talking about me. I'm about to tell them to go fuck themselves, then I remember I'm here as the revered head of the family and decide to behave accordingly, and smilingly turn to Tobias and Jamel and Angelina and start to teach them a bit of radical political history.

"Do you know what's special about today, kids?" I ask them.

"It's Saturday," says Jamel, who despite the trillions Alice has spent on his education isn't I suspect destined to be one of the world's intellectuals.

"Yes Jamel, it's Saturday," I smile encouragingly. "But it's also a really important day, called May Day. Do you know what May Day is?"

"It's maypoles and shit," says Tobias in a really bored voice.

"Yes Tobias, brilliant!" Frankly I'm astonished by how much he's matured in the last fortnight and feel a glow of pride at his precocious use of bad language. "But May Day is also famous for being a day of left-wing political demonstrations around the world, which is why it's sometimes known as International Workers' Day, because what happens then affects us all ... What's that, Tobias?" I smile. "Is there something you want to add?"

"International means abroad, doesn't it?" he says even more wearily.

"Yes it does, very good!"

"But you never go abroad, Grandad, and you don't work either, so it doesn't affect you at all, does it?"

Alice snorts and stuffs her napkin in her mouth while the other right-wing bastards just laugh their tits off.

While they're being immature I use the opportunity to get the wine and fill my glass properly and manage to have my first decent drink of the day. Then I retreat into the living room with the bottle before anyone has a chance to stop me.

4.15 p.m.

Falling asleep in front of other people's TVs is never as good as doing it at home. So when darling son Roger shakes me awake I am I confess a little grumpy. And when he kneels in front of me and gives me a concerned smile I have a huge desire to whack him over the head with the now empty bottle of (extremely good) wine.

"It's great to have you here again, Dad," he smiles.

"And it's great to be here with all of you. We should do it more often!"

"Yes we must," he smiles, and I start to get a panic attack in case he means it. But he hasn't finished. "It's so important that kids grow up with a proper sense of family, isn't it? Kelly and I have talked about it and we think it's really vital they get a sense of where they come from. And Alice and Quentin think so too of course. He's such a great uncle, isn't he?! We're all really keen that they develop a proper understanding of their family history and heritage."

"Why?"

"What do you mean why?"

"Why can't you leave the poor little tossers alone with their iBoxes and their iPads and whatever it is Angelina gets up to?"

"Because it's *important,* Dad."

"Why?"

"Well, because most people think it is, that's why!"

I smile understandingly. "You've been watching Who Do You Think You Are, haven't you? Typical BBC1 crap."

"Look I'm talking about real life here, Dad, not the telly. I sometimes wonder if you can tell the difference between the two!"

"Well *that* puts me in my place, doesn't it?!" I exclaim. "Well, Roger I'm terribly sorry I've not got the money to play golf and go skiing and buy multi-million pound houses in Barnes and that the only entertainment I can afford in my impoverished state is the telly..."

"Sorry yes you're right, you're right, that's so insensitive of me..."

"I'm afraid the disgusting amount of money you earn cocoons you from the harsh realities of life most of us have to put up with Roger!"

"You're right, you're so right. Fred the Shred and I were discussing it at Gleneagles only last weekend – isn't that odd? Anyway, can we get back to the family thing now?"

"You know an iPhone would be really useful."

"What?"

"To keep me in touch with the family."

He stares at me coldly, and I stare straight back into his eyes and suddenly see the ruthless City financier carefully calculating what it's worth.

"OK Dad," he smiles. "If I get you an iPhone will you come with Alice and me and the kids to see Auntie Edith?"

"Edith?" What a price to pay! Still, a visit won't take that long and an iPhone's for life. "OK," I say grudgingly, "it's a deal."

"Fantastic. You know, the kids didn't even know who Auntie Edith was, Dad," he laughs. "They didn't even know you *had* a cousin! My fault as much as anyone's, of course. I mean none of us have seen here for years."

"That's because she's a cow, Roger."

"She's not a cow, Dad," he frowns, "she's a piece of living history."

"Barely living from what I hear. So when would you like this fiasco to take place?"

"This Thursday."

"This Thursday?! But that's election day!"

"I am aware of that."

"Why does it have to be this Thursday? I might have things to do this Thursday."

"Because all the kids are free this Thursday. Alice's kids' prep school is being used as a polling station, and Angelina's play school assistant is off helping the UKIP candidate. We'll have a really great family day out, I promise! I'll go and phone Auntie Edith right now..."

"Yeah great. With a bit of luck she might peg out before Thursday."

"That's not funny, Dad."

"It wasn't meant to be."

He pauses, and smiles back at me. "Anyway, if she pegs out you won't get your iPhone."

"Ha ha."

"It wasn't a joke, Dad."

Sunday 2nd May

11.00 a.m.

Am lying in bed dreaming about the Galloping Gastro in the halycon days before homicidal Alsatians and gangs of tousle-haired old Etonians ruined it when the doorbell rings. I have a very strong suspicion who it is, but guilt makes me get up and put on my dressing gown and answer the door.

Yes, it's Lizzie.

Oddly enough, she makes no attempt to lunge at me, though I can't believe she's not tempted because my knackers are hanging loose beneath a flimsy covering of M & S polyester. For some moments she doesn't even look at me, which is even odder, though to be fair she's absorbed in daubing her wrinkly lips with crimson lipstick and squinting at how she looks in the mirror of her powder compact.

Then she snaps the compact shut and gives me a belated twinkle. "I'm terribly sorry, it's so common doing your make-up in public, isn't it?! But I'm late for Anthea's do and I forgot to pass on her message. Well no actually I didn't forget, I rang your doorbell endless times, but you kept pretending you weren't in so in the end I gave up!"

I decide pretending ignorance is the best policy so I smile and say, "I don't know what the fuck you're talking about, Lizzie."

This sets her off gurgling. "Oh how scrumptious! Say some more oiky stuff, Arnold, *please*, I've missed it!"

"What's Anthea's message?"

"Oh yes..." She looks disappointed but pulls herself together. "Well she's having her pre-election beano for her online mag today and she asked me to invite you personally because your contributions have been so crucial to its success and she's desperate for you to do more."

"So why didn't she ask me herself?"

She twinkles meaningfully. "I think you know why."

"Why would I fucking ask if I did?"

This sets her off gurgling again, but when she's stopped she puts on a solemn look. "I think she thought you wouldn't be very friendly after she wriggled out of doing naughties with you."

I'm appalled. Don't women have any respect for privacy anymore? "The last time Anthea and I met was for purely professional purposes," I say tersely.

"Yes and I'm the King of China," she gurgles. "Now I'm leaving in five minutes so are you coming or not?"

"No hankie-pankie though," I say firmly.

"Oh *really,* dear," she says as if the idea has never crossed her mind, and stays where she is on the doorstep.

I look at her warily, then turn to go in and get dressed and as I do so a gust of wind flaps at my dressing gown, and there's a tinkle of geriatric laughter.

"You know, I've only seen you in your dressing gown twice, Arnold, and both times I've seen your lunchbox!"

I pretend I haven't heard and slam the door behind me.

2.30 p.m.

You have to give it to Anthea, she's really got her ear to the ground and her finger on the pulse of recession-hit London. Her pre-election beano for her online mag is a pop-up party in a posh office on the eighteenth floor of Centre Point. A bit different from suburban sodding Barnes, I think to myself.

The invitation says "Only oldies-who-won't-admit-they-are are welcome!" and to get in we have to sneak through a broken fire door at the back and up the emergency stairs. In the office there's the usual cheapo wine and crispy things but there are also piles of cigarettes and other substances and big notices saying PLEASE SMOKE.

Lizzie instantly enters into the spirit of things and totters off to get some ganja, which leaves me free to grab a glass and mingle. Frankly, I've never seen such a gathering. Lulu is there, looking considerably younger than she did at fifteen. And Phil Collins, who's trying to chat her up by talking about all his failed marriages and not getting very far. Then I see a stick-thin figure sucking on a cigarette and wearing a ridiculously inappropriate T-shirt and with a face that makes W H Auden's look wrinkle-free, and immediately recognise Ronnie Wood. Now I happen to know Ronnie is just a year older than me, because I googled him the second he left his totally hot wife Jo for a twenty-year-old Russian bird. But on seeing him in the flesh all I can say is, some men in their sixties can wear T-shirts and some can't. Not that I'm trying to compete with a Rolling Stone, I'm not stupid, but let's face it he's clearly not interested in anyone over twenty-one anymore, so maybe I should give Jo a bell. I'm wondering how I can tactfully ask him for her number when my hairy doppelganger, Noel Edmonds, wanders by with a perma-tanned Des O'Connor, exchanging jokes and laughing uproariously and slapping each other on the back a lot. Then Trevor Nunn comes up and tries to join in but they've clearly no idea who he is so he stalks off in a huff.

As I go to refill my glass I notice Lionel Blair and Brucie having a tap-dancing competition while their wives stand patiently waiting to catch them when they fall.

It's amazing, everywhere I look there are celebs! Before I can get my drink, Anthea appears out of nowhere and flings her arms round me and says "How great to see you, sweetie!" And introduces me to Anne Robinson, who looks half her real age and says she recognised my name at once, and she's read both my brilliant online articles. "And you do look *so* good for ninety," she murmurs.

"He certainly does, doesn't he?" Anthea beams. "I told you you'd be impressed! Anne is going to write lots and lots of articles for me, sweetie. But she's terribly busy doing her telly thing at the mo so we wondered if you could do the actually boring writing bit for her."

"Yeah possibly, if the money's right..."

Anthea shrieks with laughter, while Anne looks me up and down in that contemptuously sexy way she does on The Weakest Link. Then she murmurs again, "Why don't we meet at one of my luxurious homes and toss a few ideas around?" And gives me that knowing wink she does on the telly. "If you can stay alive that long..." Then she rudely turns her back on me – just like on the telly again! – and is gone.

Meanwhile Anthea has spied Sir Richard Branson, who's just come in and is busy picking stuff out of his beard. When I ask her what he's doing she says he planned to make an amazing entrance at the start of the party by bungee-jumping in from the top of Centre Point. Apparently he's been trying for the bungee-jumping world record for years now and keeps failing. As he did today, when he misjudged the window and had to be rushed to A and E to get the glass extracted and has only just got back.

"He's promised to write all about it for my mag," she

enthuses, then has another brainwave. "*I know* – why don't you help him write it?!"

It's clearly time to stand on my dignity. "Anne Robinson is one thing, Anthea, but if you seriously think I'm going to be a ghostwriter for a dyslexic right-wing billionaire..."

"Why not? You're my top star writer and no one could do it better!"

"Yeah, yeah, yeah," I say cynically. "And while we're about it, why not make it into a series? We could call it 'Wealthy Old Tory Wankers' – how about that?!"

"That's so childish and pathetic, Arnold, really..." And I see her eyes widen and I swear I can see the little cogs whirring round inside. "Which is what makes it so brilliant! You're on, you're so totally the best, sweetie! Just let me go and help Richard with his beard..."

I watch her scurry over to Sir Richard and feel a twinge of jealousy. As I gaze at her enthusiastically picking away at his facial hair I wonder if the grinning trillionaire entrepreneur is now her hero instead of me. Despite her protestations, I have the feeling I shouldn't rely too much on Anthea and her online activities in future. In fact, I start to wonder if maybe the staid old world of proper magazines like Sudoku Weekly and GQ still has an appeal after all.

I'm about to sneak off home but the words "staid" and "old" remind me of Lizzie, and I wonder if she's all right and if I can get a free lift off her.

I can't see her anywhere, and am about to leave when I see a wizened figure tap-dancing away with Brucie. I go closer – and yes it's Lizzie. Brucie's glamorous wife tells me that Lionel Blair collapsed ages ago but the two irrepressible old-timers have been dancing the afternoon away. I ask her if she's jealous and she hoots with derisive laughter. I suppose her response is understandable, but it makes me feel oddly protective towards my geriatric but spunky neighbour.

5.50 p.m.

As I finally manage to drag Lizzie out we pass Ronnie Wood and his supposed best mate Rod Stewart rolling round on the floor kicking and punching each other. When I try to separate them they say they're play-fighting so fuck off. Their childish behaviour makes me feel really quite mature. Which is oddly disturbing.

Monday 3rd May

11.00 a.m

Spend the morning watching the general election campaign on every channel that I can find, because refuse to watch it solely on hopelessly biased BBC. By the end have got a pretty clear overall picture of what's happening, and three things are obvious – Gordon Brown has met his Waterloo in Rochdale with Bigotgate, and David Cameron is screwed because Simon Cowell has decided to back him, therefore by Friday Nick Clegg will be prime minister.

2.00 p.m.

Spend the afternoon thinking about the family. Come to the conclusion that I'm seeing far too much of them.

5.45 p.m.

Dismayed to discover that stressful combination of thinking about general election and family has seriously depleted wine supply. Only have one bottle of Tesco reddo left! Check my wallet and pockets and find I have one five pound note and 48p in coins. Enough for a single bottle of Tesco reddo and a Toblerone (if still on special offer) but not enough for a large glass of house Rioja at the Galloping Gastro.

This is the nightmare I have always feared. The slippery slope from which there is no return. Feel panic attack coming on and wonder if should spend more time with family after all.

Resist temptation to open the final bottle of reddo, and masochistically log on to online bank account to check my overdraft, and discover that enormous payment from GQ has arrived. *Result!*

Tuesday 9th May

Now I'm in funds, am able to enjoy a relaxed and civilised start to my day just for once. Lie in bed till midday instead of eleven, then have a leisurely breakfast of stale everything – stale pitta bread, stale "fresh" coffee with a sprinkling of stale Bird's custard powder which has an expiry date of 2005 (because out of milk and condensed milk). Afterwards stroll down to Tesco and take a hundred out of the cash machine and print out my impressive bank balance. Then go into Tesco and buy new case of 3 for £10 reddo and a carton of milk and a jar of Gold Blend and a tin of corned beef (need to eat sometimes!) and stagger back home with them.

6.45 p.m.

Seem to have fallen asleep at kitchen table after celebratory glass or two of reddo. Am woken by mobile beeping. It's text message from Wills. Am about to delete it unread just in case he wants to come and stay and bore the arse off me again, but feel warm and caring towards fellow humanity today so don't.

Him – hi just checking ur ok for joe allen tomorrow
Me – yeah
Him – great great great got lots to tell u bye!

Am so pissed off that almost text back and cancel. How come he's now allowed to talk about himself instead of me talking about me? When did this totally unacceptable reversal occur? Decide to take my mind off personal problems by going to www.quickshag.com and having a look at some pictures. Turn on computer and check emails first. There's one from GQ magazine. Probably another commission, great!

Dear Mr Appleforth,

Mr Jones has asked me to inform you that he's very distressed to discover you're not dead after all. Nothing personal but he wants all the money back that he's just coughed up for your appallingly puerile article, and if he doesn't get it pronto he's going to take legal action.

Screw you.

Sebastian Youngbottom (now head of financial affairs)

PS He'd still like to meet your sister though.

Am now so traumatised that can't concentrate on anything, not even www.quickshag.com.

Try to take my mind off imminent financial ruin by opening another bottle and watching Midsomer Murders on ITV3. But even that doesn't work. Switch to E4 to watch Friends because Jennifer Aniston doesn't send me to sleep but definitely does it for me in other ways, but this evening not even perky blonde Jen with her really short skirts can distract me. In desperation turn on the PVR and try to fall asleep in front of Inspector Dalgleish in his toupée, then when that fails have a go with the depressed looking actor in Foyle's War.

But nothing works.

As a last resort I search through living room cupboard. Find Rosemary Conley Ultimate Whole Body Workout DVD, Jane Fonda Lean Routine Workout DVD, Emanuelle, Black

Emanuelle and Emanuelle In Space DVDs, plus box set of Poirot. Too exhausted for the others so put Poirot on. David Suchet minces into view and smirks and twitches his greasy moustache and speaks in that camp French accent, and as always I'm amazed that no one else in the world has noticed his Poirot is a gay version of that bloke behind the bar in Allo Allo. What's his name...? René. Yes, clearly *un homage* to René in Allo Allo. Can feel myself relaxing at last. Fortunately, the story is as soothingly incomprehensible as ever, right up there with Midsomer Murders. Just what I want, no idea at all what's going on. I feel my eyelids flickering. Love TV detectives, brilliant, best thing ever. As I drift off I wonder if David Suchet walks like Larry Grayson in real life, or if it's proper acting...

Wednesday 5th May

1.35 p.m.

As I walk down the steps into the cosy womb-like gloom of Joe Allen I sigh with relief that it's not the poncy Garlic Club. I see Wills sitting at our usual table reading the menu with the help of his finger like he always does, and for a moment I forget my desperate financial state and everything seems right with the world.

He sees me approaching and his simple face lights up and he leaps to his feet and we high-five each other, just like we've done almost every Wednesday for the past thirty-six years.

"Hi Cuntface," I say warmly. And we sit down and I'm touched to see there's a litre of the vino reddo de la maison ready and waiting on the table. I pour a glass and feel such a surge of gratitude towards good old Wills that I decide I'll let him do the wanking joke instead of me just for once.

"So what have you been up to since I saw you last?" I say.

He frowns as he tries to remember what the punchline is, then finally gets there. "Apart from wanking, you mean?" And his simple face breaks into a grin of relief that he's got it right.

I'm tempted to tell him his comic delivery is about as funny as Margaret Thatcher's, but decide to let it pass.

He leans across the table confidingly. "Actually I haven't been doing any wanking for ages," he says eagerly. "I haven't had the time! Since I saw you last week Mary and Penelope and I have been so busy working on our relationships that –"

"You don't have to explain, Wills, it's just a *joke!*"

"No, no, no, I need to talk to someone, I need to share

what's been happening to me and you see there isn't anyone else who'd understand!"

"Christ you must be desperate," I say, thinking he sounds just like Quentin. The trouble is I can't tell him to shut the fuck up because he's still my best mate, and as you get older you realize how precious friendship is. Plus, I've written some great new quizzes for Sudoku Weekly – they're about Barbara Windsor and he'll love them, and if he doesn't I'm screwed. So I concentrate really hard and finally come up with a meaningful question, just to show I'm listening. "So are you still shagging nine or ten times a week, or was that a one-off?"

"Things are fine in that direction, thank you," he replies evasively.

"And what about getting Mary to understand you like passing your prick round amongst your mates? How are you doing with that one?"

"Are you by any chance trying to mock the pain I've been going through recently, Arnold?"

"Not at all, that's what you told me, Wills!"

He gazes at me thoughtfully for a moment, then says, "Actually, Mary is going to vagina awareness classes and they've been a great help."

I nod. "And, er, Penelope…?"

He hesitates, then smiles smugly. "No, no Penelope has no need of anything like that – not at all!"

I don't want to hear any of this, but some masochistic force pushes me on. "So you're not down to six or seven yet then?" I ask, fearing the worst.

He sips some water and I suddenly realize he's not been drinking any of the vino. "Put it like this," he smiles.

"Penelope is a dedicated follower of Kali and an Ayurvedic vegetarian, which means no booze of course, but believe me the effects are extraordinary – for both of us. Sadly, Mary's had a bit of a blip sexually speaking, but we had a really good talk and she's agreed to go with Pen on a weekend retreat to unblock her chakras."

"Then you'll all be at it like rabbits again?"

He shrugs serenely. "If Kali wishes it. It's entirely out of my hands..."

"Who is this guy Kali? I want to join."

"She's a Hindu goddess and I'm afraid it doesn't work like that, Arnold."

I sense he's being obstructive. "So what if I give up meat and booze? Will I get more totty that way?"

He smiles condescendingly. "I doubt it. In your case I strongly suspect your body would go into such deep trauma that I'd have to re-do my obituary."

"Ha ha. Well keep me posted on the shagging stakes. Now let's get back to me..." And I give him a quick rundown on Dylan Jones threatening to sue me to get his money back, though just to save time I don't bother to mention his correspondence with my imaginary sister.

"I'll give Dylan a bell," says Wills airily, "I'm sure I can sort it out. I've known him for years, you know. We magazine editors stick together, you see."

"So he's another one of your best mates, is he?" I ask pointedly. "Along with Dawn French and Lord Trevor of Wicked?!"

Before Wills can wriggle out of that one, the waiter arrives. I order Caesar salad and cheeseburger well done and chips, like I've done almost every Wednesday for thirty-six years.

And Wills orders green vegetables and lentils for a change, and when they politely remind him they serve American food in Joe Allen he cancels the lentils.

I'm about to mock his new Ayurvedic diet when he remembers something. "By the way I've got some great news for you," he says. "You're going to love this." He beams across the table. "Word on the street is that John Nettles is about to leave Midsomer Murders."

I stare at him, speechless.

"What are you looking like that for? I thought you'd be delighted, you're always saying how much you hate John Nettles!"

"So which street did you hear this on, Wills?" I ask unsteadily.

"Well the Radio Times again, actually. The word in the Radio Times is he's definitely leaving Midsomer Murders."

"I'm devastated."

He frowns. "But why? You mean you don't hate him really?"

"Of course I do. But don't you understand anything about the complexity of life? Is everything really that simple and straightforward for you? You see, they'll get someone to replace him, and I might *like* the new one, I might really want to stay awake and watch him – and then what'll I do?!"

He gazes at me, still frowning. "I think I see what you're driving at. Sort of."

I try to escape from the pit of depression his information has thrown me into, and finally force a smile. "Oh well, I'll just have to get used to falling asleep in front of Poirot instead..."

"I hate to tell you, but they're getting rid of Poirot soon too."

"Don't mess with me Wills, I'm not in the mood for your pathetic attempts at humour."

"It's true! And Heartbeat as well. I'm afraid all you're going to be left with soon is Miss Marple, mate."

For a moment I can't speak. Then I finish my glass and decide to put a brave face on it. "Well it's not the end of the world, is it, Wills, not quite. I'm sure the miracle of multi-channel telly will come to my rescue! After all, even when ITV3 finally tires of John Nettles and Heartbeat, if they ever do, I'm sure I'll be able to find them somewhere, in some obscure nook or cranny of the digital universe – and even if the terrible day finally comes when I can't, well there are always second-hand box-sets from Amazon!"

He smiles at me. "That's the spirit, mate. Don't let the bastards get you down."

"I won't, Wills. Believe me. And don't fucking call me mate."

Thursday 6th May

10.20 a.m.

Wake up early and am about to nod off again when remember it's the General Election today. Go back to sleep for an hour.

Then lie there wondering what to wear for the five-yearly ritual of spoiling my ballot paper. In the end put on "Che Guevara wears David Cameron T-shirts" T-shirt even though it still smells of sick, because sometimes in life the obvious solution is the right one.

Am about to set off for the polling station when I notice the answerphone is flashing. It's a message from Wills.

"Sorry to let you down mate but I've talked to Dylan Jones and it's no go. But he says if you'd like to submit a style feature on what the elderly bankrupt is wearing in the new Tory Britain he'll look at it sympathetically, and might even knock a few quid off what he's going to sue you for. By the way, have you got any idea who I should vote for? Do you think Sudoku Weekly's readership is mainly Labour or Tory or Lib Dem?"

Am about to ring and tell him they're too thick to vote at all, then decide that's not a very left wing attitude, so sit down and draft an abusive email to Dylan Jones. Then make a cup of tea (with real milk this time!) and have a brunch of corned beef and completely inedible pitta bread and suddenly remember I didn't give the Barbara Windsor quizzes to Wills. Go back to computer to email them to him, then have a brilliant left-field thought of the sort that's come to my rescue so often over the years, and re-read abusive email to Dylan

Jones and make a few quick changes, and do the same to the Barbara Windsor quizzes so it's more his sort of thing.

Hi Dylan!

Delighted to hear you're keen to see a piece from me on older guys' outfits. Will get down to it as soon as poss, but in the meantime I've got something I'm sure will be right up your strasse.

It's a quiz page about a really cool GQ-type celeb who's married to a fashion icon and wears Nicole Farhi and has also written a few plays. (It might need a few tiny rejigs but you'll get the gist!)

The GQ Celeb Quiz Page

This month's quiz page stars the much-loved blonde and bubbly left-wing star of stage and screen Sir David Hare.

1. *In which famous "Carry On" film did Sir David Hare bare his breasts?*
   a. *Carry On Camping*
   b. *Carry On Up The Kazi*
   c. *EastEnders*

2. *Which really famous pair of gangsters was Sir David Hare friends with when younger?*
   a. *The Kray twins*
   b. *Den and Angie*
   c. *Harold Pinter and Antonia Fraser*

3. *Which long-running soap opera beginning with E has Sir David Hare successfully starred in for some years?*
   a. *EastEnders*
   b. *Emmerdale*
   c. *Endless plays about the Iraq War*

4. *Which highly respected British artist turned down a knighthood because it was a load of elitist right-wing wank?*
   a. Barbara Windsor
   b. Sir David Hare
   c. Alan Bennett

Re-read it and think the political satire is spot on, right up there with my hard-hitting Private Eye pieces in the '80s, and the rest is pretty shit hot too. So email it off. If Dylan Jones doesn't like it, sod him, I'll rejig it back to the Barbara Windsor version and flog it to Wills for Sudoku Weekly next Wednesday.

Want to make my contribution to the democratic process before I forget, so hurry off to the polling station and get my name checked on the list of residents and go into a little booth and spend a creative five minutes drawing rude pictures on my ballot paper.

As I turn to leave, an ancient over-powdered face peers at me over the partition. "Coo-eee, I knew it was you, I can smell you a mile away! Do you want to come to our party tonight?"

"What party?"

"Our victory party of course."

"Victory for who?"

She gives a peal of laughter. "Don't be a silly boy!"

"Listen to me, Lizzie, Nick Clegg is going to win, it's a fucking no-brainer!"

"You do make me laugh! Anyway who cares who wins? You like free shampoo don't you, well there's going to be oodles of it! I'm afraid it'll all be in big oiky beer glasses because Georgie Osborne has said we've all got to pretend we drink bitter or whatever it's called, you know like the hoi-polloi do, but that's just part of the fun really, isn't it?"

"I'm appalled to hear such cynical talk. And I wouldn't dream of coming."

But I don't want to fall out with the old dear so I generously suggest we walk home together, and by way of small-talk tell her about Dylan Jones and my obituary and how he's going to sue me.

"Another silly boy," she says severely. "Just so impetuous sometimes! Don't you worry your little head, I'll get Dave to put a stop to it, I'll talk to him as soon as I get in."

"Dave?"

"David Cameron. He and Dylan love each other to bits you see, they *keep* writing books about each other, and I've known them both for yonks of course!"

"Won't David Cameron be a tiny bit busy today?"

She gurgles away. "You're so sweet and innocent. No he's got *staff* to do the busy bits! And even if he didn't, he'd find time for me!"

I'm not convinced even Lizzie can wield quite that much influence. But if she can, well she's a miracle worker.

As we approach our houses I hear a car horn hooting loudly and realize it's coming from a vulgarly ostentatious Range Rover parked outside my flat. I'm thinking it looks vaguely familiar when Roger and Alice get out and their scarily unrepressed kids jump out too and make straight for us. Lizzie looks at them in horror and murmurs, "Thanks heavens I had my tubes tied," and totters off into her house as fast as she can.

Roger and Alice look at me accusingly and say, "What sort of time do you call this?" And I realize it had completely slipped my mind that today is the day we're having our lovely bonding family day out to see cousin Edith.

2.40 p.m.

The long drive to the dreary bit of Sussex coast where Edith lives is a nightmare. Alice insists on sitting in the front with Roger, so I'm sandwiched in the back between a grizzling Angelina and an out-of-control Tobias and Jamel, who think holding their noses and going "poo poo poo poo poo" for two hours is the wittiest thing since Oscar Wilde. Roger and Alice pointedly ignore my repeated suggestion of stopping for lunch so there's not even the chance of a dose of reddo to calm the frazzled nerves.

When we reach the care home where Edith resides a Hattie Jacques-like matron opens the door and lets us in. She leads us through a cavernous badly lit room full of the living dead, all of them staring blankly ahead and ignoring Midsomer Murders (what else?) on the television. It crosses my mind they've probably been sitting there not watching John Nettles ever since he was doing Bergerac.

Surprisingly, Roger and Alice don't seem to find the place nearly as depressing as I do. In fact, they seem weirdly eager to see the best of everything and keep pointing things out excitedly.

"Look, Dad, a forty-eight-inch plasma screen. How state of the art is that then?!"

"Oh, wow, what a fantastic view. Isn't that knockout? Better than anything in Barnes or Brook Green even, eh?!"

Edith is in bed in her little room and doesn't move when we come in. Nor does she move when Roger tells her who we all are, and Alice gives her a box of chocolates and some flowers and says how lovely it is to see her again and how well she looks! Nor when Angelina prods her experimentally, and Jamel says you've got a funny smell like grandad, is that old people's smell? Nor when Tobias says of course it is, you thicko, and they fight viciously till Roger steps in and separates them (because Alice doesn't believe in being interventionist).

I gaze at Edith's mask-like face and ponder the transience of life and wonder if I've been unfair about her – perhaps she wasn't that hideous really. As I look at her I remember those sunny childhood summers when we were thrown together for weeks on end, and were free to roam the fields and woods and play hide and seek, and have picnics of crisps and jam sandwiches and Tizer and she'd sit on me and make me eat her bogies because she was stronger than me. And as I gaze down at her corpse-like visage I can't help thinking yes this is a big improvement on how she used to be.

My reverie is interrupted by Alice being manically cheerful again. "Isn't it lovely, Dad, look, she's got her own TV!"

"She's too gaga to watch it," I say.

"No she's not, she's lovely, she's just resting, aren't you Edith? Anyway she's obviously really happy here!"

"You know, the matron told me they've got lots of box sets too," Roger chips in brightly, "and everyone can borrow them. Isn't that great? If you ask me this place has got everything!"

3.30 p.m.

Much though they keep saying they love the place, Roger and Alice manage to get us in and out in twenty minutes flat. And I wonder if they're not having quite as good a time as they say when Roger pulls into the first crappy hostelry we pass and downs two brandies, and instead of her usual Diet Coke Alice pushes out the boat and orders one with sugar in it. I get Roger to get me a large glass of the house red and a packet of smoky bacon crisps. The kids sip their glasses of tap water and look at the crisps enviously because none of them is allowed to eat stuff with E numbers or anything nice in it. Roger and Alice go off and have a whispered conversation about God knows what, and while they're gone I do a trade-off with the little bastards, and in exchange for the rest of the crisps they promise to let me sleep peacefully all the way home.

5.40 p.m.

When I wake up I'm taken aback to find we're driving up to Roger's home, not mine.

Kelly opens the front door, and I'm surprised to see Quentin by her side. Kelly smilingly takes my hand – which is weird, considering she hates me – and leads me into the dining room where there's a freshly opened bottle of wine on the extendable oiled oak dining table which was only £1295 from Heals, as she tells me for the second time. She pours me a large glass while Quentin pulls out a chair for me and says, "So how did you like seeing Auntie Edith in her care home, Dad? I hear she's extremely happy there."

"Hard to tell really as all she can do is dribble," I say, and take a swig, then look up and realize they're all sitting round the table with me. All three of my darling children, plus Kelly, all sitting round the table smiling at me.

"It comes to us all in the end, Dad, I'm afraid," says Alice.

"If you're lucky enough to live long enough," smiles Roger.

"You know, we've got your best interests at heart, Dad, we really have," says Quentin.

I stare round at them. Maybe I'm getting as gaga as Edith, but it's only then that I realize what they're up to.

"I'm not going into a home," I say. "Forget it."

Roger smiles sympathetically. "Look we can't force you, of course we can't! But we've thought about it really hard, Dad, and we've weighed up all the pros and cons, and while the last thing we want is to take away your independence I'm sure that after we've discussed it calmly you'll agree it's the best solution."

"You need looking after," says Alice bluntly. "And sure as hell I'm not doing it."

"It's really peaceful there, Dad," says Quentin, "It's a really lovely little seaside town! Not that I've ever been there but I'm told it is. My friends say it's just like Brighton, but without the horrid noisy shops and pubs and restaurants and people of course."

"Anyway you can't go on like you are," says Alice with relish, and I can't help feeling this is pay-back time for her. "Your flat is filthy and your personal hygiene's appalling and you're a terrible influence on the children."

"Not to mention the drinking," adds Kelly nastily.

I gaze round at my nearest and dearest, plus Kelly, and feel a mixture of rage and righteous indignation, and jump to my feet. "I know what this is about really! You just want to get hold of my money!"

"You haven't got any money," says Roger, "you're permanently overdrawn."

I glare at him. "You just want all the capital from my flat!"

"But you rent it, Dad."

"Don't be fucking pedantic!" And I grab the bottle of wine and run off, ignoring their pathetic demands for me to grow up and be reasonable and admit I just can't cope on my own any more.

As I hurry down the streets of Barnes, shocked and traumatised by their treachery, I seem to see strange blue-rosetted figures coming at me from every corner, then I spy a solitary red-rosetted figure being thrown to the ground and kicked and spat on by an enthusiastic group of silver-haired ladies. At first I assume I'm hallucinating, then I realize I'd forgotten it's election day.

6.40 p.m.

Never have I felt so glad to get back to the security of my own home. I lock the front door and have a pee and look forward to a healing evening slumbering in front of ITV3 with the remains of the (excellent) bottle of red I pinched from Roger's. As I cross the living room the phone rings but I turn on the TV and ignore it. It's Monarch of the Glen – perfect! – and I'm just settling down to Susan Hampshire twinkling away to Richard Briers when my answerphone clicks on. The voice of my treacherous daughter cuts through the innocent Scottish idyll.

"You know you can't escape the truth by running away, Dad. Your life is out of control and you're a walking health risk. You know we all just want what's best for you…"

I don't listen to any more but get my coat and hurry out, deeply disturbed that there's no escape from these monsters even in my own home. As the front door slams behind me I panic about where to go. But I don't really have any choice. I'm so stressed that only a glass of house Rioja will calm me so will have to brave the Galloping Gastro's murderous mutt yet again.

As I approach my one-time favourite hostelry I wonder if it's such a good ideal after all. My sexual choices might have diminished recently, but there's still the Nando lady and www.quickshag.com so there's still hope, but a quick well-aimed snap of canine teeth and even those desperate last resorts might be denied me.

I'm about to turn back when I hear a familiar shrill voice ahead. It's Lizzie, standing outside the Galloping Gastro tearing a strip off the angry young guy from behind the bar because his Alsatian has dared to growl at her dogs. I hide in a doorway so as not to interrupt. "Do you want me to have the foul slobbering creature put down? *Do you?* Because I'm Vice-President of the League Against Violent Dogs, young man, and if I give the word they'll be round in their van *just like that!*" I watch her click her fingers in his face, and suddenly he's not angry any more, in fact his lips are quivering and he's saying *"No please, not Benjie, no please…!"* and I swear I can see the tears glistening in his eyes. She lets him grovel abjectly for a while, then tells him to bugger off and not bother her ever again, and he hurries back into the pub as fast as he can, pulling the bewildered Benjie after him.

I step out from the doorway. "I didn't know you were Vice-President of the League Against Violent Dogs, Lizzie.

I'm really impressed!"

"Of course I'm not, dear," she beams. "It's lovely that you're always so naïve, I do like that in a man! Now let's have a little soupçon of something to celebrate."

"To celebrate what, the end of Benjie?"

"No, silly, the Tory landslide of course!" And before I can explain to her how deluded she is because Simon Cowell's totally screwed it for Cameron by saying he's voting for him she's dragging me and her doggies after her into the pub.

The angry young guy sees her come in and is still so scared by her threats that he insists on buying us drinks. I look round to check-out Benjie but he's nowhere to be seen, so I lean across the bar and say, "Some pistachio nuts wouldn't go amiss, squire," and give him a wink and a smirk. He glares at me and is about to respond when he catches Lizzie's steely gaze and stammers, "Yes of course. And I'll get you some Mini Cheddars too, on the house naturally!" and hurriedly retreats. *Result!*

So Lizzie sits nursing her double Drambuie and ice while I sip my large glass of house Rioja and eat my bowls of pistachios and Mini Cheddars and ignore her doggies gazing greedily up at me – and I have to say, it's an idyllic little scene. And it's about to get even better.

"I almost forgot," she says brightly. "Dave has had a word with Dylan, and he's terribly apologetic and insists he was only joking and of course he never had any intention of suing you, and of course he doesn't want the money back either. Oh yes and he really likes your quizzy thingy, he says he just loves your quirkily whimsical sense of humour!"

"What does he mean mean quirkily fucking whimsical?" I say. "It's bitingly fucking satirical!"

I'd forgotten how much she loves me talking dirty so conversation stops for a minute while she gurgles helpessly.

"What else did the little tosser say?" I ask eventually, moderating my language to avoid more delays.

"Nothing really. Oh yes! He asked Dave to tell me to tell you that the new cheque's in the post, so to speak. Not *actually* in the post because I believe it's whizzing through cyberspace to the bank of Arthur Scargill as we speak!"

"The what?"

"Your bank, dear, the Co-op. Sorry, my little joke!"

Despite this pathetic piece of right-wing so-called humour, I gaze at her in awe at what she's achieved on my behalf. She really is superhuman.

She meets my gaze and flickers her heavily mascaraed eyelashes flirtatiously. "What are you staring at me like that for, Arnold?" And straightens the jacket of her powder-blue two-piece and fondles her pearls provocatively.

"Nothing. I was just wondering why you're looking so smart," I reply quickly, because I don't want to sound too grateful or Christ knows what she'll expect from me. "Oh yeah, of course, you're off to your Tory bloody beano!"

Before I can stop her she's taken my hand in her gnarled paw. "Now don't be boring, dear, why don't you come? You know you want to really."

"If you seriously think I'd spend five minutes with a group of over-privileged wankers who probably don't even agree what a shithead Margaret Thatcher was, well, all I can say is you know me less well than I think you do, Lizzie."

This provokes another gurgling fit. While she's spluttering and snorting I hear my mobile beep. It's a text from my treacherous son Roger (who hasn't even given me the iPhone he promised me).

theres no point trying 2 hide dad we no all ur haunts and uv only got one friend and we just want a nice chat

I smile warmly at Lizzie even though she's in mid-splutter. "On second thoughts, Lizzie, I don't want to be a spoilsport and far be it from me to be judgmental, so yeah I'd love to come!"

"Oh goodie, that *will* be jolly!" And she immediately gets up and gathers her doggies and puts an arm firmly through mine, then sniffs and takes it away again.

As we leave the pub she whispers rather loudly, "I don't want to sound like one of those ghastly suburban types, dear, but a little bit of a wash might help. And by the way you can't wear a T-shirt tonight, sorry."

"But I thought you were a libertarian – live and let live?" I say, because I can hardly believe I'm hearing this. "Well if you and your tossing Tory mates can't accept me as I am, then I'm not coming!"

"Well that's very sad, but you see it's a really special night, to celebrate our country coming to its senses and restoring a proper blue-blooded natural born leader to power at last – someone with a sense of entitlement! And I'm very sorry but I'm afraid people who support proper blue-blooded leaders with a sense of entitlement simply don't wear pongy T-shirts. Nor do their close chums, Arnold."

"Well I have to beg to differ on that one, Lizzie," I say haughtily, trying to hide how betrayed I feel. "And I'm afraid we seem to have come across an irreconcilable ideological stumbling block. So I'll just have to say goodnight."

"Night night, dear."

We both take out our keys and start to open our front doors and as we do so my mobile beeps. It's another text from Roger.

good news dad! theyve just rung 2 say the lady next 2 edith has died so theres a room free but not for long! On our way 2 pick u up just for a little chat!

I turn back to Lizzie, who fortunately is still struggling to find the keyhole. "Look on consideration Lizzie I don't want to be over-rigid and intolerant, and what do clothes matter anyway, it's the human being inside that counts, isn't it?"

"Absolutely."

"See you in five minutes."

I've never washed and dressed so quickly in my life.

Four and a half minutes later I stand in front of the bedroom mirror in my Next suit and tie and shiny shoes that I never got round to flogging on eBay, and I'm disgusted by what I see. Reflected back at me is nothing less than a class traitor. Even worse, a not very successful one.

Still, needs must.

I hurry next door and of course Lizzie is really impressed, but like many women before her can't resist trying to improve me. Even though I'm keen to get away I patiently put up with her straightening my tie, but when she spits on her hankie and starts scrubbing toothpaste off my face I curtly insist we leave straightaway.

My assertiveness only seems to excite the old boot because as she drives off I feel a hand wandering up my thigh. "Just feeling the material, dear," she smiles when I try to remove it. And flirtation nearly leads to disaster as she almost collides with a vulgarly ostentatious Range Rover that's racing down the street in the opposite direction and screeches to a halt outside my flat.

9.00 p.m.

The party is at the Chelsea townhouse of a billionaire Tory donor who Lizzie tells me sadly can't be there because he's on such an amazing tax dodge they only allow him in the country three days a year. She totters off "to network" so I grab a pint of shampoo – in one of the manly beer glasses Lizzie mentioned earlier – and a foie gras butty and have a look around. I don't notice many leaders of men, or politicians of any sort for that matter, but everyone else is certainly there, and I briefly wonder if Hello! magazine is sponsoring the evening, like it did Robbie Williams' wedding. It crosses my mind that if Wills was with me he'd be having an orgasm over so many celebs (if he had any orgasms to spare, that is, which I doubt). Clearly show biz has taken over the Conservative Party just like it has the rest of the world.

I wander past Brucie (*again!* I don't know how he does it!) and am distressed to hear him chatting to Tarbie about handicaps. Equally distressing is the sight of the fearless adventurer Sir Richard Branson (yes him again too!) standing on his own picking at the plasters that now cover the few bits of his face that aren't covered with hair. On a healthier note, I overhear Sir Cliff Richard talking to Tim Henman about tennis. Then there's Sir Tim Rice talking to Sir Mick Jagger about cricket. And Madonna's ex, Guy Thingy, chatting away to Marco Pierre White about grouse shooting. No one is talking about the election, presumably because they know they're going to get such a thrashing.

I think to myself how sadly typical that these right-wing celebs don't have anything better to talk about than sport – what about culture for fuck's sake? And just as I'm thinking it, I pass Lord Lloyd Webber chatting away to Jim Davidson about the Pre-Raphaelites, and chuckle to myself as I realize how unwise it is to generalize.

But who's this? No, I don't believe it, it's the Beverley Sisters! I go closer just to check, and no it's not the Beverley sisters, it's Trinny and Susannah chatting to Carol Vorderman. How weird, I reflect, I've never met any of them but because of the unique power of television it feels like I'm bumping into old friends! Anyway, it's clearly now or never Carol-wise, so I quickly finish my pint of shampoo to give me confidence and go up and introduce myself. The three of them stare at me blankly, so I just chuckle, then wink at Carol and jokily ask her if she's free for a bit of multiplication later. She gives me a look that frankly makes Anne Robinson seem friendly, so I cross the rude cow off my three-in-the-morning fantasy list and ask the other two what they're up to. They cackle helplessly and tell me to go fuck myself, in those hideous Sloaney voices that sum up everything I truly detest about the upper classes but that really give me the horn.

I go for a little stroll to calm Mr Stiffie down and when I get back the Beverley Sisters have done a bunk. Lizzie comes and "rescues" me, as she puts it, and asks me who that oiky chap is who's been talking to Lord Lloyd Webber because he's just asked her to come for a dirty weekend in Dubai. I say it's Jim Davidson, a vulgar and tasteless alcoholic misogynistic so-called comedian, and she says oh that does sound lovely, just like you dear! I briefly wonder if she's trying to make me jealous, but before I can confront her she drags me over to meet her best buddy.

It's Sir Michael Caine, who gazes at me through his glasses in that scary unblinking way he has. I turn to Lizzie to rescue me but she's already buggered off and is busy doing air kisses with Georgie Osborne, who's just popped in to check on the supplies of shampoo and foie gras and keeps yelling excitedly, "There's going to be lots more where that came from, just wait till I put up VAT!"

I turn from the pampered deluded fool back to Sir Michael, who at least had to fight his way up from nothing, just like me.

"So how long have you known Lizzie?" I ask.

"Oh, you know, Lizzie and I – we go way back…" he says in that famously flat voice. "Bloody way back – know what I mean?" And he gives me his hooded look, which is remarkably similar to the scary unblinking look, but which finally convinces me, if I still had any lingering doubt, that far from being a lezzie, Lizzie was in her time a goer of heroic proportions.

"How interesting," I smile back.

"It is a bit, yeah." He puts a matey but threatening arm round my shoulder. "So what do you think about voluntary national service, Arthur?"

"Arnold."

"And while we're chatting, what about bloody layabouts on benefits then, eh, Arthur?"

"It's Arnold."

He gives me the hooded look and the scary unblinking look both at the same time, which is quite something. "So what would you say to joining a youth cadet group I'm setting up in the Elephant and Castle, Arthur? Cos that's where I come from and I wanna give something back to this great country of ours. Mind you, if that bloody Osborne puts the taxes up to fifty-one per cent I'll be out of here faster than shit off a bloody shovel, believe me."

Of course, I'm flattered to be asked to join his cadet group, but I'm also surprised because while I pride myself on being young at heart I can't deny that I'm not quite in the first flush of youth. Then I realize that Sir Michael's arm round my shoulder is getting heavier. And I find myself wondering if he put it there not to be threatening after all but simply so I can hold him up. Perhaps the tragic truth is that the iconic star of Alfie is now so ancient that by his standards I am indeed a mere stripling.

If so, what a humbling lesson in life that is.

And how old does it make Lizzie, for God's sake?

Friday 7th May

1.10 a.m.

The Tories have just made their first gain from Labour. The sight of Lizzie and Georgie Osborne hugging each other and jumping up and down is nauseating but I manage to contain myself. But when she tries to drag me into the hugathon that really is a step too far, and I brusquely tell her I'm leaving immediately, whether she comes or not.

She really loves me being assertive, and to my surprise totters happily after me and we then spend twenty-five minutes trying to find her car.

"By the way, Georgie told me he knows your gay son *very* well!" she tells me cheerily as I collapse into the passenger seat. "Apparently they got up to all sorts of things at St Pauls!"

"Did he go into specifics?" I ask hopefully as she careers off into the night.

"Of course he did, silly – Georgie always tells me everything!"

"Would you mind getting him to repeat it to me?" I ask casually, wondering how cheaply I can buy a hidden microphone and how I can get it into The News Of The World by Sunday week at the latest. "Just for my diary of course!"

"Certainly not," she frowns disapprovingly. "Noblesse oblige, Arnold, Georgie's mum Lady Osborne and I play poker at the Paddington Pool And Poker Club every Wednesday."

"What's that got to do with anything?"

She sails through a red light and glances at me fondly. "It means I don't want you having anything to do with gutter journalism, dear, just in case that was in your mind. After all, if we're going to become an item I really want to be proud of you."

"If we're *what?*"

4.00 a.m. (ish)

The impossible finally happens.

Hard though it is to believe, Lizzie and I come to an agreement about politics.

Not straightaway though. First, we sprawl on her decadent Tory bed watching the results on her posh TV and drinking the Dom Perignon she's got in for the occasion, and she keeps cheering and I keep not cheering. But in the end we're forced to agree we've both got it wrong – the Tories aren't going to get a landslide, and no one likes the Lib Dems any more than they ever did.

In between discussing politics, we have sex. Lots and lots. And it's really dirty, just like I knew it would be with a Tory.

In between discussing politics and having sex I discover something else that's great.

Lizzie is someone I can reveal my innermost worries and insecurities to without fear of mockery or retribution.

I first realize this when we're having a pause and indulging in a bit of pillow-talk and I ask her if she's really a hundred and eighty-three.

She doesn't answer for a few minutes, then coyly asks how old I am.

"Sixty-one and five months in a fortnight," I reveal, "but I like to think I look younger."

She nods and smiles, obviously agreeing with me. Then beams apologetically and says, "Well I'm four months older than you, dear. But I've been out in the sun an awful lot."

Later on we're having another break, and I'm so relaxed with her now that I hear myself owning up to my fear of change. It all comes gushing out – how everything feels so impermanent, and recent events have only made it worse...

"Like Gordon Brown and John Nettles! I mean much though I hate them, the thought of one of them leaving Downing Street and the other Midsomer Murders really freaks me out. Why can't anyone leave anything alone ever?! Why can't things stay like they were?!"

Of course, being a Tory, she understands this entirely. And all this confessional stuff makes us both really horny and basically we only stop when we hear that no one has voted for Esther Rantzen in Luton South, which not only brings us together politically but makes us laugh uncontrollably.

That's another great thing – we share a sense of humour!

And during the night we discuss the delicate issue of political differences in some depth. In the end we agree that yes we have very different belief systems, but when it comes down to it who gives a toss because let's face it most of it's about nurture rather than nature really, isn't it? (Or is it the other way round?)

Anyway, I'm really beginning to think we're soulmates. Plus, Lizzie says she's got oodles of money and she just loves giving it to lost causes.

Perhaps this is love. Who'd have thought it?!

3.30 p.m.

Finally get back home and double-lock the front door just in case the kids try to get in. Give bollocks a wash then change into my "This T-shirt would look great on your bedroom floor" T-shirt so that I can keep Lizzie on the boil later. (Over the years have become increasingly sensitive to the risk of letting the novelty go out of one's sexual relationship).

Then pour a glass of Tesco 3 for £10 reddo and collapse knackered in front of the TV, which is still burbling on about the election.

Ponder the extraordinary unprecedented events of the last 24 hours. And spend a few moments thinking about the election as well.

Switch over to ITV3, which am disgusted to find is showing Dr Quinn, Medicine Woman. An American programme on ITV3 – whatever next?! Then force myself to calm down and realize things could be worse. At least it's starring Jane Seymour, who's English, or was many years ago.

Can't be arsed to change channels. Feel eyelids flickering pleasantly, and decide I can't be arsed to continue with magnum opus any longer either...

Great sense of freedom. Fall happily asleep...

5.10 p.m.

Wake up feeling groggy with red wine all over my "This T-shirt would look great on your bedroom floor" T-shirt. Am enraged at the unfairness of life and the fact that everything goes right for everyone else, specially smug so-called best friend Wills, but never for me and I have no career and no money and no one in the world cares for me so might as well kill myself because can't even afford new fucking T-shirt.

Then remember I don't need to feel any of that any more.

Weird feeling. Not sure I like it.

William Humble has written a number of highly-acclaimed films for BBC TV, including the Emmy award-winning *On Giant's Shoulders* starring Judi Dench, and the BAFTA-nominated *Hancock*, with Alfred Molina as Tony Hancock. He wrote *Virtuoso* about the concert pianist John Ogdon, also with Alfred Molina, as well as Alison Steadman. Other BBC films include *Ex*, a comedy starring Griff Rhys Jones; and another comedy, *Royal Celebration*; also *Poppyland* and *Talk To Me*, both starring Alan Howard.

For ITV, he wrote the film *Whatever Love Means*, with Laurence Fox, and *Too Good To Be True*, a psychological thriller with Peter Davison and Niamh Cusack. He dramatised Mary Wesley's *The Vacillations of Poppy Carew*, Rosie Thomas's *Every Woman Knows A Secret*, and wrote two series based on novels by P.D.James – *An Unsuitable Job For A Woman*, and *The Black Tower*. He has also written for

Churchill – the Wilderness Years, *Poirot* and *Maigret* starring Michael Gambon.

His stage plays include: *What a Performance*, with David Suchet as comedian Sid Field and *Façades*, with Frances de la Tour as Edith Sitwell. He has also written several radio plays and – a million years ago – a novel.

He is married and has two alarmingly grown-up children and lives in London, embarrassingly close to where Arnold Appleforth used to hang out.

URBANE